THE GAMBLER'S CHASE

The Chase Fulton Novels Series
Book One: *The Opening Chase*
Book Two: *The Broken Chase*
Book Three: *The Stronger Chase*
Book Four: *The Unending Chase*
Book Five: *The Distant Chase*
Book Six: *The Entangled Chase*
Book Seven: *The Devil's Chase*
Book Eight: *The Angel's Chase*
Book Nine: *The Forgotten Chase*
Book Ten: *The Emerald Chase*
Book Eleven: *The Polar Chase*
Book Twelve: *The Burning Chase*
Book Thirteen: *The Poison Chase*
Book Fourteen: *The Bitter Chase*
Book Fifteen: *The Blind Chase*
Book Sixteen: *The Smuggler's Chase*
Book Seventeen: *The Hollow Chase*
Book Eighteen: *The Sunken Chase*
Book Nineteen: *The Darker Chase*
Book Twenty: *The Abandoned Chase*
Book Twenty-One: *The Gambler's Chase*
Book Twenty-Two: *The Arctic Chase*

The Avenging Angel – Seven Deadly Sins Series
Book One: *The Russian's Pride*
Book Two: *The Russian's Greed*
Book Three: *The Russian's Gluttony*
Book Four: *The Russian's Lust*
Book Five: *The Russian's Sloth* (2023)

Stand Alone Novels
We Were Brave

Novellas
The Chase Is On
I Am Gypsy

THE GAMBLER'S CHASE

CHASE FULTON NOVEL #21

CAP DANIELS

ANCHOR WATCH
PUBLISHING
** USA **

The Gambler's Chase
Chase Fulton Novel #21
Cap Daniels

This is a work of fiction. Names, characters, places, historical events, and incidents are the product of the author's imagination or have been used fictitiously. Although many locations such as marinas, airports, hotels, restaurants, etc. used in this work actually exist, they are used fictitiously and may have been relocated, exaggerated, or otherwise modified by creative license for the purpose of this work. Although many characters are based on personalities, physical attributes, skills, or intellect of actual individuals, all the characters in this work are products of the author's imagination.

Published by:

ANCHOR WATCH
—— PUBLISHING ——
** USA **

13 Digit ISBN: 978-1-951021-42-9
Library of Congress Control Number: 2023903386

Cover Design: German Creative

Printed in the United States of America

The Gambler's Chase

CAP DANIELS

Chapter 1
The Grey Ghost

Fall 2009, Savannah, GA

The man beneath the salt-and-pepper receding hairline stood from behind his desk and pulled on his jacket boasting a pair of gold aviator's wings above the left breast pocket. "I'm Micky De-Long. Welcome to the Gulfstream family, gentlemen. Let's go have a look at your new chariot, shall we?"

I stuck out a hand. "Nice to meet you, Mr. DeLong. I'm Chase Fulton."

"Pleasure," he said as he pumped my hand.

I motioned toward my handler and former Green Beret. "This is Clark Johnson."

Shakes and pleasantries ensued, and Disco reached for De-Long's offered hand. "Just call me Disco. It's my job to keep these guys current and capable."

Delong said, "That must make you the chief pilot."

"It's good work if you can get it, Mr. DeLong."

We followed him from his office to the gleaming floor of the massive Gulfstream Aerospace hangar. The space seemed to be devoted to a single enormous Gulfstream business jet with swarms of technicians in white coveralls hard at work on various sections of the stunning aircraft.

Clark, Disco, and I froze in place, staring up at the gleaming behemoth, and DeLong chuckled. "I'm afraid this one isn't yours."

Disco sighed. "Not yet."

"Indeed," DeLong said. "This, as you may know, is the new G-Six-Fifty, the largest, fastest, most capable business jet we've ever produced. She taxied under her own power for the first time, and we held our public rollout ceremony in September of this year. She'll make her maiden flight in late October, and we plan high-speed flight testing for spring of two thousand ten."

"How much?" I whispered before I realized the words had escaped my lips.

"Sixty-five million is the projected sticker price, but a Gulfstream Four would account for a very nice trade-in allowance."

"She's magnificent," Clark said.

DeLong slapped Clark on the back. "Thank you, Mr. Johnson. I'll be sure to let the design team know you approve. Yours is next door," he said as he motioned across the apron and toward the open doors of a second hangar not quite as glamorous as the first. "As you can see, the jets in this hangar, except for yours, of course, are all in some state of refurbishment. While you were in the simulators for your qualification training, we were putting the finishing touches on your new member of the family."

I walked beneath the fuselage and slid my palm against the glass-like finish of the belly. "I like the grey."

DeLong said, "That's the original *Grey Ghost* paint scheme for the military version, except without the government markings, of course."

We walked every inch of the exterior as DeLong narrated the tour. "We retained the starboard-side, military cargo door just as you requested. I'm curious, though . . . What sort of flying missions do you anticipate for the aircraft?"

Disco and Clark turned to me as if I'd suddenly become the official spokesman, so I had a little fun. Checking over each shoulder, I leaned close and whispered, "You see, Mr. DeLong, we're spies, and we plan to save the world with this baby."

His eyes grew into softballs, and he swallowed hard the instant before the three of us burst into uproarious laughter. Clark threw an arm around the corporate rep. "Relax, Micky. We're a humanitarian aid organization. You know, digging wells and doctors without boundaries . . . stuff like that."

"Borders," DeLong said. "You mean Doctors Without Borders."

Clark shrugged. "If you say so."

With the question adequately evaded, I said, "Let's have a look inside."

We climbed the airstairs, and I turned right as the remainder of my posse turned left into the cockpit.

DeLong slid a hand across the first luxurious leather captain's chair. "Have a seat, Chase. I'll tell you about the interior."

I slid into the plush seat and pressed the button to swivel toward the rear of the cabin. "This is nice."

He situated himself across the aisle in a matching seat. "This is the executive configuration—twelve identical captain's chairs, fully articulating, Wi-Fi, secure satellite communication per the specifications, service galley, spacious lav, and of course everything is finished with only the finest materials and craftsmanship."

"I'm without words, Mr. DeLong. It's spectacular, but this isn't the interior configuration we expected."

He put on a smile. "This is just one of the configurations. Come with me."

We stepped from the plane and back onto the polished floor of the hangar. DeLong waved for a woman in coveralls and a hard hat. She raised her chin, clearly awaiting instructions from the boss, and my tour guide shot a thumb toward the plane and held up two fingers.

In minutes, the cargo door was open, the executive seating was lifted from the plane on the tongues of a forklift, and in went what DeLong called the cargo-pax configuration. Eight durable seats mounted to a pallet went in first, and a pair of technicians secured the pallet in place. Next, two cargo pallets stacked with netted boxes made their way through the wide cargo hatch.

"This is the interior you requested," he said. "In addition to the crew, you can comfortably seat eight and carry two pallets of cargo anywhere in the world. If the seating isn't required, a third pallet can take its place."

It was my turn to smile. "Now, that's the right interior."

"That's not all," DeLong said. "The configurations are limited only by your imagination. We have a medivac pack, a caged animal pallet, and even a package we call the max-pax. It's thirty-four— not particularly comfortable—seats for humanitarian evacuation missions."

"I don't know how many humanitarian evacuation missions you've flown, but I'd imagine an empty plane with no seats would qualify as the max-pax platform."

He raised both hands. "You're the experts. I'm simply giving you options, Chase. All of the configurations we discussed are part of the package, and they'll be delivered with the airplane as long as you have adequate storage for them. If not, we can arrange for—"

I stopped him. "We have plenty of room, but we'll need the training to change configurations."

"Of course. That's all part of the package."

I checked my watch. "It's been three weeks since we've seen the rest of our family, so I'd like to make the flight test and get out of your hair so you can attend to your project in the other hangar."

DeLong said, "Of course. Our chief test pilot is waiting for you in his office. If I don't see you again today, I'm confident we'll see each other again soon."

I thanked him for the tour before knocking on the test pilot's door.

A voice from the other side said, "Please come in."

When we stepped through the door, I was almost disappointed. Instead of a Hollywood-style fighter pilot, the man standing behind a neatly arranged desk resembled an accountant more than a jet jockey.

I suppose the look on my face betrayed me, and the man chuckled. "Don't worry. I get that look a lot. My logbook looks a little more impressive than my gut, but what can I say? The wife is an excellent cook."

I stammered. "That's not . . . I mean . . . I'm Chase, and this is Clark and our chief pilot, Disco."

"Jim Gladwell. Pleased to meet you. And Disco sounds like a call sign. At least I hope it's not your real name."

"Former A-Ten driver," Disco said.

Gladwell grabbed his headset from the credenza behind him. "In that case, Disco, prepare to be disappointed by the Gulf-stream."

Our chief pilot laughed. "No airplane in which I can stand up and go to the bathroom disappoints me."

Gladwell gave him a thumbs-up. "Excellent point. Empty water bottles in the cockpit have come in handy far too many times in my life."

Disco went first while Clark and I luxuriated in the interior of the plane and Gladwell demonstrated the limits of the Gulfstream's capabilities. When my turn at the controls finally rolled around, I leapt into the left seat like a kid with a brand-new driver's license. Ten minutes into the session, I was amazed how much the real thing felt and behaved just like the simulators we'd been flying for three days. I felt immediately comfortable at the controls of the impressive machine and couldn't wait to put her to work.

We thanked Gladwell and arranged for the delivery of our additional interiors. "We'll have them trucked to St. Marys when you're ready to receive them."

I flipped through my phone's calendar. "We'll put your people in touch with our man at the airport, and they can work out the times. We'll be overseas for a few days. We've worked hard enough to deserve a little R and R."

We shook hands and climbed aboard our newest magic carpet. The only problem arose when all three of us tried to turn left into the cockpit.

I took a step back and surrendered. "Fine. You two can have this leg, but I'm up front next time we light the fires."

Disco slid into the captain's seat on the left, and Clark crawled into the right. The twelve-minute flight put us on the ground in St. Marys long before the plane could stretch her legs, and we stepped onto the tarmac and right into the anticipation of the rest of our team.

Mongo was first to push his way aboard, and his massive girth darkened the doorway. "This is nice. Even I fit in here."

Singer, our Southern Baptist sniper, was next through the door, and in his typical style, he had nothing to say, but the grin on his face was approval enough.

Tony, our former rescue swimmer turned master painter, said, "I may have to give up painting old ships of war and take up modern business jets. This is astonishing. The girls are going to love it."

"Speaking of the girls," I said. "I recommend we load up a little gear just in case we run into an opportunity to put out a fire and head for the Mediterranean. I'm afraid they'll forget we exist if we don't show up soon."

My idea was welcomed with exuberance, and less than an hour later, we picked up our international clearance from Jacksonville Center, and we were on our way to Ibiza, Spain, with a fuel stop in the Azores. Since I was smart enough to defer my cockpit seat on the flight home from Savannah, it was Clark's turn to sit in the well-cushioned seats in the back while Disco and I pulled our new Gulfstream off the ground. We were wheels up, headed for a rendezvous with the women we loved.

The *Grey Ghost* performed beautifully on the climb out—especially considering the tanks were completely full of fuel and we had Mongo aboard—but in that moment, I couldn't have known that we'd never reach our cruising altitude for the flight.

Chapter 2
7-5-0-0

As we climbed at nearly four thousand feet per minute over the coast of the Atlantic, the workload in the cockpit lightened until Disco and I were little more than systems monitors and computer operators. Our Citation had been a wonderful airplane, but the Gulfstream felt like an entirely new league of luxury and capability.

Climbing through twenty-four thousand feet, the Jacksonville Center air traffic controller said something I'd never heard before that moment. "Down Island one-six-five, verify squawking seven-five-zero-zero."

Disco jerked his head toward me. "Did he say seventy-five hundred? That's the hijack code."

"It sure is," I said. "When was the last time you heard of a hijacking?"

He turned up the volume on the radio, and we listened intently.

"Uh, Jacksonville, Down Island one-six-five, affirmative, seven-five-zero-zero. We're diverting to Nassau, Yankee-Golf-Fox. Uh, that's all we have for now, Center."

Before the Down Island pilot released the push-to-talk button, an accented voice inside the cockpit yelled, "No more radio!"

"Those guys are in trouble," Disco whispered almost to himself.

I slid my seat all the way back so I could reach the cockpit door. "Clark, come up here."

He forced himself from his plush surroundings and ambled to the cockpit door. "What is it, College Boy?"

"Have you ever heard of Down Island Air?"

"Yeah. They come in and out of Miami regularly. It's a little regional airline. I think they fly RJ-two-hundreds, mostly. Why?"

"Somebody just hijacked one of them, and they're diverting to Nassau."

He took a knee in the doorway. "Where are they now?"

I shrugged. "I don't know. We just heard it on the radio."

Disco held up a finger. "I'm on a discrete frequency with JAX Center."

I handed a headset to Clark and asked, "Are we going?"

"You better believe we're going. There's nobody on the ground in Nassau who can do what we can."

Disco keyed his mic. "JAX Center, November Two One Golf Romeo is now Grey Ghost One, and we're diverting to Nassau for a precautionary landing."

The controller said, "Roger, Two One Golf Romeo. Say nature of emergency."

"It's not our emergency, Center. We're responding to yours. If you need any more information, call the Pentagon."

Silence filled our headsets while the controller processed what Disco said. Finally, she said, "Grey Ghost One cleared direct Grand Bahama International Airport. Say requested altitude."

Disco said, "Grey Ghost One is turning direct Nassau and passing flight level three-one-oh, but we'll take whatever works best for you on the altitude."

"Roger, Grey Ghost One. Descend and maintain flight level two-three-oh."

Disco transformed from his typical mild-mannered corporate pilot persona into the gritty A-10 Warthog driver he'd been for two decades. "Grey Ghost is out of thirty-one for twenty-one. Get me on the ground first, Center."

The controller said, "You'll be with Miami Center shortly, and I relayed your request for expedited service. They understand the situation."

"Thank you, JAX. We're standing by for the handoff."

Clark closed his eyes as if he were praying, but I suspected he was planning instead. When he opened his eyes, he said, "We need Skipper."

I slid my seat forward. "Maybe not. Tony might be able to play Skipper for this one."

Without another word, he disappeared and returned several minutes later. "Okay, here's the plan. You were right about Tony. He can get us rolling. I've been on the line with the Board, and they approved our involvement. They're paving the way with the Bahamian authorities. If we can get on deck and in position before the hijackers, we'll have a huge advantage. Do you think that's possible?"

JAX Center said, "Grey Ghost One, contact Miami Center on one-two-four point one. Godspeed."

Disco keyed up. "Thanks, JAX. We're off to Miami Center."

I handed Clark the headset, and he pulled it on just as Disco checked in with Miami. "Miami Center, Grey Ghost One, level two-one-oh and en route for the seventy-five hundred code."

"Good morning, Grey Ghost One. Miami Center. Advise ready for descent into Nassau. There will be no delay."

Disco said, "Roger, we'll expect no delay. Do you have an ETA for the other aircraft?"

"Affirmative, sir. You'll be on the ground about twenty minutes before they arrive. That's the best we can do unless you can increase your speed."

"We're at max cruise," Disco said. "But we'd like to stay up high as long as you'll let us."

The controller said, "Roger, advise ready for the descent."

"Did you hear that?" Disco asked.

Clark said, "Yeah, I got it. Twenty minutes ahead. We're going to gear up, and I'll have two kits built for you and Chase. Tony is coordinating with the locals on the sat-phone."

My heart pounded as I played through the possible outcomes for the afternoon, and Disco noticed my distraction.

He tapped the panel in front of me with his fingertips. "I need you to focus on flying the airplane right now. We'll deal with the ground when we get every piece of this thing stopped, but as long as we're moving, you're a pilot and not a commando."

I brushed his hand away. "That's exactly why you're the chief pilot and I'm just a knuckle-dragger."

He chuckled. "Yeah . . . that's you, ole knuckle-dragger. Seriously though, I've never had any training for hostage rescue on an airliner. I'll do whatever you tell me, but I don't know how much help I'll be."

"Don't worry," I said. "The rest of us have been to the Israeli school. Their technique tends to leave bad guys piled up like cordwood. We'll handle the insertion and trigger-pulling. We need you for the things you know about airplanes."

He lowered his chin. "Don't think I'm not willing to hit and get hit. I just don't want to be in your way."

"I know you're just as short on fear as the rest of us. I'm the commander when we hit the ground, and I'm not taking anyone onto that airplane with me who hasn't been trained and drilled into the ground on how to do it perfectly. I know exactly what I need from you."

He scanned the panel as the captain of a jet airplane should. "So, what is it? What do you want from me?"

"I said *need*, not *want*. What I need from you is for you to mentally put yourself in the cockpit of that airliner. I need you inside the heads of that crew. What would you want me to do from the ground in Nassau?"

He pulled off his sunglasses and slid them into his shirt pocket. "I'd want you to keep my passengers alive, regardless of what happened to me."

I laid a hand on his shoulder. "That's noble, but the guys in the front seat of that airliner probably aren't retired, well-decorated combat pilots with a team of commandos at their side. They're probably scared kids, and we've all been one of those at some point."

His eyes were those of a man trying to put himself in shoes that weren't his, and I let him go.

A few minutes later, Miami Center called. "Grey Ghost One, descend at pilot's discretion to maintain one-one-thousand."

Disco slid his glasses back onto his face. "Grey Ghost One is out of flight level two-one-oh for one-one-thousand."

I set the altitude preselect, and the autopilot initiated our descent.

Disco nodded toward the cockpit door. "Go back there and check your kit. I know Clark said he'd have it ready for you, but you'll want to make sure it's perfect when we hit the tarmac. I've got the airplane for the descent."

I slid the seat back and headed down the aisle. My kit was draped around the back of one of the leather seats, and I slid it across my shoulders. My pistol was precisely where it should've been. My knife was situated for easy access for me, but not for an opponent, and my rifle sling was adjusted exactly as if I'd done it myself.

I gave Clark the thumbs-up, and he said, "You don't have to check my work. You may have traded me in for Hunter, but I still know how you like your gear."

Without another word, I planted myself back in the cockpit and scanned the horizon for the airport. When it appeared like a white spot on an endless blue ocean, I pointed through the windscreen. "There it is."

Disco said, "It's all yours if you want to fly the approach and landing. Just remember . . . we're heavy and full of fuel, so the landing roll will be longer than you think. Try to stay off the brakes." He paused and then put on the face of a man who'd just come up with a plan.

"What is it?" I asked.

"I'll tell you what I'd want if I were the captain of Down Island Air flight one-six-five. I'd want somebody to force me to lock the brakes after landing and let the smoke pour off the rubber tires as they melt to the runway."

"You're a genius, Captain Disco . . . A genius, I tell you."

We greased the landing and taxied to the general aviation terminal, where Tony had arranged our first meeting with the local police commander.

We wasted no time hitting the ground at the bottom of the airstairs, where a man in a formal police uniform waited.

I stuck my hand in his. "Chase Fulton, U.S Secret Service. I'm the interdiction team commander."

The officer shook my hand. "Chief Superintendent of Airport Division Police Melvin Conroe." His Bahamian patois rested just beneath his formal tone.

"Nice to meet you, Chief, but the pleasantries will have to wait. How far out is the Down Island flight?"

"Dey should be on da groun' in 'bout twenty minutes maybe."

Tony bounded down the stairs with laptops and sat-phones hanging from every appendage.

I said, "This is Tony, our ops officer. I need him in a quiet office with plenty of electrical outlets. Can you manage that?"

Chief Conroe snapped his fingers twice, and another over-dressed officer materialized at his side. The young officer led Tony away, and the chief asked, "What else, Mr. Fulton?"

"I need a crippled airplane—preferably something big—at least two hundred feet of cable strong enough to tow the crippled aircraft, and a motorized tug."

I grabbed Disco by the collar and yanked him into our conversation. "I need this guy in the control tower and in radio comms with the tug operator." I spun on a heel and drove a finger through the air toward Singer, our sniper. "I need that guy on top of the control tower."

Clark, Mongo, and Hunter joined my huddle with Chief Conroe, and I said, "The four of us need turnout gear, including helmets and face shields, and a ride on the biggest fire truck you've got."

Chief Conroe blinked in rapid succession. "It will take some time for all of dis, and I do not have any big, damaged airplanes."

I took a step toward the chief and pointed toward the runway. "There are at least fifty terrified, innocent people on the next plane that will land on that runway, and I intend to keep every one of them alive. Either you help me do that or get out of my way. We don't have island time. We need to move now!"

My insistence worked, and Singer and Disco were headed to the control tower in seconds.

Conroe said, "Firemen are coming wit gear and trucks, but I still have no crippled airplane for you."

"Use mine," I said. "Just get me a tug with all the cable you can find."

With our unit comms in place, I called Disco. "What's the ETA?"

"Eight minutes," he said. "I don't think we've got time for the tug."

My mind reeled until finally, the reality of what had to be done settled on my shoulders. I turned to Clark. "You're leading the boarding party. I'm taxiing the *Ghost*."

He grabbed my shirt with both hands and shook me. "We can buy another airplane, College Boy, but you're impossible to re-place. Don't get yourself killed."

I brushed him off. "I'd kinda like it if you stayed alive, too."

The fire truck arrived, and my team donned the turnout gear. The Bahamian fire service didn't own anything in Mongo's size, so we stuffed him into the biggest fire coat they had.

With my team resembling firemen, they situated themselves on the truck while I fired up the Gulfstream, still brimming with jet fuel.

Disco's voice crackled in our earpieces. "Six minutes, guys."

I said, "Roger. We're moving. What do you have for us, Tony?"

Our temporary analyst said, "The airspace is sterile, and the air-port is closed. The U.S. ambassador is smoothing things over with the prime minister, and I'm working on keeping our presence out of tomorrow's newspaper."

"At this point," I said, "I'm working to keep our presence out of the obituary section of that paper."

"Four minutes," Disco called.

I taxied the Gulfstream to a taxiway positioned forty-five hun-dred feet from the spot where the hijacked airliner would likely touch down, and I held short of the runway. Waiting for the airliner to come into sight, I called Tony. "Do we have a head count yet?"

He said, "Forty-seven passengers, three crew, and three hijackers have made themselves known. We have no way to know if there are sleeper agents still in their seats."

"Did you copy that, Clark?" I asked.

Clark said, "Roger. At least three bad guys. If our plan works, they likely won't be able to stay on their feet, so that might give us a momentary advantage."

Disco said, "The tower controller just cleared them to land. They'll be on the ground in two minutes. Chase, please don't break my airplane."

I saw the regional jet turn onto final approach and align itself with the runway centerline. The gear was down, and the approach looked perfect from my seat nearly halfway down the runway. I held the brakes of the Gulfstream and spun up the turbines. The *Grey Ghost* was ready to lunge, and all I needed was perfect timing.

I watched the nose of the airliner rise slightly as it crossed the landing threshold. The pilots were committed to landing at that point, so I released the brakes and taxied onto the runway in front of them. Everything about the maneuver felt unthinkably wrong. I was willing to risk our new Gulfstream if the now-terrified pilots of the regional jet weren't able to get their machine stopped in time, but I prayed they wouldn't add power and take off again. The only other option was to taxi the airliner off the runway and onto the grass. That would be almost as good as melting the tires but riskier for the passengers and crew.

The telltale white puffs of smoke from the main landing gear said they'd touched down, but the billowing plumes of smoke told me our plan was working perfectly and the pilots were standing on the brakes. Blowing the tires would've been enough to prevent the airliner from taking off again, but luck or divine intervention was on our side that day. Not only did all four main tires blow, but the friction also started a pair of bright orange fires beneath the belly of the jet.

With no tires left to roll, the crippled jet came to a stop far closer to the Gulfstream than I wanted, but thankfully, the *Grey Ghost* lived to fight another day.

I shut down the turbines and sprinted down the airstairs.

The firetruck carrying three deadly commandos raced past the Gulfstream and directly toward the now-crippled airplane. The crew aboard the fire truck hit the cockpit and cabin windows with a blast of foam to blind the occupants to the commotion outside. The white foam covered my approach on foot, and my team dismounted the truck just behind the left wing. Clark and Hunter leapt atop the wing while Mongo skirted beneath the belly of the jet and climbed onto the right wing.

In unison, Clark and Mongo pressed shaped charges of C-4 around the perimeter of the emergency escape panel above each wing as I propelled myself onto the wing with Mongo. The giant looked up as if to ask permission to blow the hatch, and I gave him a nod.

"Fire in the hole!" came his reply, and both emergency exits shuddered and disappeared into the interior of the airplane.

Hunter and I were first through the openings. I turned toward the rear of the plane and heard Hunter's suppressed rifle hiss four times through the screams of the frightened passengers.

"Clear to the rear," I yelled the same instant Mongo and Clark came through the hatches, weapons raised and eyes patrolling for targets.

A woman on the aisle in row four forced a finger toward the cockpit door and yelled, "The third one is in there!"

Hunter and Clark moved forward with weapons trained on the cockpit door, just as we'd been trained by the Israelis, while Mongo and I shoved passengers through the blown hatches and onto the wings. Noise inside the cabin subsided a little more with each passenger who exited the cabin.

Singer's voice pierced the chaos that remained. "There's a scuffle in the cockpit. I can see enough through the foam to make the shot if you say the word."

"Send it," I said.

Clark and Hunter froze, not wanting to catch any shrapnel Singer's shot might send through the cockpit door.

Ten seconds passed like hours until Singer said, "No shot. One of the pilots is on his feet, and the angle is no good."

Clark said, "Roger. We're moving through the cockpit door."

"Holding fire," Singer said in his calm baritone.

With three strides remaining before Hunter reached the cockpit, sounds of a fight pierced through the door. The fuselage of the RJ-200 was cramped, and the taper of the cockpit made that space even tighter.

Clark said, "Get that door open, and I'll take him down."

Hunter reached for the broken handle, but before he could grasp it, the door exploded outward, sending Clark and Hunter sidestepping to clear the aisle and gain an angle of fire on the hijacker. I took a knee in the center of the aisle and trained my rifle on the ever-widening cockpit opening. The scene unfolding in front of me was almost impossible to comprehend.

The captain of the airplane stood over the body of the hijacker, and he was tugging on the handle of the crash axe, its blade buried deep in the bandit's chest. Hunter planted a boot on the man's shoulder, stabilizing the corpse enough for the captain to accomplish his desire. The blade slipped from the man's sternum with the sickening sound of suction and fluid. To my surprise, the captain wasn't finished. He landed two more torturous blows to the dead man's torso before Hunter could wrestle the axe from his white-knuckle grip, but even disarmed, his rage wouldn't die.

"How dare you attack my airplane, you miserable piece of trash!" As his assault continued, the captain landed more kicks to the corpse than I could count.

Finally, the first officer pulled his captain from his stupor. "Greg! Stop! He's dead. Come on, man. Stop it."

The captain jerked away from his first officer, pulled his tie loose, and took a long breath. "Sorry. I was just . . . Are the passengers okay? What about Leslie?"

Clark and Hunter stepped aside, and I said, "Look. Everyone's off the plane except the hijackers. Everyone's okay."

"What about Leslie?" he asked again.

"Is she the flight attendant?"

The captain nodded. "Yeah, she's the flight attendant, and she's my . . ."

The first officer said, "Nobody's supposed to know, but they're, you know, kinda dating or whatever. Never mind that. Thank you, guys—whoever you are—for . . . this."

"You're welcome," I said. "But we were never here. When you talk to the press, be sure to thank the efforts of Chief Superintendent Melvin Conroe and his officers."

The captain appeared to reclaim his composure. "But you guys are Americans. What are you doing here?"

I gave him a shrug. "We just happened to be in the neighborhood and thought we'd lend a hand."

"What are you guys?" he asked.

I shook my head. "As I said, we were never here. Your crew and passengers are alive thanks to the heroic efforts of Chief Superintendent of Airport Division Police Melvin Conroe. Don't forget that name, okay?"

The captain kicked the foot of the dead hijacker on the deck. "What about him? How do we explain that?"

I stared at the name tag on his bloody shirt. "You can chalk that one up to the heroic actions of Captain Greg LaMonte. It looks like you have a promising future as an axman on a logging crew if you ever decide to give up the flying thing. By the way, thanks for not hitting our Gulfstream."

He ducked and looked through the windshield. "That's yours?"

I shook my head again. "Nope. That doesn't exist, and it was never here, either."

Chapter 3
Every Penny

After a fuel stop in the Azores, we arrived at Ibiza's international airport and into the arms of the rest of our family we'd not seen in what felt like an eternity. The reunion led to stories too fantastic to be true—for anyone else—but for us, it was all just another day in the life of our team, the people we love, our family.

After a few days on the island, enjoying the warm, dry life and not on our toes expecting incoming fire, my brothers-in-arms and I settled into a condition we'd rarely known. We truly relaxed and treasured our time together without a war to fight or an enemy to quash.

Ibiza has no shortage of three things: beautiful sunshine, beautiful people, and lavish resorts. Ours was no exception, and one of my favorite corners of the island retreat was the casino. The cards weren't exactly stacked against me, but I was suffering some punishing losses on a night that cradled a full moon over the Mediterranean Sea as if the darkened sky never wanted to let the glowing orb depart her embrace. I felt exactly the same about the beautiful woman sitting beside me with her hand draped delicately across my thigh. The stakes of her game, in many ways, were far higher than mine, but I had no way of understanding just how much she stood to lose in the coming hours.

On the soft green felt of the table beneath my fingertips lay an eight and a four. The dealer, only three feet away, showed a king atop her down card. "Hit me."

The dealer slipped a card from the shoe and flipped it over, landing the five beside my cards. The five made my hand a seventeen, and I raised my palm to wave off another card. Nobody hits seventeen.

"*Ty dolzhen vzyat' kartu. Ochen' malen'kiy.*"

There are places on Earth where hearing the Russian language isn't surprising. Ibiza, Spain, is *not* one of those places.

I turned to face the man at the end of the table. His shirt clung to his body like a second skin, and his arms bulged as if electrically charged. I hadn't spoken Russian in so long that I feared my mouth could no longer create the hard Slavic sounds, but I gave it my best shot. "You think I should take the hit?"

He nodded. "*Da.*"

I counted the chips stacked in the colored circle beside my cards. *Five hundred dollars.* I tapped the felt, and the dealer called over her shoulder. "Player hitting hard seventeen."

The pit boss, dressed in a stylish, well-cut jacket and tie, stepped beside the dealer and asked in Spanish, "You want to hit your seventeen, sir?"

I shot a look at my new Russian friend, and he gave me a nod. I returned my gaze to the pit boss. "*Sí, señor.*"

"Deal the card," he said to the dealer.

She drew another card from the shoe and turned up a four of diamonds. Everyone at the table gasped except the Russian and me.

The dealer slowly slid a stack of chips behind the ones already standing in his betting circle and held up one finger. "Double down." The three and eight lying beside his two-thousand-dollar bet waited patiently as if even the cards themselves knew a ten was coming . . . and come it did. A jack of spades landed on top of his eleven, giving him twenty-one on a double-down bet.

Neither of us could lose the hand. The worst possible outcome would be the dealer making twenty-one, pushing the hand with no loss or gain, but when the dealer revealed her down card, the six of hearts, the steroidal Russki relaxed and raised a finger for the cocktail waitress. He seemed to know what would happen even without watching the table.

The dealer turned up a seven, giving herself twenty-three and busting the hand. The Russian won two grand, and I enjoyed watching my stack of five hundred become a thousand.

Turning to the man, I stumbled through the question in Russian. "How did you know?"

"I didn't know you would draw a four, but I knew it wouldn't be the ten I needed."

"So, you didn't care what happened to my hand. You were only concerned about yours."

He sipped his cocktail. "Such is the way of the world, Mr. Fulton."

My attempt to avoid reacting was wasted because Penny made no effort to hide her surprise. She locked eyes with the Russian. "What did you say?"

Suddenly, the man seemed to remember he spoke English. "I wasn't talking to you. I was talking to your husband."

As if materializing from thin air, my partner, Stone W. Hunter, appeared behind the muscle-bound Eastern European. No one— certainly no one from the Rodina—should've known I was on Ibiza, but even with my hackles up, the coming seconds required careful navigation.

The Russian and I locked stares, and he slid his entire stack of chips forward.

The dealer asked, "Color up?"

The man mumbled, "Bet it all."

The dealer unstacked the chips and restacked them in counted columns. "It's twenty-five thousand, sir. The table maximum is ten thousand."

The Russian grunted. "Bet it all."

I studied his gaze and felt Penny's hand slip from my thigh and onto the table. She pushed all of our chips forward and said, "Us too."

The dealer counted our stacks. "I'm sorry, sir, but the table maximum is ten thousand, and you have fifteen thousand five hundred."

The Russian motioned toward the man beside the dealer. "He will approve no limit."

The pit boss said, "Okay, we'll make the table no limit, but only for one hand."

The other players at the table raked their chips from the betting circles to the rail, and the dealer dealt only to the Russian and me. I received a pair of eights, and the Russian drew a nine and a two. The dealer's up card was a beautiful, perfectly timed six of clubs.

I reached for my wallet, but Penny beat me to it. She pulled a card from her purse and tossed it onto the table as I motioned to split my eights into two hands.

The dealer glanced at the pit boss, who nodded. She dealt me a three to turn my first eight into an eleven, and it was my turn to petition the manager.

He said, "It is no limit for this hand, sir. And your credit is good."

I held up one finger to call for the double down, making my first hand worth thirty thousand dollars. The dealer laid a nine on top of my eleven, giving me a twenty.

I waved her off and pointed toward my second single eight. She dealt another eight, and I motioned to split again. By the time the splitting and doubling down was complete, I had three hands on the table in front of me—a twenty and two nineteens worth a total of seventy-five thousand dollars.

The Russian raised one finger, indicating a double down on his eleven. The pit boss nodded, and the dealer laid a six on the table, giving the Russian a seventeen.

To my surprise, he smiled, leaned back, and tilted his glass to his lips. I'd never wagered anything near the total that lay in front of me on the spotless green felt, but I felt confident with my hands, especially since the dealer was showing a bust card. Either my new friend had more money than the casino, or he was the best actor in Europe.

The dealer revealed her hole card to be a five, and my heart sank. If she drew a ten, she'd make twenty-one, and I'd lose seventy-five thousand dollars.

She tapped the table, drew another card, and I held my breath. She turned up a three, and my confidence was restored. Anything bigger than a seven would mean a bust for the dealer, and the Russian and I would win a total of one hundred twenty-five thousand dollars.

Her next card was a two, giving her a total of sixteen. Casino rules dictated that the dealer must continue taking cards until their hand reached a total of seventeen or greater. With sixteen on the table in front of her, she drew one final card from the shoe, and the Russian leapt to his feet.

"Stop!" he demanded.

The dealer froze, still having not revealed the final card.

The Russian gambler held out a hand toward the dealer. "Lay card facedown on table." He leaned toward me with the stench of cigarette smoke lingering on his skin. "I will bet you one million American dollars she does not bust."

I recounted the dealer's hand. It was still sixteen, and a face card was long overdue from the shoe. Stalling while trying to piece together the Russian's motivation, I said, "Why only one million?"

He laughed and leaned on the table. "Tell your man behind me to move away. I am not afraid of him, but I am afraid of what I might do to him if he tries to detain me."

It was my turn to laugh. "You might be able to bench-press a statue of Lenin, but I'd bet every penny I have that you wouldn't survive fifteen seconds against the man standing behind you."

"Every penny?" he asked.

I nodded. "Every penny."

He pointed at my wife. "Including *that* Penny?"

Hunter threw an arm around the Russian's neck faster than I could get to my feet. Before I closed the distance between us, Hunter had the man pinned facedown on the multicolored carpet of the casino.

I landed a knee on the man's lower back and twisted his muscled arm behind him. "Challenging me is one thing, Boris, or whatever your name is, but when you challenge my wife, you've crossed a line I will always defend. What are you trying to prove?"

Long before casino security arrived, Clark, Singer, and Mongo surrounded Hunter and me. Disco, the final combatant on my team of tier-one operators, took Penny by the arm and led her away.

When a pair of armed security officers arrived and tried to step between my team and the well-grounded bodybuilder, they quickly learned the two of them weren't enough. Radio conversations in rapid-fire Spanish ensued, and soon, four more officers arrived and Clark stepped back to give them access to our prisoner. When the officers identified the man beneath my knee, they froze and turned immediately to the pit boss, who said, "Help him to his suite."

Hunter and I pulled back, and the officers helped the Russian to his feet and encouraged him to follow them.

He yanked his arms from their grasp and yelled at the dealer. "Turn over card!"

I glanced back at the table just as the dealer turned over a two, giving herself eighteen. She raked the Russian's chips from the table and stacked seventy-five thousand dollars in front of my winning hands.

Chapter 4
Working Nine to Five

As security led the Russian away from the table, I raised a finger toward the pit boss. "Have someone lock that up for me, please. And I'd like to speak with you privately."

He whispered something in the dealer's ear and motioned for me to follow him. We stepped through a door beside the cashier's cage, and in excellent English, he said, "What happened back there?"

"That's what I was going to ask you. Who's the Russian? Is he a regular?"

"No. As far as I know, this is his first time in the casino. According to his registration, he is Dmitri Dmitrievich Barkov."

"Barkov?" I asked. "Are you certain?"

"That's how he's registered, and all guests must present a passport to verify their identity. What caused the gentleman to pull Mr. Barkov from his seat?"

"You didn't hear it?" I asked.

"No, sir. I was watching the no-limit hands."

I scratched my head, unsure how much to divulge. "Mr. Barkov—if that is his name—insulted my wife, and my security intervened."

He raised an eyebrow. "Your security?"

"Yes. Only a fool would play with that much money on the table without security."

The pit boss cleared his throat. "The casino has excellent security, sir. There's no reason for you to—"

"With all due respect, your *excellent* security neither heard nor intervened when Barkov threatened my wife."

He said, "A moment ago, you said Mr. Barkov *insulted* your wife. Are you now saying he *threatened* her?"

"Do you not find threats to be insulting?"

"Your point is taken, Mr. Fulton. Your markers are clear. Please feel free to return to the table anytime you'd like. Simply present your player's card, and the dealer will dispense your chips."

"Thank you," I said. "But I think we'll get some air."

He laid a hand against my arm. "There's just one more thing, Mr. Fulton. In the future, please announce your security to our security chief or casino manager."

"Are you the casino manager?"

"No, sir, but I will make sure the manager knows you have personal security while you're here."

I offered my hand with a one-hundred-dollar bill folded in my palm, and he shook it. I said, "Thank you for your kindness."

He checked the camera above the door before opening it for me, and I tried to appear unhurried when I stepped through.

Clark, Hunter, Mongo, and Singer stood near a bank of electronic slot machines and surveying the room. Without a word, I raised my eyes toward the ceiling, and Clark nodded.

Four minutes later, we assembled in our suite, where Penny and Disco were having cocktails on the balcony.

"You've got to stop doing that," Penny said.

"Doing what?"

"Having Disco whisk me away every time it gets weird. I'm not that delicate."

"I know you can take care of yourself," I said, "but there was too much wrong with that situation to leave you in the casino. And now I know why." I instantly had everyone's attention. "The pit boss said the Russian's name is Dmitri Dmitrievich Barkov."

Clark shrugged. "Okay, so the guy was Russian. I understand getting Penny out of there, but who's Dmitri Dmitrievich Barkov?"

I said, "When you and I first met, it was on the heels of my first real mission in Havana. Prior to that mission, I was involved in a mission to protect a racehorse at the Belmont Stakes with an operator named Dutch. Do you know anything about that op?"

Clark shook his head, so I continued. "The horse's name was Silent Storm, and he was owned by none other than Dmitri Barkov."

Clark spun on a heel. "I'm clearly gonna need a drink."

Singer huffed. "If this is going where I think it's going, I may need a drink, and I don't even touch the stuff."

I groaned. "I'm afraid we're all going to need several drinks by the time I finish this story. Barkov not only owned the horse that won the Triple Crown that year, but he was also on the yacht in Havana Harbor when I killed Suslik. In fact, I put a nine-millimeter bullet in Barkov's shoulder that night."

Hunter squinted. "Wait a minute. The musclehead at the table —the guy we put on the ground—he owns a racehorse, and you shot him in the shoulder?"

"No, I think the guy at the table may be Barkov's son."

Hunter asked, "And you think he's after you to square the deal with the bullet in his poppa's shoulder?"

I held up a hand. "As Clark would say, you're putting the cart before the gift horse's mouth. Try to be patient, and I'll bring all this together."

Clark took his first sip. "That's stupid. I'd never say anything like that."

I ignored him. "So, yes, I shot Barkov senior in the shoulder in Havana, but that wasn't the end of the story. As crazy as this sounds, it turned out that Barkov—still the senior Barkov—killed Anya's mother, Katerina Burinkova, because he was in love with her."

Hunter said, "Now I need a drink. Russians are screwed-up people, but this guy, Barkov, killed a woman because he was in love with her? That's messed up in any country."

"No, that's not why he killed her. He cut her heart out in front of Anya when she was four years old because Katerina was in love with Anya's real father, Dr. Robert Richter."

Hunter shuddered. "I'm still not putting it together. Why would Barkov's son show up at the same table as you and run his mouth about Penny?"

"Keep listening," I said. "Here's the important detail you don't know yet. Anya and I killed Dmitri Barkov and sank him in the Strait of Florida." I paused, replaying the fateful afternoon off the Florida Keys. "No, that's not exactly right. Anya killed him, and I helped her sink his body."

"Why?" Hunter asked.

"Why what?"

He cocked his head. "Why were you involved at all? I mean, I get that Anya would want to kill him because he killed her mother, but that doesn't have anything to do with you."

I let his wisdom sink in for a long moment. "You're right, but at the time, it seemed to make sense. Barkov and Dr. Richter were, apparently, old Cold War nemeses. They butted heads over far more than just Anya's mother. Barkov was high-ranking KGB, and Dr. Richter was, well . . . whatever he was. Ultimately, though, he's dead because he was trying to kill us."

Hunter nodded. "That clears it up, regardless of the history. If he was shooting at you, you had to shoot back."

I said, "The shooting was over by the time Barkov and Anya faced off. She put a knife through his chest and growled, 'I am Katerina's heart.'"

Hunter sighed. "She's scary."

I nodded slowly. "Sometimes."

Clark's tumbler was dry when he said, "None of that matters. What matters is the fact that a guy who *could* be Dmitri Barkov's son showed up on Ibiza at the same blackjack table as you and made a wisecrack about Penny."

I said, "There's no question this guy is Dmitri Barkov's son. That's how names work in Russia. A boy takes the masculine form of his father's first name as his middle name. The pit boss said Muscle Boy's name was Dmitri Dmitrievich Barkov. That means his father was Dmitri. The only remaining question is whether his father is *the* Dmitri in question."

Clark said, "I think it's safe to assume we know the lineage. Now, we need to know what Dmitri Junior wants."

"Let's go ask him," I said.

Hunter chuckled. "Just like that, huh? We're going to prance up to his room, knock on his door, and ask him why he's picking on Penny. Is that the plan?"

I said, "I wasn't going to prance, but we have to confront him. Ignoring him isn't going to accomplish anything, and it certainly won't make him go away."

Everyone turned to Clark, and he threw up his hands. "Why's everybody looking at me? I'm the handler. If I get an assignment from above, I pass it down to you. That's the extent of my job."

I rolled my eyes. "Pretend for just a minute that you're still a door-kicker. Do you know of any doors that need to be kicked?"

"Oh," he said. "We know a door needs some good kicking. We just need to know which door is his."

Skipper, our analyst, spoke up for the first time. "Is he staying here?"

I said, "I think so."

She pulled her laptop from the coffee table and stroked a few keys. "Dmitri Barkov is booked in room . . . Oh, get this. He's in suite seventeen seventy-six."

I laughed. "I'm sure the irony is lost on him, but it amuses me. Let's go rattle his cage and show him what a few British traitors started a couple hundred years ago."

"Not so fast," Skipper said. "Let me do a little snooping before you go barging in on God knows who or what." Her fingers disappeared into a blur as she plunged into her keyboard. A couple minutes later, she leaned back and sighed. "Okay, he's definitely not alone. He arrived on a private jet five days ago. It was a chartered jet, though, and not registered to him. It belongs to a company called European Express. That's a charter service out of Helsinki, but that doesn't matter except to say Barkov obviously doesn't have his own jet."

"That's interesting," I said. "If this guy is the Barkov in question, I assume he would've inherited his daddy's fortune. I thought Barkov senior was loaded—like the billionaires' club kind of loaded."

Skipper twisted her mouth. "That *is* interesting. I'm still working on the passenger manifest, but there were four other people on the plane, not counting the flight crew."

"How long will it take to get their names?"

"It depends. It's possible I'll never get their names. Travel in Western Europe is so crazy these days. Sometimes you need a passport, and sometimes nobody cares. It looks like Barkov and his passengers' flight originated in Vilnius. It departed Helsinki before that, but with only three souls on board. That's likely the flight crew—two pilots and a flight attendant."

I said, "Okay, I'll be the one to ask. Where on Earth is Vilnius?"

Skipper and Mongo laughed, and our giant said, "It's the capital of Lithuania, near the border with Belarus."

I said, "And Belarus shares a nice long friendly border with Russia, right?"

"Don't put the pieces together just because you think they fit," Skipper said. "The four other people could be his wife, mother-in-law, and two kids. We don't know yet."

I lowered my chin. "And we'll never know if you don't get to work on it."

"Oh, really? If that's how it's going to be, I get off at five and come back to work at nine tomorrow morning."

Chapter 5
That Doesn't Exist

After some labor and working-condition negotiations, Skipper reconsidered her position and put in a little overtime. In my world, labor relations are primarily made up of extensive begging on my part, and once again, it worked.

"Scooch in and take a look at this," Skipper said as she spun her laptop toward the rest of us.

"Scooch?" I said. "Is that a real word, or did you make it up?"

She grinned. "Just like when Clark speaks in whatever language he speaks, you knew what I meant."

We scooched, and Skipper narrated. "I couldn't find anything through immigration on the charter manifest, but I did manage to sneak my way into the resort's security camera footage archive, and look what I found."

I leaned in as the video played in fast-forward. When our Russian friend appeared at the check-in counter, Skipper returned the video to actual speed. He presented a card and signed an electronic screen.

"That only shows Dmitri," I said.

"Keep your pants on, Dr. Impatient. Count the key cards the clerk slides across the desk."

She slowed the video, and I watched the cards hit the desk. "I see six."

Skipper said, "Yep, me too. That likely means three rooms if they issue two keys per room. I'm only guessing at that, of course, but wait . . . there's more."

The camera angle changed, and we were suddenly looking at the lobby door of the resort. Dmitri led the way through the door with four other men who made him look like a dwarf.

Skipper said, "Watch the split."

The four men following Dmitri spread out and positioned themselves perfectly throughout the lobby to cover every angle.

I leaned back. "It looks like we're dealing with pros."

Hunter nodded. "Yep, but I'm not intimidated. Are you?"

"Not intimidated," I said. "Just a little more cautious. Any guesses at who or what they are?"

Clark said, "I've got one, but it's a little dark."

"Let's hear it," I said.

"It could be wet work."

"On me?" I asked. "If they're here to kill me, why would they give me a warning at the blackjack table? Wouldn't a professional Russian hit squad just stick me with a dart or put a bullet in my skull and vanish?"

"Maybe. But maybe Dmitri is an egomaniac and needs you to know who's hitting you."

I let my eyes climb the wall and explore the ornate ceiling. "Why would he threaten Penny?"

Hunter asked, "Was it really a threat? What I heard was something about a bet, and he wanted to know if you were willing to bet her."

"Yeah, but he knew her name."

Clark said, "Back to the ego thing. This guy probably wanted to make an impression."

I laughed. "I think we were the ones who made the impression."

Skipper palmed her forehead. "That's exactly what it was!"

I said, "What?"

"The threat on Penny wasn't real. He did that for one reason . . . To get a reaction out of you and us. He wanted to see how many of us were waiting and ready to jump into the fight. Dmitri was doing his groundwork."

I let out a long breath. "I'm afraid you may be right, and now he knows everybody's face."

Clark said, "Let's hit him and find out. I'm up for a little friendly Q and A. How 'bout the rest of you?"

Hunter leapt to his feet. "Let's do it."

"Not so fast," I said. "I'm thinking about going alone but wired for sound. You know, a little man-to-man chat. What do you think?"

Penny tossed in her two cents' worth. "I don't like it. If these guys are what you think they are, is it really a good idea to go in there alone?"

"I understand your hesitance," I said, "but I'm not easy to kill, and these guys will be right outside the door. I think Dmitri is far more likely to show me his hand, one-on-one, than with a mob breathing down his neck."

"As always, it's up to you, but I don't like it."

Hunter said, "I'll go in alone if you don't want Chase out on a limb."

Penny shook her head. "No, I don't like the idea of any of you going in alone. What if all five of them are in that room?"

Singer spoke up in his subdued baritone. "Head counts are easy. Show me the window, and I'll tell you how many bedbugs are under the mattress."

"I don't care about bedbugs," I said. "But a good head count would come in handy. If they're rolling deep up there, we'll hit them hard, but if Barkov is alone, I'll look him in the eye and get the truth out of him."

"Now, that makes me happy," Penny said.

Skipper rattled the keys of her laptop and spun around a few seconds later. "Suite seventeen seventy-six is on the northeast corner. You can't miss it."

Singer pulled his cell phone from a pocket and checked the screen. "I've got plenty of charge. All I need is a pair of binoculars and ten minutes."

Clark tossed the binoculars to our sniper, and he headed out the door.

Right on time, Skipper's phone rang ten minutes later. She punched the speaker button. "Let's have it."

Singer said, "The Russian has good taste. Why can't you get us a suite like that?"

"I can book it, but Chase has to write the check, and you know how he is."

"Yep, he's tight for sure. I've got your head count. It's three, but two of them appear to be hourly rentals. Dmitri probably won't appreciate the interruption, but the girls look like they're bored, so they'll likely welcome a visitor."

Singer was back before I thought it possible. "How did you get off the roof so fast?"

"I wasn't on the roof. I'd love to claim I did something spectacular like scale the outside of the building and parachute off the top, but I'll stick with the boring truth. There's an observation deck on the eighteenth floor of that hotel." He pointed through the window. "I just rode the elevator up, took a peek, and headed home. Nothing to it."

"Nicely done. Giving me the layout would be spectacular, so let's do that."

Skipper slid a blank sheet of paper and a pencil across the table, and Singer sketched the suite.

I studied the rough drawing. "Now, all we need is a key."

"Already on it," Skipper said. "By the time Clark gets you wired up, I'll have the door unlocked."

I pulled off my shirt, and my handler wired me for sound.

"You're ready to go," he said.

I buttoned my shirt, stuck my holstered pistol in place over my appendix, and grabbed a pair of bathrobes from behind the bathroom door.

"What are those for?" Clark asked.

"Just in case."

"In case of what?"

The rest of the team slipped their earpieces in place, and we did a comms check.

I gave Skipper the eye, and she said, "Tell me when you're in place, and listen for the click."

"You're the best," I said.

"I'm better than that."

We took the stairs two at a time so we could get an idea of what we'd face if we had to exfiltrate back down that route. Stairways in huge buildings tend to collect people and discarded detritus. Knowing what to expect on an exfil route is always a handy piece of intel.

When we reached the seventeenth floor, I turned to the team. "Everybody ready?"

Heads nodded, and Clark said, "Let's do it."

Trying to appear harmless, Clark, Hunter, Singer, Disco, Mongo, and I poured through the heavy metal doorway and into the corridor. Thankfully, no one was there to see us except the collection of cameras mounted in the ceiling.

I stepped in front of the door to suite 1776 and said, "Open sesame."

The lock clicked, and I twisted the handle. Slowly pushing the door inward, I peered through the crack to find the swing arm security latch in place. Hunter stepped beside me and slid a pair of miniature bolt cutters through the crack. He made short work of the arm, and I stepped through the door.

The foyer was empty and dark, but the suite was beautiful. The elegant fixtures and oversized furniture made our rooms look like the Happy Family Motor Lodge.

Singer's sketch was spot-on, and I moved silently through the space. The bedroom door was ajar, though not open far enough to see the occupants of the room, but seeing them wasn't necessary. I made out three distinct voices in the jumble of sounds, and only one of them sounded remotely Russian.

I raised my shirt enough to grip my pistol with my right hand as I held the robes in my left. I pushed the bedroom door open until it stopped against the wall. In an instant, I crossed the room and took my stand at the foot of Dmitri's bed.

The blonde was the first to notice me, and she screamed as if she'd been shot. The brunette followed her friend's gaze to my six-foot-four-inch, two hundred twenty–pound frame standing only a few feet away. She didn't scream but stepped from the bed and held out her hand. I laid a robe across her fingers and tossed the second one to the blonde.

Dmitri looked up without a hint of surprise. "Is okay, girls. I will have talk with man, and you will come back in quarter of hour."

The women slinked out of the room, and I wondered how challenging it would be for my team, waiting just beyond the door, to convince the women to keep the invasion to themselves. The last thing we needed was a pair of ambitious young police officers trying to figure out what six armed Americans and one naked Russian billionaire were doing in a luxury suite in Ibiza.

I lifted a towel from the floor and tossed it toward Dmitri. "Put some clothes on. We need to talk."

He slipped from the bed and pulled on a pair of boxer shorts and a T-shirt, never taking his eyes from mine. "You have minor upper hand for moment, Chase Fulton, but this will change soon. You made terrible mistake of judgment coming into my room tonight."

"Why's that, Dmitri Barkov?"

He hung a thumb in the arm of his shirt, stretched the material over his bicep, and nodded. "I am impressed. Perhaps you are better at this game than maybe I believed. Congratulations for knowing already my name. This is very quick for clumsy American."

"Let's take a walk," I said.

He raised his sculpted shoulders. "This is for me fine. Where are we going?"

"To the living room. I'll stand by the window, and you'll sit on the center of the sofa."

Dmitri smiled. "This detailed instruction is for waiting team outside, yes? So, if they come inside quickly, they will shoot only me and not you, no?"

"You catch on quickly, comrade."

He narrowed his gaze. "And you are coward who is afraid to face one man without team to save you from fight."

I followed the Russian through the door and into the living room. A glance at the door of the suite showed me a tiny fiberoptic camera lens and microphone protruding just above the threshold.

With the lens and mic in place, I tore open my shirt and peeled the commo gear from my chest. "There you go. There's the coward's commo. Now, sit down anywhere you want."

His demeanor changed, and he watched my feet—an old KGB technique to predict an opponent's coming movement.

He finally planted himself in an oversized chair and lit a cigarette. "What do you want, Chase Fulton?"

"That's not the question. The question is, what do you want? Why are you here, Dmitri?"

"I will tell to you what I want." He pulled the cigarette from his mouth and dusted the ash on the carpet. "I am here for one of two possible solutions. Both you and I know you killed my father. For this, there is international warrant."

"So, that's it. You're here to arrest me?"

He examined his cigarette. "If this is necessary, yes, but I have also one other possibility."

"Let me guess . . . You'd rather kill me."

He dropped the cigarette onto the carpet and ground it beneath his bare foot. "This is why America is weak and Soviet Union will—"

"The Soviet Union doesn't exist, Dmitri."

He smiled. "This is one more reason America will beg for us to remove our Soviet heel from your neck. You believe we are gone because we have name of only Russia and no longer Soviet Union. Ha! You are fool. Arrogant fool."

"Get off your soapbox, Lenin. You're dreaming." I stuck out my hands. "If you're going to arrest me, do it. Let's get it out of the way. What are you? FSB? GRU?"

His smile turned to laughter. "You think you know so much, but you are foolish child. If you think you are strong enough to survive inside Black Dolphin Prison, you are more than foolish. No one leaves Black Dolphin alive."

I reseated my pistol deep into its holster and motioned toward the sofa. "Mind if I sit down while you're making up fairy tales?"

"What is this fairy tales?" he growled.

"The Dolphin," I said. "I just happen to know someone who escaped alive and is doing quite well in the free world."

Dmitri buried his fingernails into the arm of his chair. "When this is over, I will kill you with bare hands."

I held up my palms. "With my bare hands . . . or yours? Your English isn't great, Dmitri. You should really work on that. But if you'd feel more comfortable threatening me in Russian, my Russian is a lot better than your English."

"Is not threat, *Amerikanets*. Is to you prophecy. Now, shut up with silly games. You must now make choice."

"What choice, Dmitri? I'm the only one in this room with a gun and clothes. I have all the choices in the world. You're the one with limited options here."

He laughed. "Even you are not stupid enough to kill me inside hotel room with your face inside security cameras in hallway and elevator."

"Oh, Dmitri . . . how naïve you are. The Cold War is over, and the good guys won. We've come a long way since the days of dead drops and cyanide capsules. We have control of every camera in the building, and I took the stairs for a little exercise. You're right about one thing, though. I probably won't shoot you unless there's no other option, but if I think you're a genuine threat when this conversation is over, I'll throw you off that balcony."

"Stop making me laugh. You are puny little man. I will tear you into pieces if you try to touch me."

"Let's get back to these choices you seem to think I have. So far, you've only come up with one, and even though I'm not afraid of your little prison, I'd love to see what's behind door number two."

"First choice is arrest on international warrant and trial inside Russia for murder of my father. This choice will have only two possible endings. You will be shot by firing squad or spend rest of short life inside prison." He resituated himself in the chair. "Second is partnership."

"Partnership? With whom?"

"With *Sluzhba Vneshney Razvedki Rossiyskoy Federatsii*."

"Oh, that explains it. You must be a lowly SVR corporal or file clerk."

He exploded from his seat and drove a finger through the air. "What I am is *Oprichnik*, and you are tiny worm beneath my boot!"

I threw a short kick to his kneecap with the heel of my robotic foot, and he melted to the ground. As he rolled on the carpet with his knee cradled in his palms, I said, "Next time you come at me, I'll drill holes through your chest. *Ponyat'*, comrade?"

He growled like a furious bear. "*Idi na khuy!*"

I planted a heel against his forehead and shoved him backward against the chair he'd occupied only seconds before. "Watch your mouth, Dmitri. If you're going to arrest me, get up, put some clothes on, and do it. Otherwise, get on your rented airplane and fly back to your beloved Soviet Union . . . that doesn't exist."

Chapter 6
That's the Question

I left Dmitri on the floor of his luxurious suite and strolled through the door as if nothing had happened inside. Everything about the time spent with Barkov was surprising, but not as much as what I saw—or rather, didn't see—when I stepped into the hallway.

Instead of five teammates holding two ladies of the evening, I found only Disco and Hunter.

"Where's everybody else, and why did they leave?"

Hunter said, "If you hadn't ripped your comms off, you'd know Dmitri activated a panic alarm, launching his henchmen into action."

"Henchmen, you say?"

He made a face. "Okay, I don't really know what a henchman is, but you get the picture. Clark decided to cut the "ladies" loose since they weren't likely to call the cops. Disco was smart enough to bring the fiberoptic gear, so we could see and hear you, but not vice-versa."

"So, what about the rest of the team?"

"They were playing patty-cake with Dmitri's men, but they got bored, so they're on their way back to our *lesser* suite."

"Fair enough," I said. "Let's go. We've got a lot to discuss."

Back in our suite, Clark took charge of the meeting. "Here's what we know. Barkov's men aren't exactly Spetsnaz. They were way too easy to put down. We left them bound and gagged, but the important question is, what happened with dear old Dmitri?"

I said, "I dismissed his entertainment for the evening and listened to him tell me how I was either going to spy for the SVR, or he was going to send me to the Black Dolphin Prison. He kept saying he had an international arrest warrant for me for killing his father."

Skipper said, "Yeah, I caught that, and I'm on it, but I can't find any warrants, international or otherwise. And if I can't find it, it probably doesn't exist. It's more likely he's using the term 'international warrant,' when, in reality, it's just a local warrant from some Russian judge, if it exists at all."

I scratched my chin. "This is starting to sound like a pretty good opportunity to feed some high-quality disinformation to the SVR. All I have to do now is find a way to surrender and take Barkov's deal without sounding too eager."

Clark grunted. "Easy there, College Boy. I love your aggresivosity, but you can't jump in bed with Barkov without running it up the chain of command. This thing is too big for us to call an audible in the field. I'll brief the Board, and we'll see what they think."

"Aggression," I said.

Clark frowned. "What?"

"The word you were looking for is *aggression*, not *aggresivosity*. Your English is only slightly better than Barkov's."

He drew his phone and gave me a look. "I'll show you some aggresivosity *and* aggression if you don't stop hounding me about how I talk."

I held out a hand. "Hmm . . . I wonder why it's not shaking. You didn't expect that to actually scare me, did you?"

Before he could play any more verbal judo with me, someone answered his call. "Good evening, sir. Clark Johnson here. Do you have ten minutes to hear an operational opportunity?"

Apparently, the voice said, "Yes," so Clark spent the next several minutes detailing the events of the previous hours. When he was finished, he listened for a few seconds and said, "Roger, sir. Talk to you then."

With the phone call ended and the vocabulary lesson well forgotten, Clark turned to Skipper. "Set up a video conference call in one hour."

She looked up. "With whom?"

He tossed his phone to her. "The details will arrive in a text message within ten minutes."

She caught the phone. "Consider it done."

"What did they say?" I asked.

He plopped himself onto a stool. "They didn't say anything, College Boy. *They* is plural, and I was only talking to *one* person. You meant to ask, what did *he* say?"

I couldn't resist grinning. "Actually, it's more complicated than that, but you're on the right track. What did *he* say?"

"He said to have Skipper set up a video conference call so our whole team could see the entire Board when the orders come down. It looks like they're making good on their promise to be more transparent. I guess we'll see how long that lasts."

The text message came, and Skipper went to work arranging the camera and seating for the whole team. In the middle of her scrambling, she stopped and stood erect. "Uh, what about the others?"

"What others?" I asked.

"You know, Penny and Irina."

"Good question. Give me a minute." I pondered the question and came to a conclusion. "Let's include them, but let's do it invisibly and silently."

Skipper said, "No problem. I'll put them behind the camera and tell them to be quiet."

"Not just quiet. Silent."

The hour passed, and the scene was set. Clark and I filled the center of the screen with the team arranged in a semicircle around us.

Penny pointed toward the left side of our arrangement. "That area is in shadow. You'll want some lighting over there."

Skipper raised an eyebrow. "Remember that thing I said about being silent? It started two minutes ago. We're not shooting a movie, Ms. Hollywood. We're briefing an initial tactical action plan. How many of those have you filmed?"

Penny ducked her head, and Skipper said, "That's what I thought. Now, plant your pretty little butt in that pretty little chair, and don't start believing it's a director's throne. It's not."

To my surprise, Penny did precisely as she was told, but I made a mental note never to try Skipper's technique with my wife.

With everything and everyone in place, Skipper said, "If we're ready, I'll make the connection."

"Let's do it," I said.

She spun in her seat, and seconds later, the full Board appeared on the oversized monitor, and introductions were made.

Bradford Rawlings III appeared to be the voice of the Board. "I've briefed my colleagues on what Mr. Johnson told me, but we'd like to hear it directly from Dr. Fulton, if that wouldn't be too much trouble."

Clark turned to me as if surrendering the floor, and I told the story of how Barkov, Penny, and I ended up at the same blackjack table, and every detail of the interaction.

I paused to give the members of the Board who were taking notes time to catch up.

Rawlings said, "Please continue."

"We decided to confront Barkov in his suite, and that's exactly what we did. As is almost always the case in situations like that, the environment and outcome were a little different than we expected. There's no need to brief the details other than to say, things got a little physical, but we prevailed."

"We would expect nothing less," Rawlings said.

I continued. "Ultimately, Barkov stuck to his story about having an international warrant for my arrest in connection with his father's disappearance."

"Disappearance?" Rawlings asked.

"Barkov actually said murder, but there was no body to recover, and there were certainly no witnesses."

Rawlings cleared his throat. "Forgive me, Chase . . . if I may call you Chase."

"Of course.

"Forgive me, but the way I read the after-action report, it was clear that you were not the elder Barkov's killer, but were, in fact, a witness to his termination. Is my recollection inaccurate?"

I played the scene through my mind from a dozen years before when Anya Burinkova thrust her knife through Barkov's chest and growled, "*YA serdtse Kateriny.*"

After gathering my composure, I said, "No, sir. Your recollection is correct. I didn't actually kill Barkov. Anastasia Burinkova terminated him, at least partially to avenge her mother's murder by Barkov's hand. He cut out her heart in front of her when she was only four years old. I'm sure that's what she meant when she declared herself to be 'Katerina's heart.'"

Seemingly unmoved by my description of Barkov's final seconds on Earth, Rawlings said, "So, your only alibi is Anya Burinkova, who actually committed the act for which you are being pursued. This creates an interesting legal quagmire. Even if you *were* arrested and tried inside the former Soviet Union for

Barkov's murder, the only person who could save you from execution or life in prison is a Russian SVR officer turned defector who the Kremlin may believe is dead. Is that accurate, Dr. Fulton?"

"Please call me Chase. And yes, Anya is the only person who could testify that I did not kill Barkov. There's no chance she would return to Russia in any official capacity. Before she could take the stand to clear my name, she'd be arrested, taken to Yasenevo, and likely placed in front of a firing squad before the sun went down."

"I'm not sure that's an accurate assessment of how modern Russia would deal with a dissident."

I shot a look at Clark, and the two of us burst into laughter. "Mr. Rawlings, with all due respect, how many Russians have you stood toe to toe with in the last twenty years?"

He offered a slight bow of his head. "Forgive me for discounting your experience with the Russians. I must admit that my time behind the Iron Curtain happened when Ronald Reagan was still an actor and not yet our president."

As he spoke, the wheels turned inside my skull.

Skipper noticed and whispered, "Are you okay?"

I mouthed, "Maybe."

I turned my back to the camera and hid Clark from the lens. "We have to talk to Anya."

He nodded. "You're right."

Having neither seen nor heard our conversation, Skipper raised a finger. "I'm on it."

Clark took command of the meeting. "Gentlemen, forgive me, but something has come up that directly affects this potential operation, and we have to deal with it. As much as I hate to cut you short, we'll have to reconvene later."

Rawlings said, "We're not as incompetent as you might expect, Mr. Johnson. We've already tried, and Anya cannot be found. It seems as if she's dropped off the face of the Earth."

Skipper peered into the camera. "But I've not tried yet."

Rawlings smiled. "If we can't find Anya, I doubt you'll be able to do any better, but please feel free to shake all the trees you want. I am curious about one thing, though. What are you going to ask her if and when you do find her?"

Clark and Skipper turned to me, and I said, "I think we need to know if she's interested in terminating another Barkov."

Chapter 7
A Better Idea

"Can you find her?" I asked the second she cut the feed with the Board.

Skipper rolled her eyes. "If she's alive and on the planet, I can."

"Do you think you have methods and access the Board doesn't?"

The eye rolling continued. "I've got methods and access *nobody* else has. Now, leave me alone. I've got work to do."

Penny timidly rose from her non-director's chair. "You're not really thinking of having Anya waltz in and kill this guy, are you?"

I slid my hand onto the small of her back. That was one of my hand's favorite spots. "No, I'm not thinking of having anyone waltz in and kill him. I don't even want to kill him. I just want to get to the bottom of all this without getting locked up in a Russian prison."

"That's not a real possibility, is it?"

I pulled her toward me. "No, sweetheart. It's just a threat from a lunatic. As Clark might say, we're going to take the lemons Barkov hands us and turn them into cheeseburgers."

She squinted. "What?"

"See? Welcome to my world. I never know what he's talking about, either."

Skipper leaned closer to her laptop and adjusted her glasses. That wasn't her typical posture.

"What's wrong?" I asked.

She held up a finger and dived back into the keyboard. "Give me a minute."

Clark jumped into the mix. "So, what's next, College Boy? Are you going to turn yourself in to Barkov and let him haul you off to the gulag?"

"Not just yet," I said. "I'm intrigued by the Board's interest in who actually killed the senior Barkov and who was there to witness the thing."

"Why could any of that matter?" he asked.

"I don't know, but something about it doesn't smell right. I'm trying to put my head into a space it was never meant to go. I'm trying to think like the son of a murdered Russian oligarch. I need to know why he thinks I had anything to do with his dear old daddy's death. But that's not the big question. What I really want to know is why he thinks I'd believe his story about an international warrant."

"I get that," he said. "But what's his play going to be if you call his bluff on the warrant?"

"Right now, I believe he's trying to get into—or back into—the good graces of the SVR at Yasenevo by recruiting an American operative as a spy. He suspects I had something to do with his father's disappearance, so he probably thinks he can scare me enough to convince me to spill my guts."

Clark pulled the toothpick from his mouth and waved the wet end toward me. "You know something, College Boy? You're pretty bright sometimes."

"I try, but I could be wrong about all of this. Maybe he does have something he believes is a real warrant. Who am I to say? The thing that has me concerned is how close Skipper's face is to that screen. She's struggling, and that can only mean one of two things. She either can't find Anya, or she found her and doesn't like where she found her."

Clark looked around me and at our analyst. "So, ask her."

I huffed. "She told me to give her a minute, and when that happens, I give her three."

Irina stepped between Clark and me. "Forgive interruption, but I have for you maybe idea you have not thought of."

Her English skills had grown exponentially since she came to America, but the use of articles was still years away.

"Tell me your idea," I said.

"Is maybe not best idea, but is idea from inside head of only Russian person in room. Maybe *order na arrest* is not for you. Maybe is for Anya. Tell to me exactly what Barkov said to you when he claims to have *order na arrest*."

"The word you're looking for is arrest warrant," I said.

"Yes, of course. Sometimes, my mouth only works in Russian, but think hard, and remember exactly what he said."

I followed her order and replayed the scenario with Barkov. "He said, 'Both you and I know you killed my father. For this, there is international warrant.'"

She widened both eyes. "See? Russian language is better language than English. Is precise language, but does not always translate with precision. Think about what he said."

I replayed the scene a dozen times, but it never changed. "I don't know where you're taking me, so I'm going to need some help."

"Is simple. Barkov did not say to you, 'I have arrest warrant for you.' He said, 'For *this* there is international warrant.' You understand difference?"

I shook my head. "I'm sorry, but I'm still not getting it."

She laid a palm on my cheek. "Close eyes, and listen in Russian."

She spoke the two phrases in her native language as I listened intently. My Russian was rusty, but played side by side, the two sentences weren't remotely similar.

I palmed my forehead. "He wasn't saying that *he* has an international arrest warrant for me. He was saying there was a price on his father's head. It's the difference between an arrest warrant and a hit contract. He's not lying. He's just translating poorly into a language he doesn't understand very well."

She touched the tip of her nose with her index finger and smiled. "*Tochno!*"

I smiled. "Exactly, indeed."

Before I could celebrate the epiphany, Skipper said, "Uh, we've got a problem. The Board was right. Anya is gone."

Penny was the first to speak. "If you had any idea how many times I thought that was true, you wouldn't be worried. Just relax and wait. She always comes back."

I wondered if I was the only person in the room who felt the blade slide beneath my ribs. "What do you mean she's gone?"

Skipper leaned back in her chair and motioned toward the laptop with both hands. "She's gone. Just . . . gone."

"What about that agent at the DOJ?" I asked.

She looked up. "Ray White?"

"No, the other one. The woman. I can't remember her name."

She hit the keyboard with several shots from her fingertips, and a woman who looked like she could've been a stunt double for Jessica Alba filled the screen. "This one?"

"I don't know. I've never seen her."

Skipper said, "Her name is Gwynn Davis, and she's Anya's partner at the DOJ while they're on field missions. It seems like they're pretty good friends outside of work, too. That's why I started my search with her, but she's not seen or heard from Anya in almost two weeks."

"Is that unusual?"

"It's not rare when taken by itself," she said, "But there's a lot more. Anya's last cell phone ping was in Daugavpils, Latvia."

"Latvia? What's in Latvia?"

Skipper shrugged. "How should I know?"

"How long was she there?"

"There's no way to know. Her phone was there for thirty-six hours before it died. After that, I have no idea."

I said, "Bring up a map of Northern Europe." Soon, the screen was full of the region, and I leaned in. "Now, show me Daugavpils."

Skipper slid her mouse over the city in extreme Southern Latvia. "It's right here."

"And remind me where Barkov and his buddies climbed aboard their chartered jet."

Skipper closed her eyes and let her head fall backward until she was facing the ceiling. "Oh, my God. They got on in Vilnius, Lithuania, less than a hundred miles away from Daugavpils."

"Let's look at this objectively," I said. "If the SVR dispatched Barkov—and maybe others—to round up Barkov senior's killers, they're after me and Anya. The cell phone pings put the younger Barkov and Anya within a hundred miles of each other less than a week ago. Is it a stretch for us to assume Barkov had something to do with Anya's disappearance?"

Skipper said, "Wait a minute! It's too early to call it a disappearance. She's done this before, and she's very good at it. I've simply not found her yet, but I will."

I groaned. "But if the Russians got to her, you may find her on a prison roll, or even worse, in the obituaries."

I tried to avoid looking directly at Penny. I didn't want to see her reaction. Our situation was serious enough without pouring a steaming pile of emotions on top of it.

"So, what do you recommend?" Skipper asked.

"I don't know yet, but I'm open to suggestions."

Mongo wasted no time in spitting out his opinion. "I say we go upstairs and hang that steroid weasel off the balcony until he tells us where Anya is."

Mine wasn't the only attention Mongo's suggestion caught. Irina glared at the giant as if she were on the verge of sticking a dagger through his sternum. In some combination of Russian and English, she said, "And just what makes you so concerned about Anya when it is Chase who is target for this man Barkov?"

Mongo took a step back. "It's . . . I know it's Chase . . . Okay, forget the balcony idea."

Irina couldn't maintain the icy Russian glare any longer and burst into uncontrollable giggling.

Penny joined her and said, "It's fun messing with them, isn't it?"

Mongo stared at me, but I was smart enough to keep my mouth shut. As the giggling died, the big man whispered, "Does that mean we can still hang him over the balcony?"

"I've got a better idea," I said. "I think we should let him dangle me over the balcony."

Clark said, "I don't know what you're talking about, but I don't like it."

"Relax. Skipper says there's no warrant. Irina says it's a translation thing. I say it's a bluff. Let's find out who's right."

"I still don't like it," Clark said. "But I see where you're headed. Are we rolling deep, or are you going in alone?"

"Alone? Ha. If that guy gets me in his hands, he'll wring me like a dishrag, and I'm not interested in taking that chance. He's probably discovered his hog-tied friends by now, and they're likely lining up to hit us head-to-head. I say we go in strong, hold our ground, and see if he flinches."

Skipper looked up. "You're going to hit him twice in one night?"

"Sure, why not? He'd never expect it, and that alone would give us a tremendous advantage. You know how much I love an enemy on his heels."

"Whatever. You're the boss. Just tell me when to pop the lock."

My glance toward Clark garnered the expected response. "Go get 'em, College Boy."

My team was on their feet and stuffing micro speakers into their ears in seconds. Press-checks to ensure our weapons were loaded followed, and we were out the door in less than a minute. The climb went quickly as our footfalls echoed through the chamber of the stairwell.

At the seventeenth floor, I held up a hand. "Is everybody good?" Nods followed, and I said, "Keep your heads down. I'll be first through the door. I want Hunter in the slot in front of Singer and Mongo."

We slipped through the heavy steel door and into the carpeted hallway, where our strides were silent and perfectly in sync. We passed suite 1774, and I said, "Hit the door, Skipper."

The instant we stepped in front of Barkov's suite, the light above the handle turned from red to green, and I twisted the knob. My team and I had made thousands of multiple-man tactical entries in both training and real-world situations, so every man knew precisely what every other man would do in every situation. The action was muscle memory with zero hesitation. An instant of indecision could leave an operator spilling his own blood all over the floor instead of making the bad guys lose theirs. If blood was going to flow that day, it wouldn't be ours.

I cleared the doorway with my pistol just below my field of vision. In an instant, I could raise the weapon and deliver lethal punishment against any adversary, but in the tenths of seconds during which I scanned the room, no targets of any kind presented themselves. My feet carried me into the room and to the right without conscious thought, but my eyes detected a distinctive change from the last time I was in the room.

Hunter brushed past me as he moved left an instant after breaking the plane of the door, and I didn't have to look to know that Mongo and Singer were moving forward into the open space of the suite.

Our dynamic entry into the room would typically involve no effort to move quietly. We would burst into the room with demanding voices and aggressive movement, leaving little doubt that we commanded the environment, but the empty room dictated that we retain the element of surprise by moving as quietly as possible. When we encountered a target, we'd bark orders and demonstrate our willingness to inflict harm on anyone who resisted, but for the moment, silence was king.

With the main room clear, the team morphed into a new configuration with Singer on point, Hunter still number two, and Mongo behind me. Putting Mongo's enormous frame in front of anyone eliminated that shooter's ability to see anything in front of him, so the big man would always bring up the rear.

The small corridor leading to the pair of bedrooms was the perfect choke point. Once we were inside that fatal funnel, an ambush would be nothing short of catastrophic for us, so Mongo and I slowed our pace to avoid putting all four of us inside the kill zone at once. Singer and Hunter spent less than a second in the corridor and pushed their way into the room on the left.

I led Mongo through the door on the right, making an almost silent entry, but what came next was anything but quiet. Terror filled the woman's eyes, and she screamed as if she'd seen the devil himself. I had already begun my move to the right so Mongo could clear the left side of the room. Seeing the giant consume the space in front of her, the woman froze in terrified, shuddering silence, her scream muffled by her own horror.

I felt, more than heard, Hunter and Singer step into the room behind us, and the woman wilted to the floor from the shock of seeing four armed commandos only feet away with weapons drawn.

"I've got her," Singer said as he took a knee beside the trembling woman. "It's okay, ma'am. We're not going to hurt you. We just need to know where the man who's staying in this suite went."

She swallowed hard and couldn't stop her eyes from darting wildly around the room.

Singer spoke in a soothing voice I would love to be able to produce. "Listen to me, ma'am. Just look at me. Everything is going to be fine. What's your name?"

"Tabitha." The word escaped her lips like those of a whimpering child.

"It's okay, Tabitha. No one is going to hurt you. We're here for the man who rented this room. Can you tell me where he is?"

The word seemed to stick in her throat, so she shook her head in short, choppy motions.

Singer brushed a strand of hair from her face. "There's no reason to be afraid. You're perfectly safe. Just tell us where he is."

She sobbed and labored for her next breath. "He's gone. I don't know where. He checked out, and he's gone. I'm only cleaning the room. That's all. Please don't hurt me."

Singer cradled her hands in his. "Come on. Let me help you stand up. I'm sorry we frightened you."

He helped her to the edge of the bed. "You're okay now. It's important that you understand we need to find this man before he hurts anyone else. Are you certain you don't know where he went?"

She licked her lips, and her shoulders relaxed. "No, I don't know where he went. I'm just here to clean the room. That's all. Maybe the front desk can tell you where he went. Are you police officers or something?"

"Yes, ma'am. That's right. And that's why it's so important that you not tell anyone we were here. This man is extremely dangerous, and if you tell anyone you saw us, it's possible someone could tip him off that we're coming, and you don't want that, do you?"

She shook her head, this time much more confidently. "I have to tell my supervisor. She knows how long it takes me to clean a room, and I'll be in trouble."

Singer pressed a pair of folded bills into her palm. "What's your supervisor's name? We'll take care of everything. Just keep this between us, okay?"

Chapter 8
Little Russian Princess

Back in our suite, Skipper labored furiously in search of Barkov and his group. "I don't understand it. They're just gone."

"What about the charter company?" I asked. "Have you tried them?"

"I've tried everything," she said. "There are no jets from European Express anywhere near Ibiza, and I can't find Barkov's name on any manifests off the island."

"How about the ferry back to the mainland?"

She cocked her head. "Which one? The one to Valencia, Gandía, Dénia, or the nice long one up to Barcelona? There's, of course, another option. There are three ferries per day that run from Ibiza to Mallorca, and then dozens to the mainland from there. Oh, and by the way, there's no manifest for any of the ferries. It's simply a matter of buying a ticket—or stealing a pass—and driving or walking aboard."

Clark let out a long, low whistle. "So, we're chasing a puff of smoke in a cumulous cloud."

Skipper nodded. "I couldn't have said it better myself, but I have a hunch we shouldn't worry about finding Barkov."

I gave our analyst a look, and she said, "He's not running from us. I think he's regrouping to take another shot at us. Or, more specifically, another shot at *you*."

I chewed on my bottom lip. "I think you're right, but I'd prefer having the home-field advantage next time he makes a run at us."

Penny slid onto the corner of the desk and lifted the phone from its cradle. Ten minutes later, a pair of armed, uniformed men arrived in our suite with a briefcase.

"Can I help you?" I asked.

The first man thrust the briefcase toward me. "We're from the casino, Mr. Fulton. Your wife asked us to close your account. Congratulations on your winnings."

I relieved him of the case, slid it onto a side table, and popped the latches. Opening the lid revealed stacks of banded one-hundred-dollar bills with a settlement statement lying on top. I pulled a pair of bills from the case and handed each man a tip. "Thank you. I guess the house doesn't always win, huh?"

The first man pocketed his bill and scanned the room. With an excellent imitation of Clark's crooked grin, the man said, "Well, Mr. Fulton, there appears to be a dozen people in your suite, and you're the only one receiving a briefcase full of cash. I'd say the house did just fine. Thank you again for joining us. We look forward to seeing you again soon."

By the time we divided the contents of the briefcase, almost everyone's casino losses were covered, but my winnings were left unpaid.

"Let's break camp and head for Bonaventure," I said. "I miss Kenny and Earl. The new boathouse and gazebo should be almost finished."

Disco said, "Those two are a strange pair, aren't they?"

"There's someone for everyone. Speaking of somebodies . . . How are things with your somebody?"

He almost blushed. "Lonely at the moment. It's been a while since I've seen Ronda No-H, as you goofballs like to call her. She's loving life on the ship, but long-distance relationships are tough."

Penny slid onto the sofa beside me. "Tell me about it. I was getting used to having Chase home all the time while he was playing psychotherapist."

I gave her a playful shove. "Why does everybody keep saying that? I wasn't *playing* anything. I've got a license."

She giggled. "We keep saying it because it gets under your skin and makes us laugh, so psychoanalyze that, Dr. Fulton."

Clark said, "I love anything that gets under his skin. And speaking of skin, are you sure it's a good idea to lead Barkov back to Bonaventure?"

"I don't know what that's got to do with skin, but it's not like I'm blowing him off or anything. I think he's serious, but if we don't have any way to find him, there's not much we can do until he pops his little weasel head back out of his hole."

Skipper chimed in. "I didn't say I couldn't find him. I just said I couldn't tell you how or exactly when he left Ibiza. You can bet your butt I'll find him, but that's not my major concern. I want to know why he scampered out of here in such a hurry."

I said, "I'm sticking with my regrouping theory. He underestimated us, so I think he's retreating long enough to come up with the manpower and a plan to get me harnessed up and spying for the Kremlin . . . which isn't going to happen."

Clark laid his feet on the coffee table. "Oh, it's going to happen. What better way is there for us to feed the Russians a cargo ship full of disinformation? We can play with their heads for twenty years with the garbage you're going to make them swallow."

"I didn't mean I wasn't going to do it. I meant it wasn't going to happen the way Barkov wants. There are a lot of factors in this sort of thing. You and I both know espionage never plays out the way it's designed."

"What do you know about espionage, College Boy? You played sucky-face with one Russian defector, so now you think you're James Bond?"

Penny leaned forward, untied my boot, and pulled the lace from the leather. I didn't know what was about to happen, but I was intrigued. As if taking a Sunday-afternoon stroll, she stood, rounded the couch, and dangled my bootlace around Clark's neck. Pulling the ends of the lace as if it were a garrote, she hissed, "If you ever mention Chase playing kissy-face—or any other body part—with anybody besides me, the bootlace becomes a piano wire. Capisce?"

He ran a thumb beneath the cord and turned his head. "I didn't say *kissy-face*. I said *sucky-face*."

She pulled the lace tighter against the flesh of his neck, and he flinched. "Okay! I got it."

She gave one final tug for good measure. "Good."

I laughed, and she turned to me with an equally fierce glare. "And as for you, buddy boy . . . If you ever decide to take a walk down Memoriskia Lane, or whatever it's called in Russian, you'll wish for a strand of piano wire around your neck instead of where you'll find it in the middle of some dark night when you *thought* I was asleep."

I threw up both hands in surrender. "Penny Lane is the only walk I'll be taking."

My wife wadded the lace into a ball and threw it at me.

I snatched it from the air and set about re-lacing my boot. "See what you did? You got us both in trouble."

Clark chuckled. "I'm not the one in trouble, Hop Along. I never developed a taste for Slavic stew."

"I think they call it borscht."

He shook his head. "I wasn't talking about the soup, and you know it."

I closed my eyes. "Can we please talk about anything else?"

Disco came to my rescue. "We sure can. Which one of you is my co-pilot for this little Sunday-afternoon drive?"

I hesitated just long enough for Clark to say, "It's my turn."

My argument was just strong enough to sound sincere, but I ultimately surrendered the driver's seat to my handler.

With bags packed and everyone ready to be on the western edge of the Atlantic, someone rang our doorbell. Believing it would be the bellmen coming for our luggage, I threw open the door and said, "Come on in!"

Instead of a pair of tuxedoed bellmen, a petite Spanish lady in a stylish blue suit stood with an envelope in her hand. "Señor Fulton?"

"Yes."

"*Esto es para usted.*"

I took the envelope and studied it carefully. "*Gracias.*"

The young lady smiled and turned to go. "*De nada.*"

In my best Spanish, I said, "Wait. Before you go . . . Who is this from?"

She shrugged, "I don't know. It was left for you with the concierge."

"And you're sure you don't know who left it?"

"No, sir. I'm sorry."

I twisted the bolt on the door and let it fall against the jamb so the bellmen could come inside when they arrived. Waving the envelope toward Clark, I said, "Somebody left a note for us."

"What does it say?"

I tossed the envelope to him. "I don't know, but I'm not opening it."

He shook it, sniffed it, and held it up to the light. "Maybe it's a cashier's check for the rest of our winnings."

Skipper snatched it from his hand and slid a fingernail beneath the flap. A single photograph fell from the envelope and onto her palm.

"What is it?" I demanded. "You look like you've seen a ghost."

Skipper stared in frozen disbelief at the picture until I slid it from her hand. It took only seconds for the image to bore a tunnel through my brain.

"What?" Penny asked, reaching for the photograph.

I reluctantly surrendered the picture of Anya Burinkova bound, gagged, and beaten. Her blonde hair lay pasted to her flesh by her own blood, and her once flawless skin bore the blackened bruises of hours, if not days, of torture at the hands of someone who knew the darkest of arts all too well.

As Penny stared down at the picture, the anticipation in the room grew heavy, and she whispered, "Not again."

Hunter leaned in. "You're killing us. What's in the picture?"

Instead of answering, she handed the photograph to Mongo's wife, Irina.

Penny said, "Our men are going off to rescue their little Russian princess . . . again."

Chapter 9
The Wrong Decision

I held out a hand, wordlessly asking Penny to return the picture, and she did. Her stare met mine, and I said, "That's not what we do."

She ducked her chin and glared up at me. "Is that the story you're sticking with? If so, I'm prepared to rattle off the list of times you've done it before."

"You didn't let me finish. We don't run off to rescue people who aren't in danger."

Her ire morphed into inquisition. "What do you mean, not in danger? Look at her. She's practically dead in that picture."

I held the picture up in front of her. "You could be correct. In fact, if this picture were authentic, she'd likely be dead by now, but take a look at her right hand."

Penny, along with everyone else in the room, squinted and focused on Anya's hands tightly bound behind her back.

Clark plucked the toothpick from his mouth and examined the splintered tip. "Did you teach her to dive?"

"No, the Russkies taught her to breathe underwater, but I taught her the international hand signal for 'I'm okay.'"

Barely visible among the cotton rope surrounding her wrists and hands, her thumb and index finger formed a beautiful circle.

"Shut up!" Skipper plunged her way through the crowd. "Are you saying the picture is a fake?"

I floated the photograph through the air, and she caught it. "I'm not saying it's a fake. It could be real—the blood, the bruises, everything—but if it is, even in that condition, the human hand doesn't accidentally form that signal. It's up to you to determine if the picture is faked, but I'm certain Anya was one hundred percent in charge of the situation, whenever and wherever that picture was taken."

As if she'd forgotten we had been only moments away from flying home, Skipper leapt back onto her chair and opened her laptop. She scanned the picture and zoomed in until Anya's features were enormous. She brought the focus to her bound hands and leaned back in satisfaction. "Penny, come check this out."

My wife weaved her way between Clark and me and settled on one knee beside Skipper. "What am I looking for? Oh! Never mind. I see it. Have a look at her nails."

I leaned in. "They're perfect."

Penny gave my shoulder a slap. "It'd be better if I never heard you use that word to describe anything about her ever again. Okay?"

I tried to ignore her. "There's absolutely zero chance that any person or team of people could catch, hog-tie, and torture Anya without her getting in at least a few blows of her own. Fingernails like that don't survive the kind of fight she'd put up."

Before Penny could scold me again, Skipper said, "You're right, but there are a couple of variables you're not considering. They could've stuck her with one of those darts she loves so much, or more likely, they could've spiked a drink. If she was unconscious, she wouldn't put up a fight."

I considered Skipper's idea. "That's true, but they wouldn't have beaten her up while she was unconscious. If she wasn't bound when they got physical, she would've fought back, but if she was bound, she would've clawed at the ropes. Either way, the clean, *not* perfect fingernails would've suffered."

Our analyst said, "That leaves us with the okay sign. If we rule out the possibility of it being accidental, which I think we can safely do, she's either saying she has the situation under control, or she wants us to know the whole scenario is a setup. Either of those two possibilities leads us to the same conclusion. She doesn't need or want our help."

I lifted the picture from the scanner. "I hope you're right."

I'll never know what made me do it, but I spun the picture between my fingers and noticed, for the first time, a small line of handwritten text on the back of the shot. I laid it on the table and read the Cyrillic script. "*Teper' ty gotov sdelat' to, chto ya khochu?*"

Penny said, "Can somebody tell me what that means in English?"

Irina said, "It means, are you now ready to do what I want?"

Skipper straightened her glasses. "Oh, that changes things."

"Does it?" I asked. "How? If Barkov has Anya, as this picture seems to prove, all he's done is sign his own death warrant. He's done his homework. Surely he knows we're not the kind of people who respond well to threats of violence. If he's trying to lure us into a trap, that's a worse plan than trying to intimidate us. We hurt people who play games like that."

Penny laid a hand on my back. "Chase, it could mean something else completely."

"What could?"

"If Barkov is trying to lure us in, Anya's okay signal could mean 'don't fall for it.' If there's one thing I know about Anya, it's that she's still in love with you."

"Wait a minute," I said. "That's not—"

Penny squeezed my arm. "Don't get so defensive. Everybody, including you, knows that's true, and that's the one thing she and I have in common. I know if I were kidnapped, bound, gagged, and beaten to a pulp, you'd be the one person on Earth I'd want coming to rescue me."

"You don't understand. Anya isn't—"

She squeezed again. "This time, *you* didn't let *me* finish. If I were in that position and knew you couldn't survive the trap they'd set for you, I'd gladly take the beatings and anything else they put me through to keep you from stepping into that trap. And Anya would do exactly the same."

I let her wisdom churn inside my head, and I turned to Skipper.

Before I could open my mouth, our analyst looked up. "She's right, Chase. I'd do the same, even though I don't love you with the same kind of love those two have for you."

When the implosion of one's life decisions begins, stopping the crumbling from inside is like trying to climb a waterfall. Finding someone on the outside to pull me from the cascading tumult was my only hope, and like so many times before, the hand that stretched into the depths of my self-created calamity was attached to the arm of the deadliest sniper I'd ever know . . . and also the truest heart I'd ever experience.

Jimmy "Singer" Grossmann laid an arm across my shoulders. "Let's take a walk while the others lump our gear downstairs."

The endless blue of the Mediterranean spread out before us as we walked in silence along a footpath leading to a row of palm-frond umbrellas over brilliantly colorful wooden chairs facing the sea.

Singer slid onto a chair and pulled off his cap. "It's not exactly the gazebo at Bonaventure, but it'll have to do. Tell me what you're thinking."

He was right. The chairs weren't nearly as comfortable as the Adirondacks in the gazebo had been before they were reduced to charred skeletons of their former selves.

"I'm thinking I wish I'd done the rehab."

He examined the lining of his hat. "What rehab?"

I watched a diving pelican pierce the surface of the azure plane that was the sea. She emerged victorious with her head held high and her beak pointing skyward. The catch of the day was likely still alive when it slid down her gullet. "The rehab to play ball again. I could've done it, you know. I could've hit the gym and clawed my way up through the minor leagues. I was good enough back then. Sometimes, I lie awake and pretend I can hear the crowd jump to their feet and cheer as I slug my first big-league home run over the Chick-fil-A cow at Turner Field."

He gave me a long, appraising look, replaced his cap on his head, and stood. Four strides toward the water, he motioned toward the chair he'd abandoned. "What do you see?"

"An empty chair."

He stepped aside and pointed to the next one. "And what about here? What do you see?"

I narrowed my gaze in anticipation of the life lesson that lay only a few seconds into my future. "Another empty chair."

He pointed toward the next seat, and I said, "Yet, a third empty seat, but I get the feeling I don't see what you want me to see."

In a demonstration of emotion I'd never seen from our sniper, Singer lifted the third chair and threw it with enormous effort toward the placid water. It crashed to the sand in a heap of splintered color. Before the disbelief left my face, he hefted the second chair over his head and drove it into the trunk of a tree a dozen feet behind me. Mesmerized, I stared at the most peaceful man I've ever known as he drove his booted foot through the chair nearest my side. Everything about the powerful display was one hundred eighty degrees out of character for the man of God.

He knelt beside me, took my scarred hand in his, and flattened my palm against his chest. Staring through every inch of my soul, he said, "Chase, if you had done the rehab, Clark, Mongo, and I would've died, and our bodies would've frozen to the ground at the top of the Khyber Pass. You didn't let that happen, though. You came for us, and you're the reason we're alive . . . All three of us. You're the reason those three chairs are necessary. You're the reason Irina and Maebelle have husbands. And you're the reason I get to kneel at the altar in my church and pray with men and women whose souls cry out for mercy. No matter what decisions you made in your past, whether those decisions involved Anya or walking away from baseball, it's those decisions that brought a ragtag group of people together and made us all fall in love with each other. You're the reason this family of ours exists. Now, do you really wish you could trade what we have just so you can hear a few thousand baseball fans cheering for you?"

I shriveled in my seat as the awesome power of his wisdom washed over me.

In an instant, the ferocity that destroyed three perfectly good chairs turned to unmatched tenderness as a tear left the corner of his eye. He whispered, "Thank you for making that wrong decision, brother."

Chapter 10
Katerina's Heart

Our family climbed aboard a motor coach in front of the resort, and everything about my perspective on the world that had become mine changed as I watched the subtle interactions, smiles, playful tugs, shoves, and general mischief. I wouldn't trade my family for ten thousand home runs at Turner Field.

The Bonaventure Airport, as we'd begun calling it, welcomed us home as if we were the prodigal children. Don Maynard had cared for the airport for two decades while the city of St. Marys owned the field, but now that we owned the expansive ocean of concrete, fencing, and blue and white lights, Don worked with us, earning a comfortable salary in addition to his pension from the city. He seemed to always know what would happen at Bonaventure Field, long before anyone else. Perhaps he'd become part of the place through the years of grooming, cleaning, repairing, and loving it as he did. Almost before the *Grey Ghost* rolled to a stop in front of our main hangar, Don arrived in the fuel truck.

"She drinks a little more than the old Citation," Clark said as he stepped onto the tarmac.

Don looked up. "Yeah, but she's a beauty. How was the flight?"

"Long, but not bad. Have you noticed anything unusual around here?"

Don frowned. "Unusual? No, not really. The Gulfstream folks delivered the interior kits, but other than that, everything's been pretty quiet. I cleaned the big hangar and organized it for the new girl."

"Thanks for taking care of that, but listen. We need you to keep an eye out for anything out of the ordinary. We're having a little trouble out of some folks, and we don't want them sneaking around. If you see anyone or anything that doesn't look right, call me or Chase right away, but don't confront them."

Don double-checked the fuel connection and started the truck's pump. "You know I will. Should I get the police chief to run an extra car by here a few times an hour?"

Clark said, "No, that won't be necessary. We've got good camera coverage, but your eyes are better than any camera. You're the one person who knows exactly how things should look around here, so I trust you more than any bored police officer."

Hunter drove the forklift from the hangar, and I waved him down. "Maybe we should leave the gear on the plane, just in case."

He shrugged. "You're the boss. Take a look in the hangar. You're going to like what Don's done in there."

I stuck my head through the door to discover Don had done a lot more than just tidy up. He'd epoxied the floor of the enormous space until it shined. Everything inside was perfectly organized, making our hangar look as impressive as the Gulfstream hangars we'd seen in Savannah.

With the fuel truck refilled and nestled back into its slot, Don ambled through the hangar door and climbed aboard the tug.

I said, "Nice job on the hangar. It looks great."

He shot me a thumbs-up and headed for the *Grey Ghost*.

Back at Bonaventure, Penny and I couldn't wait to see the view from the back gallery. From our lofted position on the gallery, we saw exactly what we'd hoped for.

Penny said, "I know you love the boathouse, but it's the gazebo you really wanted back, isn't it?"

I squeezed her hand and bounded down the stairs. "It's bigger than the original, but I love it. Check out the cannon carriage."

She knelt and ran her hand across the smooth wood. "It's amazing, like it came right off a ship two hundred years ago. How did he do that?"

"I don't know, and I'm not going to ask him."

"Why not?"

"Because he's Cajun Kenny Lepine, and I can't understand a word he says."

She stood and gave me a shove. "You're terrible."

"Admit it," I said, "You can't understand him, either."

She rolled her eyes. "Let's check out the boathouse."

"Not before I test-drive one of these chairs. Singer gave me a whole new appreciation for chairs before we left Ibiza."

"What are you talking about?"

"Never mind. I wouldn't be able to do it justice."

"Give it a try," she said as she slid onto an Adirondack beside me.

"You know how conversations with Singer go. We had a talk about decisions. Even the bad ones can lead to good endings."

She took my hand. "I'm glad you have him to keep things in perspective. He's good for you."

"He is, but so are you and the rest of the inhabitants of our island of misfit toys."

"They're not misfits," she said. "They're just uniquely qualified to be exactly what you—what we—need in our lives. Even Anya."

"What?"

She drummed her fingers on the arm of her chair. "You know you have to go get her, right?"

"What are you talking about?"

"I'm talking about Anya. You can't leave her like that. I mean, we all know that if something happened to me, she'd swoop in like a hawk the second I was out of the picture, but that doesn't mean you can just let her die."

I laced my fingers between hers. "You may be the best person who's ever lived. You know that?"

"It's not about being a good person. It's just about doing the right thing. I'm not trying to make you feel bad or anything, but think about it. If that Barkov guy took her, regardless of the nails and the okay signal or whatever, he did it to get to you, so that makes it, at least a little bit, your responsibility. If there's one thing I know about you, Chase Fulton, it's that you take care of your responsibilities."

"What are you saying?"

She let out a long sigh. "I swear, sometimes I'd have more luck talking to that cannon, you hardheaded thing. I'm saying go get her. You have to. As weird as it is, I'm not sure I'd ever be able to look at you the same if you didn't. The Chase I fell in love with wouldn't leave her out there like that."

"Even if I agreed with all of that, I wouldn't know where to start. Who knows where she is? Who knows if those pictures are even real? For all I know, she could be in on the whole thing."

She cocked her head like a disappointed mother. "Really? If it were me in that picture, are you saying you wouldn't even try to find me?"

"But it's not you. It's one of the world's most highly trained assassins. She's more capable than me, or any of us, for that matter."

Penny lowered her gaze. "That doesn't mean—"

The back door of the house slammed, stopping Penny mid-sentence and catching my attention. When I looked up, Skipper was running down the stairs.

"Chase, you've got to see this, and you're not going to like it."

I pushed myself from my chair. "What is it?"

"Just come with me. Penny, you should come, too."

We followed her back into the house and up the stairs. She had the door to the op center propped open.

"Why isn't the door secured?" I asked.

"I didn't want to waste any time. You'll understand in a minute. Watch this."

She pointed to the large monitor above her workstation, and a video of an entry corridor played. The video opened up into a living room and kitchen, and Penny gasped. "That's my house in L.A."

"Shut it off," I demanded, but Skipper didn't move.

I moved toward the console. "I said, shut it off."

Skipper stopped me. "Wait, Chase. You need to see it all."

My blood boiled as I watched the scene play out. The cameraman continued through the house and into Penny's bedroom. A gloved hand extended in front of the camera and pulled down the comforter and blanket from the bed and sprayed a fine mist onto a pillow.

The video froze for a moment, and a line of Cyrillic text scrolled across the bottom.

Penny shuddered. "What does that say, Chase?"

"It says, 'Maybe it's water, or maybe it's hydrogen cyanide.'"

When the video came to life again, a folded copy of a newspaper landed on the pillow, and the shot zoomed in.

Penny squeezed my arm. "That's today's *L.A. Times*, Chase. He's in my house! When is this going to end? I'm tired of hiding."

Skipper spun in her chair and looked up at both of us. "The video isn't over."

I stared at the screen as the message scrolled across.

You will meet me alone where you first saw Katerina's Heart, and you will do so alone. I have access to every piece of your life, and the only way to stop me is to do exactly as I command.

Penny's face turned to stone. "Why is that in English and not Russian?"

I sighed. "Because he wants you to be able to read it. It's a scare tactic."

"Well, it's a good one," she said. "I'm scared."

I stared between my boots for a long moment, ignoring everything and everyone in the room. "Get Clark and the rest of the team up here."

It took less than two minutes for the team to assemble and settle into their seats around the conference table.

Clark asked, "What's all this about?"

"You'll see in a minute," I said. "Roll the video, Skipper."

We watched the cameraman walk slowly through the entry foyer.

Penny said, "That's my house in L.A., if you've not figured it out yet."

The video continued until it froze on the Cyrillic text, and I translated the line about the cyanide.

When the video ended, Clark asked, "Where's he talking about? Where did you first see Anya?"

"He's not talking about Anya," I said. "I'm pretty sure I'm the only person who's ever heard Anya call herself Katerina's heart. I think he's talking about Dr. Richter's hangar in Athens."

Disco shook his head as if clearing spiderwebs. "I'm lost. What does he mean by Katerina's heart?"

"The Mustang," I said. "Before I got it shot up playing Russian roulette with the Russkies off the coast, her name was *Katerina's Heart*. That's what Dr. Richter named her. When we put her back together, I had the nose art redone and dubbed her *Penny's Secret*."

"So, what are we waiting for?" Hunter said. "Let's get to Athens and hand this guy his butt in a paper sack."

I shook him off. "He told me to come alone."

"Who cares what he said? He doesn't dictate the rules of engagement. When he threatens Penny, he threatens all of us. Let's go."

I laid my palm on the smooth surface of the table. "I'm going alone."

Chapter 11
We've Got a Runner

Clark leapt to his feet. "The hell you are. There's no way you're going in there without us."

"You read what he wrote," I said. "He has access to every part of my life. He'll know where everybody in this room is, and I won't risk him hurting Penny."

My wife knocked on the table. "I think it's time I should get a say in when and where I go, *and* what risks my husband takes. I think you're both right. Chase has no real options here. He has to go, but you can't let him go alone."

Clark leaned back in his chair. "How do we do both? I'm all in favor of you making decisions, but nobody's going to support you going in with Chase."

I met my wife's gaze. "I'm not sure what you have in mind, but I'd like it if you stayed right here at Bonaventure until we get this cleaned up."

"I'm okay with that, but I'm tired of being whisked off like some delicate little china doll. I'm not going to live my life in fear."

Clark said, "We're getting off track, but I want to know what you meant by Chase going alone and being covered. I'm not smart enough to put that one together."

"From my perspective, you have to keep Chase alive and take down Barkov. You're the handler, right?"

Clark nodded, and Penny continued. "Then you need to *handle* some other team to shadow Chase in Athens."

Clark snapped his fingers. "Everybody out. I need the room." No one moved, and he said, "Get out. I've got to call the Board to get this authorized."

Hunter leaned back and propped both boots on the table. Everyone else positioned themselves in a similar fashion, except for Penny.

She stood and headed for the door. "I'll be right outside."

Clark's call found only one Board member. "Hello, Mr. Johnson. What can I do for you?"

Clark briefed the mission, and the man said, "I can authorize Team Eleven, or we can convene the rest of the Board if you'd prefer."

Clark looked up for my input, and I gave him a nod.

"There's no need to convene the Board. Your authorization is good enough for us. I'm sure you'll brief them up."

"Of course I will. Let us know what else you need."

Clark said, "Thank you, sir. We'll keep you posted."

Skipper cut the connection and stared at Clark.

He threw up his hands. "What?"

"I know a lot of things, but I've never heard of Team Eleven. I have no clue how to reach them."

Clark pulled out his sat-phone and pressed a pair of keys.

Seconds later, a calm, low voice came through the speaker. "Tell me you've got a mission for us."

Clark slid the phone to the center of the table. "I do, but it's a short-term gig . . . we hope."

"Short term is better than no term. Let's hear it."

Our handler said, "It's unorthodox, but I need you to cover a solo team lead for a contact at Ben Epps Field in Athens."

"When?"

Clark checked his watch. "Sixty minutes."

"Done."

Clark continued. "We need overwatch, two close support troops, and a pair of gunners in tight if it hits the fan. The meeting will be in hangar two-ten, and you have to be invisible. Got it?"

"No problem," the voice said. "Invisible is what we do best. Who's the primary?"

Clark sighed. "Chase Fulton."

"You've got to be joking."

"Do you need a headshot?" Clark asked.

The man said, "No, I figure the red cape and big S on his chest will make him pretty easy to pick out."

I said, "I wasn't planning to wear my cape this time. I'll probably be the only guy who shows up in a Mustang."

"Just to be safe," the man said, "send us a picture for our sniper."

"Wilco," Clark said. "Have you got anything to add, Chase?"

I shook my head. "Let's go to work."

* * *

Penny's Secret, my 1944 North American P-51 Mustang, glistened on the ramp and seemed to quiver with anxiety before roaring into the air. The 12-cylinder, Rolls-Royce Merlin engine belched orange fire from her exhaust stacks as I advanced the throttle and flew the tailwheel off the runway. Seconds later, her main gear was free of the confines of the earth and folding themselves into their wells. I set climb power and propeller RPM and rode my warhorse into battle.

The 40-minute flight barely gave *Penny's Secret* time to stretch her legs. As the Athens, GA, airport lay out in front of me, my mind was awash with endless memories of Dr. Robert "Rocket" Richter and the undeniable role he'd played in my life. I'd never know if some earthly force placed me in his psychology classroom at UGA all those years before, or if some cosmic force called the shots that turned me into the target of an insane Russian who was hell-bent on turning my life inside out.

I taxied to a stop at the end of a long row of hangars and shut down the Mustang. Double-checking everything, I repositioned my pistol just behind my right hip bone and my backup weapon on the inside of my left ankle. I brought my earpiece and mic to life and conducted a comms check with the op center.

Skipper's reassuring voice filled my ear. "Don't get dead, Chase. We need you around here."

"I'll do my best."

She said, "You're Bravo One on the net. The in-place team is Alpha One through Six."

"Who's the sniper?" I asked.

A calm voice, not unlike Singer's, whispered. "Alpha Four is overwatch."

I continued comm checks with the team until I heard each of their confident voices.

"Thanks for being here, guys. I'm Chase."

Alpha One said, "Roger, Bravo One. Go to work."

With the brakes locked, I climbed down from the Mustang and took my first stride toward the hangar where I'd first seen the airplane the day Dr. Richter flew me to Jekyll Island for what would become the most fateful weekend of my life. It was the weekend I was recruited into the life of an American covert operative. Even with the uncertainty and potential danger lurking just around the corner, I wouldn't have it any other way. Singer was right. We truly are the sum result of our decisions, both good and bad. I was determined to make Dmitri Barkov understand just how bad his decision to take over my life was. The haunting, natural end to the scenario played out inside my head as my mind's eye watched the junior Barkov joining his father in the pits of Hell. If he continued to threaten my family, I was well prepared to arrange the all-expenses-paid trip for him.

I expected to see a sliver of light escaping beneath the door of Dr. Richter's former hangar, but no such sliver appeared. The massive hangar became mine after my mentor's passing, but I had never put it to use. How Barkov knew it existed was beyond my comprehension.

I slid my key into the lock and turned the knob with my left hand while gripping my Glock with the right. The inward-swinging door allowed a swath of light to pierce the interior, but not enough to lift the veil of darkness over the entire space. My hand found the pair of light switches just inside the door, but flipping them changed nothing. The overhead bulbs remained dormant, either by design or the passage of time.

If anyone were inside, I was a sitting duck backlit in the kill zone of the doorway. Even the well-armed assault team covering my arrival couldn't calm the pulse I could almost feel in my throat. Alpha Four would drive a missile of lead through anyone who emerged from the hangar, but if I were lying in a puddle of my own blood three feet inside the door, it wouldn't matter who the next dead guy would be.

I whispered into my mic, "Have you seen anyone in or out?"

"Alpha Four, negative. I've been in position for fifty-three minutes. The dust from the door when you pushed it open made it appear the door hadn't been opened in a while."

The sniper's concise observation of something as subtle as dust set my mind at ease almost as much as Singer would've done.

I stepped through the opening and pivoted around the door, placing as much of the heavy steel slab between me and the rest of the hangar as I could. Flipping the switch on my weapon's light cast a beam across the expanse of the hangar, but I'd never wanted Stone Hunter at my side more than at that moment. One-man room-clearing is a skill every member of the team mastered, but we'd never practiced clearing an acre-sized airplane hangar by ourselves. My light's narrow periphery made the hangar feel like a boundless rattrap, making me the rat.

As I pressed myself farther behind the swinging door, I felt the unmistakable probe between my shoulder blades. I froze, swallowed hard, and sent up a prayer exactly as Singer had taught.

Keeping my weapon trained on the open hangar, I reached across my shoulder and grasped the probing arm in my back. The click echoed through the voluminous space, and the massive bifold door covering the mouth of the hangar began its slow rise, crushing the oppressing absence of light.

The sniper's voice reminded me I wasn't alone. "Bravo One, verify you sent the door up."

"Affirmative."

He said, "I selected a poor nest. I've only got fifty-percent coverage of the interior."

Singer wouldn't have made such an egregious error, but that day, it was forgivable. As the exterior light consumed the interior darkness, the mortal gravity of the moment waned and morphed into a pang deep within my gut. "There's nobody here. It's a bust. Stand down."

Skipper's voice replaced mine. "Belay that order and stand fast. There's movement near the plane."

I stepped from the mouth of the hangar and peered toward the Mustang. "Alpha Four, have you got eyes on my plane?"

"Affirmative, but there's no movement."

"What do you see, Skipper?"

"I've got control of the security cameras, but they're not good enough to give me a clean view. I don't know what's out there yet, but whatever it is, it's definitely moving thirty yards off the right wingtip."

The Alpha Team commander said, "Alpha Three, get close eyes on the plane."

Clark couldn't remain silent any longer. "Bravo One, are you sure the hangar's empty? Just because nobody's home right now doesn't mean somebody didn't leave a love note stuck to the refrigerator door."

"I'm on it," I said. "But don't let anybody near my airplane."

The sniper said, "I've got movement twenty yards east of the Mustang."

Clark said, "Alpha One, Ops, can you neutralize an aggressor without lethal force?"

The team commander said, "Affirmative. Alpha Two, get tight. Three, back him up."

I moved back to the hangar and scoured the interior while leaving the Alpha Team to deal with the intruder closing in on my Mustang. No footprints other than my own appeared on the dust-covered concrete, leaving me with only one conclusion: I'd given Dmitri Barkov far more credit than he deserved. He didn't know the history of my Mustang. He never knew the warbird wore the moniker of his father's unrequited love. He likely knew only of Anya's presence in Elmont, New York, at the Belmont Stakes, where she worked alongside the senior Barkov to ensure his horse's victory. Perhaps I was to meet him there, but one other possibility remained. I questioned whether he could've known I was at the race. There was no reason for him to have known. I was fresh out of training and not officially assigned to the operation. It was far more likely he knew of my interaction with Anya in Charlotte Amalie on Saint Thomas.

I wouldn't run an operation a thousand miles away from the rest of my team, no matter what Barkov threatened. I'd crush him beneath my heel, with my team at my side, if he pushed his manic agenda to its point of ultimate destruction. He may have found his antics fodder for his self-amusement, but I wouldn't play his game by his rules. It was time to do what my team and I did best. It was time to face an adversary toe to toe and drive him into the ground, one blow at a time.

The Alpha Team pulled me from my brewing ire. "Alpha One, this is Two. We've got a runner. Advise."

The team commander gave the same immediate order I would've given. "Alpha Two, pursue. Alpha Three, hold on the aircraft. The runner is likely a diversion."

"Roger," came their replies.

With my search of the hangar complete, I checked the breakers for a reason the lights wouldn't come to life and found a nest of spiders consuming the interior space of the box. I wondered if the same condition existed inside my skull. Was I being manipulated by hundreds of crawling creatures bent on short-circuiting my light?

Determined to avoid being sucked into a pit of my own creation, I pulled myself from my own thoughts. "Alpha One, Bravo One. Hangar is secure, and I'm moving back to the plane."

A winded voice echoed in my head. "Alpha One, Alpha Two. I have the target in custody."

Chapter 12
Responsibility

I let the question of who the runner could be boil inside my head before asking, "Alpha Two, Bravo One. Is the runner a single, and is he hurt?"

"Affirmative, Bravo One. He's a single and unhurt. He's a kid who swears he just wanted to see the Mustang. I shook him up pretty good, and I think he's telling the truth."

I stepped into the chain of command. "Alpha Two, Bravo One, bring him back to the plane. I'll meet you there."

"Alpha Two, this is Alpha One. Stand fast."

Clark said, "What are you doing, Chase? You're supposed to be there alone, remember?"

"I'm going to find out if the kid is part of Barkov's game."

Clark took command of the situation. "Alpha Two, Ops. Search the kid."

"Already done. One pocketknife, eight dollars, and one pair of cheap binoculars."

I ran through the inventory and wondered how many times I had a similar payload as a child. "Alpha Two, Bravo One. How old is the kid?"

"He says he's twelve, but I suspect he's at least a couple years younger."

"Bring him to the airplane," I said.

Clark followed my transmission with his own. "Take the boy to Chase."

When I reached the Mustang, a boy, no older than ten, stood in wide-eyed wonder, gazing up at the nose art of my wife, her perfect curves, and that mischievous smile of hers. Alpha Two was nowhere in sight.

Without looking away from the Mustang, the boy asked, "Is this yours, mister?"

I stared him down. "What's your name?"

"Lucas Taylor. What's yours?"

"Where do you live, Lucas Taylor?"

He pointed through the trees. "Over there. Where do you live?"

I liked the boy's curiosity, so I gave him an answer in the form of pointing in the same direction he had. "I live a little farther over there."

"Is this your plane?"

Instead of an answer, I redirected. "What do you know about the plane?"

"I know my papaw flew B-Twenty-Nines in England in World War Two, and he says the Mustangs are the greatest things on Earth—or in the sky."

"Your papaw, huh? What's his name?"

The boy cocked his head. "Papaw Taylor. Do you know him?"

I tried to contain the laughter. "Why do you have binoculars, Lucas?"

"You sure do ask a lot of questions," he said.

"Tell me about the binoculars, Lucas."

He held up the cheap plastic set. "I use 'em to look at airplanes, and Papaw says if I don't lose 'em for a whole year, he'll buy me a real set. He says I've got to learn responsibility before I can have an expensive set of my own."

"He's right," I said. "Would you like to sit in the airplane?"

His eyes turned to beachballs. "Are you serious?"

"Sure, why not?"

A day of my life had been wasted chasing a ghost, but fate handed me an opportunity to give a Georgia boy the best day of his life, and I wasn't going to throw it away.

I hefted Lucas onto the wing and pointed toward the front seat. "Go ahead. Climb in there."

"For real?"

I chuckled. "Yes, for real. Go ahead."

He stretched across the canopy rail and slid onto the seat. Silence from boys of any age is rare, but it would've been easy to believe Lucas Taylor couldn't speak as he let his fingertips glide across every instrument, gauge, and switch in the cockpit.

When he could finally speak, he asked, "Do you really know what all these things do?"

I gave him a grin. "Most of 'em."

"Can I move the stick?"

"Sure, you can."

He pushed, pulled, squeezed, and shook the stick. "Is this the trigger for the guns?"

"It used to be."

"Were you in the war with Papaw?"

It was, at that moment, impossible to contain my laughter. "No, I'm a little too young for that war, but this airplane was in it."

"Do you think it flew with Papaw?"

I shrugged. "It's possible, I suppose."

He continued soaking up the sensory overload the cockpit provided. "I wish Papaw was here."

"Do you have a phone?" I asked.

He shrank in the seat. "No. My mom says I'd lose it, but sometimes, I get to play with Papaw's."

"Do you know his phone number?"

He rattled off the number, and I pulled my phone from my pocket. "Grab the stick, and look up at me."

I snapped a couple pictures and handed the phone to Lucas. "Send your papaw those pictures."

"Really?"

Clark's voice thundered in my ear. "Uh, Chase, what are you doing? When did we start handing out phone numbers on ops?"

"You're breaking up," I said. "You can dismiss Alpha Team. We're all secure here."

"Yeah, right," he said. "Satellite comms don't break up. Get that kid out of your airplane, and get your butt back home. We've got a lot of work to do."

I boosted Lucas from the cockpit and stored Papaw Taylor's number in my phone.

The flight back to Bonaventure was uneventful, but the exhaustion from the tension of the mission set in at the worst possible moment. I rolled onto final approach, slowed toward approach speed, and eased in a notch of flaps. My speed wasn't bleeding off as it should've been, so I pulled an additional five inches of manifold pressure and trimmed the nose up.

With my speed closer to the precise numbers the Mustang demanded, the runway didn't look right. I couldn't see the approach-end numbers. My speed was close, but my attitude was all wrong. Things happen fast at 125 miles per hour, and I was falling further behind the airplane with every passing second.

What's wrong? What am I missing?

Everything was wrong, but I chalked it up to Barkov crawling around inside my brain. The closer I came to the airport, the less I liked how the airplane felt and the world in front of me looked.

I should see more runway. What's happening?

The only way to see the approach end of the runway was to lower the Mustang's massive nose, but as I pressed the stick forward, my speed increased. I could finally see the full runway, but my speed was far too high.

I shook my head, trying to clear the spiderwebs I'd seen in my breaker box, and I caught a glimpse of the most unexpected scene. I squeezed my eyelids closed and back open, trying to focus. The airport was exactly where it should've been, but the bright white fuel truck with its flashing orange light shouldn't have been barreling toward me on the centerline of the runway. I suddenly knew how the pilot of the hijacked airliner felt back on Nassau in the seconds before he melted his landing gear.

Gear! You didn't put the gear down!

Power up. I added throttle.

Pitch up. I raised the nose.

Pick up. I raised the flaps, and the Mustang and I were flying again. I'd let preoccupation with Barkov and his game destroy my concentration and sound aeronautical practice. I'd flown a screwed-up approach at screwed-up speeds with screwed-up power settings with the landing gear tucked snuggly in their wells, and Don and his fuel truck saved a million-dollar belly landing.

My second approach was flown precisely by the checklist, at exactly the correct speeds, with the gear down and locked, and without a fuel truck saving my airplane.

The landing was clean, and Don didn't say a word when he helped me down from the wing. The look on my face had to scream of my own disappointment in my poor airmanship, but Don went about his task of fueling the Mustang as if everything had gone perfectly.

Leaving the plane in his more-than-capable hands, I ran a hand across his shoulders. "Thanks, Don."

He looked up from his work and gave me a wink. "Sorry I got in your way. I must've got a little lost driving the fuel truck out to the ramp."

* * *

"You forgot to put the gear down? What were you thinking, College Boy?"

I could've avoided Clark's admonition by not telling him the story, but I was his responsibility, and hiding anything from my handler—and old friend—wasn't something I was willing to do.

"This guy's really in your head, isn't he?"

I looked away from my handler. "Yeah, he is. My whole life feels like that gear-up approach. Everything is off."

Clark said, "You're the shrink. You're supposed to know how to get out of your own head."

"Maybe I need another dose of Dr. Singer's medicine."

He huffed. "Maybe you need to get things in perspective. You're letting somebody else call the shots. Do you think General Patton ever did that?"

"General Patton? What's he got to do with any of this?"

Clark shrugged. "He's the first great leader who popped into my head, and you may've never waded ashore in the Philippines, but you're at least as good as him when it comes to taking your men to war."

"You're giving me a lot of credit."

"No, I'm putting things into perspective. You've got your hands full of a mess most people couldn't deal with, but you're not most people. Maybe Alpha One was right. Maybe it's time for you to bring out the red cape and do a little tall-building leaping, even if you can't do it in a single bound."

Chapter 13
One Particular Beach

There are few things I loved more than having Penny's head on my shoulder while lying in bed, pondering what the next sunrise would drop in my lap. That night was no different. The familiar feel of her hair brushing against my skin was like the wind on my face at *Aegis*'s helm. It reminded me I was driven by a force I couldn't see, but was, nonetheless, as powerful as any force against which I'd wage war. What remained for me was to draw my sword in the face of my enemy and beat him back with a will and determination he could never match.

The sunrise came as it had for eons, and I watched the night's possession of coastal Georgia surrender to the warmth of the light. The new gazebo Cajun Kenny rebuilt for me felt like an old friend, and I prayed I'd see ten thousand more sunrises from its embrace.

Clark stepped onto the wooden deck and placed a mug of steaming coffee in my hand. "Good morning. Did you get any sleep?"

I raised the cup. "Thanks. Yeah, I did, and I think it's time to let Barkov's steel trap taste a bite of my robot foot."

"Have you been drinking already?" Clark asked. "You're speaking in riddles, and that's supposed to be my gig."

"Just coffee so far, but the day is young. I'm saying we should let Barkov believe he's got us."

He scoffed. "It's not *us* he wants. It's *you*."

"And I say we give him what he wants because I have a suspicion there's a lot more to this whole thing than just spying for Barkov or the SVR."

He crossed his ankles and stared into his mug. "What are you thinking?"

"I don't know. But I don't think this is one of those situations when we can apply Occam's razor. On the surface, it appears this is an aggressive recruitment effort by a foreign intelligence agency, but it can't be that simple. The senior Barkov was worth a billion dollars. The son of a guy like that doesn't end up as an SVR case officer."

"I don't know who Occam is, but go on. I'm listening."

I took a sip. "I've not worked it all out yet, but think about what we know so far. Barkov's men in Ibiza weren't Line KR officers. They were too easy to put down. He may be funded or even partially directed by the SVR, but he's not using elite counterintelligence guys, so I think he's working independently."

Clark chewed on his lip and stared into the morning sky. "Are you suggesting it's a political move?"

"Maybe. If that's where this is headed, Barkov is trying to gather feathers for his hat. If he can deliver me, an American covert operator with ties to the White House, that's a pretty fancy feather. Don't you think?"

"It would be. But to what end?"

"I don't know. Prime minister. Maybe even the big-boy chair."

Clark raised an eyebrow. "You think he wants Putin's job?"

"I think he wants something big and believes delivering me on a silver platter is the key to opening that door."

He grimaced. "What about Anya?"

"What about her?"

"She's involved in this somehow. Is she part of that Occam's razor thing?"

"She's the exact opposite of Occam's razor. She complicates everything on both sides of this. Barkov believes he can get to me by using her. Penny was right about that. I have a history of pulling her little Russian butt out of the fire."

He waggled his cup at me. "You need to get that little Russian butt out of your head and start thinking with your brain instead of your—"

"I *am* thinking with my brain. I'm not concerned about Anya, but Barkov thinks I am. If he had her in custody anywhere outside of Russia, she's probably already killed a couple hundred of his guys and escaped to somewhere hot."

"Maybe," he said. "But I know you well enough to know that if she doesn't turn up, you're going to do something stupid to try to find her."

I leaned forward and propped my elbows on my knees. "I'll make a deal with you. I won't do anything on this mission that you don't directly authorize. How's that?"

He laughed. "Yeah, right. If that happens, it'll be a first."

"I'm serious," I said. "I don't always make great decisions when it comes to Anya, so I'm taking that element out of this. If it comes down to busting her out of some stronghold somewhere, that decision's on you."

He emptied his cup. "Okay. I'm holding you to this one. So, what do you want to do next?"

"That part's simple. I want to surrender."

He stood. "Oh, yeah. That sounds like a great plan. Let's get some more coffee."

Halfway up the gallery stairs, my phone chirped. "Hello, this is Chase."

Barkov's Russian accent played through the phone. "Why did you go to Athens?"

I pointed toward the phone and mouthed, "Barkov."

Clark motioned toward a pair of rockers, and we slid onto the wooden seats. He leaned close, and I turned up the volume. "That's what I thought you wanted. You told me to meet you where I first saw *Katerina's Heart*."

"What are you talking about? You are not making any sense."

Clark frowned, and I said, "You'll need to break this down for me, Dmitri. You're obviously smarter than me, so let's cut the games and do this like men."

He said, "I have you. I know everything about you, Chase Fulton. You are smart enough to understand this because you did what I told you, at least, partially, and you were wise to do this."

"I was wise to do what?"

"You made mistake in choosing location, but you came alone, as I demanded. This is show of good faith . . . or maybe fear."

"I'm not afraid of you, Dmitri, but I respect your reach. You can obviously get inside my world, and you found my weakness. If I can prevent her from being hurt—or worse—I'll do what you ask."

He laughed. "You believe you are talking about your wife, but I know this is not true. She is innocent in this, but Anastasia Burinkova is not. We are men of action, Chase Fulton. If I harm your wife, you will devote your life to killing me and everyone I care about. This would be stupid for me, and I am not stupid. You understand this, yes?"

I said, "Perhaps we understand each other better than I thought."

"There is beach on island of Saint Thomas. You know this beach, yes?"

"I do."

"Good. Two days from today, you and I will have lunch like gentlemen on this beach, and you will give to me what I ask. When you have done this, I will give also to you something of great value."

I raised a look, and Clark nodded his approval. "I'll be there, but I won't be alone."

The line clicked, and Dmitri Barkov was gone.

Clark pushed from his chair, and I asked, "Where are *you* going?"

"The same place you're going. To see if Skipper can trace that call."

* * *

"I can try," she said, "but no promises. Are you sure it was him?"

I said, "I'm sure, but I caught him in a nice little slip."

Skipper glanced over her shoulder. "Do tell."

"He thinks I was alone in Athens. He knows I went, but he doesn't know we had the Alpha Team."

"That's simple enough to explain," she said. "If he's really connected with the SVR, he can track your phone just like I can, but he probably wasn't expecting you to go to Athens, so he didn't have any surveillance on the ground."

I sighed. "I'd hoped we'd pulled a fast one on him."

Skipper rolled her eyes. "Believing you're going to outsmart this guy is a big gamble. He's been at least one step ahead of us since you kicked him around in Spain."

Clark made a noise a wounded animal might make, and Skipper asked, "Are you all right?"

"Yeah, but something just hit me. Barkov's security in Spain was too easy, and he's too much of a musclehead to let Chase push him around like he did. We're being played, and from Barkov's perspective, we look like a bunch of chumps."

Skipper said, "Maybe, but even if that's true, we can use it to our advantage. If we look like pushovers, maybe Barkov will relax and make a mistake. If he does, we have to be ready to exploit it the second it happens."

"How are you coming on the number?" I asked.

A few keystrokes later, she said, "It originated on St. Thomas, but that's not all. Remember that thing I did in The Bahamas with the old analog telephone system?"

"I remember."

She said, "The U.S. system in the Virgin Islands is only slightly more sophisticated, so getting in wasn't much of a challenge. The phone Barkov used to call you fifteen minutes ago has made a dozen calls over the last forty-eight hours, and they've all been from St. Thomas."

"So, he's camped out," Clark said.

Skipper checked her watch. "That gives us just over forty-two hours before your lunch date with Barkov. I say we have a little fun with him and remind the guy he's not playing with rookies. Who are you taking with you?"

"Singer, Hunter, and Disco."

"What about me?" Clark asked.

"I told you, I'm not doing anything you don't approve of on this one, so you make the call. Disco is a necessity, but I want Mongo here with Irina and Penny."

"Okay. I'll sit this one out until it turns into a circus, but when that happens, I'm the ringmaster."

Skipper said, "I need phones from everybody who's going."

It took half an hour to gather the team and deliver our phones into the mischievous hands of our analyst. Ten minutes later, she passed them back out. "Here you go, guys. From now on, your phones will be geographical idiots. They won't know if they're in Baltimore or Bangladesh, and neither will anybody who tries to track them."

"You're a genius," I said.

She huffed. "Yeah, tell me something I don't already know. While we're securing our network, I need to scan the airplane."

Clark lifted his phone from the table and punched a few buttons.

"Who are you calling?" Skipper asked.

He pinched the phone between his chin and shoulder. "I'm calling the geeks to get up here and scan the plane for bugs."

"Hang up," she said. "We don't need them anymore. I can do it."

Clark spoke into the mic. "Never mind. Go back to playing whatever game you and Thing Two were playing. I don't need you after all."

He didn't wait for a response before hanging up and sliding the phone back onto the table. "All right, Little Miss Do-It-All. How long will it take for you to clean the bugs out of the plane?"

"It'll take ten minutes to scan it, but I can't say how long it'll take to get them out if I find anything suspicious."

The scan took less than the prescribed ten minutes and produced no results. An hour after that, we were wheels up and headed for the islands.

Chapter 14
The Enemy of my Enemy

I stood on the sand with one of my boots in my hand and studied the remnants of the tiki bar I'd met Dutch at after my first successful mission to find and eliminate Suslik. Dutch had once been an operator with tradecraft skills second to none, but his love of the cash the Russians funneled into his pockets left him to bleed out in a cabana that had once stood less than a hundred yards from where I stood, with the toes of my only remaining flesh-and-blood foot curled into the sand.

The vision of Anya strolling along the beach, with her golden hair trailing in the wind and her sandals dangling from her fingertips, poured through my head. That had been the first time I ever saw her with my naked eyes. She'd been only a shadowy figure dressed in black through the lenses of my binoculars—before the fateful day that put the two of us on the same beach. I was there to put time and distance between me and Havana Harbor, where I'd killed Suslik, but she was there to seduce and flip the green, fresh-from-The-Ranch American who'd never been able to resist the Russian honeytrap.

"You okay, man?" Hunter asked, yanking me from the depths of my memory.

I pointed toward the shallow water just off the beach. "That's where she almost drowned me and where I shot off her toe."

"Penny?"

"No, Anya."

He gave me a shove. "She's not the one who should be dancing around in your temporal lobe."

"Temporal lobe? That's not where those kinds of memories are stored."

"Whatever. It's the only part of the brain I could think of, but you get the point."

"I do."

He said, "Good. You look like a jackass standing here with one boot on and the other one in your hand. Get yourself together, and let's get some grub."

Dinner was black beans and rice with broiled chicken and plantains.

"Why don't we eat like this more often?" Disco asked with rice falling from the corner of his mouth.

"You could've stuck with your cushy little corporate flying gig and had all the meals like this you wanted," Hunter said. "But you decided to sign up for the Apple Dumplin' Gang. Now you're stuck living with a bunch of door-kickers instead of fancy-pants charter passengers."

Disco washed down his most recent bite. "I'll take you bunch of dumplings over fancy pants any day."

Singer lifted his glass of tea in front of his mouth and whispered, "Guess who I just found."

Instinctually, the three of us turned to match our sniper's line of sight.

"Some spies you guys are," Singer said. "He's not over there, but I knew you'd look that direction. He's at my three o'clock, but don't look. It's Barkov."

I fought every instinct in my temporal lobe—and every other corner of my brain—to avoid checking Singer's three. "How far?"

Singer said, "He's across the street with three of the same goons he had in Ibiza."

"It's dark. How can you see them?"

Singer gave me a wink. "It's what I do."

Hunter asked, "Do you think we can cut him out of the herd?"

I threw some cash on the table. "Let's find out. I'd like to catch him on his heels."

We palmed a bill into a waiter's hand, who stepped aside and allowed us to leave through the kitchen.

On the street, Singer took point. "I'll cut the trail man as soon as they make a turn. Disco, you take number two, and Hunter, you and Chase should hit lead and number one simultaneously. Everybody agree?"

I said, "If you put anybody down, move forward in case this turns into a brawl. No pistols unless you're about to draw your last breath. Got it?"

Everyone nodded, and we fell into loose surveillance across the crowded street from the four men. Our prey seemed to have no fear of being trailed. None of them checked over a shoulder, serving up more questions of whether they had any security training at all. They didn't move like fighters. Instead, they carried themselves as if they feared and noticed nothing about the world around them. If their posture translated into the reality, the four of them wouldn't present much of a challenge for my team. Even Disco, our old guy, wouldn't struggle if we maintained at least some degree of surprise.

The four turned north onto the climbing grade of the disintegrating sidewalk and away from the water.

Singer said, "Cross here. I'll cut the outside corner and check for witnesses. Use hand signals if we have enough light and whistles if we don't."

Hunter, Disco, and I crossed perpendicularly and headed for the street corner while Singer sprinted ahead. From his improved vantage point, our sniper held up three fingers and pointed to his chest.

I gave him a nod and said, "Three witnesses coming toward us. Wait for them to clear."

Three tourists, who'd apparently enjoyed a few too many cocktails, staggered past, and I glanced back up to see Singer motioning a ninety-degree turn to the west.

I gave Disco a tap on the back. "Go hard!"

Singer outpaced the three of us and hooked a powerful arm around the fourth man's neck, pulling him from his feet. The sound that would've exploded from the man's mouth was muffled by our sniper's strength and practiced technique.

As if he'd been a commando from birth, Disco snagged the collar of the next man in line and yanked him backward and around the corner of the dilapidated building. Lacking Singer's hand-to-hand prowess, Disco resorted to a more primitive technique and sent the man's head crashing into the concrete wall. If the man had any will to fight, the collision depleted him of the ability.

Speed and violence of action were the core of the fighting technique Clark Johnson pounded into my head in my early days as an operator. The style had never let me down, and I didn't believe that record would change in the coming seconds.

Hunter stepped between Barkov and the only remaining man in what had been a column of security. My confidence in Hunter's ability allowed me to plow into my target with no thought of the fight behind me. I focused entirely on leaving Barkov conscious but defenseless. He would be least dangerous facedown on the sidewalk, so that's where I put him.

Straddling him like a horse, I pinned each muscled shoulder to the ground with my knees and pressed his face into the jagged concrete with a palm. "Guess who, Dmitri."

Through gritted teeth, he growled, "*Ty ubil moikh lyudey?*"

Of all the questions he could've asked, I never expected that one.

"No, Dmitri, I didn't kill your men. But I'm willing to kill *you* if you force me to."

"So, what are you going to do, hold me down on sidewalk all night?"

My lack of a plan was beginning to sting.

"I'll tell you what I'm not going to do. I'm not going to your prison, and I don't believe you have a valid warrant of any kind against me."

He groaned. "This means you will tell to me everything you know, yes?"

"That's the other thing I'm not going to do. I won't spy for you or anybody else."

He squirmed beneath me. "This leaves us in quite the predicament, no?"

"No," I said. "It leaves *you* in quite a predicament. You can walk away from me, my family, and my team, or you can die."

He turned his head far enough to speak clearly. "You will let me go if I say to you I will leave you alone, yes?"

"It's not that simple. We'll escort you to the airport, and you'll get on an airplane to anywhere you want to go in Europe. I don't care where, and you'll stay there. We'll check up on you from time to time to make sure you're living up to your end of the bargain."

"Or what?"

"Or the next time I see you, you will not see me, and you will draw your final breath. It's important for you to understand . . . I don't make threats often, and I never make idle threats."

He drew in a long breath, so I drew my pistol and pressed it against his ear. "Relax, Dmitri. I'm sanctioned by the American government to defend myself against slime like you, so if you want to turn this into an execution, go ahead and try bucking me off your back. I'll paint the sidewalk with the contents of your skull, then I'll have a cocktail and go to bed."

He relaxed beneath my weight. "We must have discussion like civilized men. None of this is what you believe it to be."

"The only discussion we're having is right here, right now, so make your decision."

He said, "My decision was made many years ago. I know what I will do, but I had to first determine if you were right American."

Hunter stepped beside me. "Everything all right, Chase?"

I glanced up at my partner. "I'm not exactly sure. Our friend here is speaking in tongues and not making any sense."

Hunter raised a foot. "My boots aren't as big as yours, but I'll bet if I introduced one of them to Mr. Barkov's face in rapid succession, he'd learn to speak some English."

Barkov said, "This is not necessary. Let me up, and we will have conversation."

I gave Hunter a nod. He retreated one step but didn't go far enough away to prevent him from ringing Barkov's bell if it became necessary.

With my hand planted firmly on Barkov's neck, encouraging him to remain calm, I climbed to my feet and stepped back toward my partner.

Dmitri kept his eyes on the two of us and slowly stood, dusting the debris from his clothes. "Where are my men?"

Hunter motioned around the corner. "They're having a little siesta on the sidewalk. Their heads are going to hurt tomorrow, and they'll be a little scuffed up, but they'll be fine."

Barkov stepped around me and onto the sidewalk beside his men, the first of whom was shaking his head and wiping blood from his mouth. Dmitri took the man's face in his hands and spoke in muffled Russian. "This is twice you have failed me when these Americans attack us. It will not happen a third time." Dmitri reached an open hand toward me. "Give to me your gun, American."

"Not a chance."

"Okay. In this case, *you* shoot this man. After all, you have authorization from American government for this."

I drew my Glock and raised it toward the man's skull.

He threw up both hands and begged in Russian. "No! Please do not do this! You do not have to do this."

Barkov held up a hand toward me and took a knee in front of his man. "If ever I see you or those two again—ever in my life—I will kill you where you stand, and I will do this with bare hands."

Almost before he'd finished the threat, he stood and planted a powerful kick to the man's chin, sending his head backward into the concrete wall and rendering him unconscious, if still alive.

Dmitri stepped back, straightened his clothes, and turned to me. "We will now have conversation like gentlemen inside someplace comfortable and quiet so you will know what all of this is about. Unless, of course, you do not wish to know. In this case, I will disappear from your life."

I gestured toward Dmitri's unconscious victim and said to Hunter, "Make sure he's still alive."

My partner knelt, felt for a pulse, and nodded.

I stared into Barkov's eyes in search of any hint of where the night might be headed but saw only placid pools of deep blue—the confidence replaced by something impossible to define. Perhaps it was resolution . . . or maybe surrender.

I motioned across the street at an obviously abandoned building with its doors hanging loosely on a pair of long rusted hinges.

Barkov scoffed. "I would like someplace more civilized."

"So would I, Dmitri, but you made this a street fight, so it's through that door or on an airplane. The choice is yours."

Inside the ramshackle structure, Dmitri Barkov and I sat on a pair of crates that had once held someone's precious cargo, now long forgotten.

"Let's hear it," I demanded.

He began. "You are correct. I have no warrant for your arrest, and even if I did, SVR officers have no police authority outside Russia."

"So, is that what you are? An SVR officer?"

He tilted his head. "Not exactly. Is more complicated than this. You would not understand."

"Try me."

"As you wish. No, I am not SVR officer. I am son of murdered man who was . . . There is no English word for *Oprichnik*. You know what this means, yes?"

I nodded once, and he continued.

"When my father was murdered, is very different inside Russia. There is no court to give to heirs what would be their property after the death of their benefactor. My father's fortune was seized by Putin, and I was given only crumbs that fell to floor from table of Kremlin."

The rage rose in his eyes, so I poked the bear.

"I guess that means you want to deliver me to Putin's doorstep with a nice little bow tied around my neck in hopes of gaining favor with the tsar. Is that about right?"

"No. I do not want favor of tsar. I want to watch him fall from his high place onto ground at my feet, and I want United States to help me do this."

I raised a finger. "Stop right there, Dmitri . . . Hunter, get the car."

The four-minute ride back to our hotel was the longest silent ride of my life. Every time Dmitri Barkov opened his mouth, I shut him up. In the solitude of our hotel suite overlooking the bay,

I sent a text message to Clark and thumbed the speed dial on my sat-phone.

Skipper answered on the third ring. "Op center."

"Clark will come through the door any minute," I said. "When he gets there—"

"He's already here. What's going on?"

"You wouldn't believe me if I told you, and I'm ashamed to admit I didn't see it coming."

Clark's impatient tone filled the air. "Spit it out, College Boy. What's going on?"

"There's no warrant. We were right about that, but we were badly wrong about everything else."

Clark said, "We're not going to play twenty questions. Now, get to the point."

I stared across the coffee table at a man who should never qualify as my ally, but was, without a doubt, an enemy of my enemy. "Barkov doesn't want me to spy for him. He wants to spy for us."

Chapter 15

Maids-a-Milking

Clark Johnson almost yelled, "What?"

I said, "He's with me now, and we're on speaker. Singer and Hunter have countersurveillance measures in place. I'll brief you later on the takedown. Right now, we're putting Barkov in harness."

Singer, the moral compass of the team and human lie detector sat beside me and studied every detail of Dmitri Barkov.

"Are you ready to get started?" I asked.

Clark said, "Go to work."

I lifted a bottle of water to my lips and tried to calm my nerves. "Look at me, Dmitri."

His eyes met mine, and the same demons I'd seen in his father's stare danced in the son's. "Before this goes any further, I have to tell you that we'll check, double-check, and check again every word you tell us for authenticity and honesty. If we catch you in a lie, any arrangement we create here tonight is over, and I will personally drop you at Vladimir Vladimirovich Putin's throne, where he will promptly arrange your reunion with your father. If you doubt anything about what I just told you, the offer to put you on an eastbound airplane still stands."

He stared at my bottle of water, and Hunter tossed one to the Russian. After a long drink, he said, "I will only lie to you to save my life."

Metering my breathing, I nodded. "We will provide you with a means to contact us twenty-four seven, so if you ever feel that your life is in peril, we can extract you or provide cover until an extraction can be made."

"You will give also to me a means of rapid chemical suicide in case I am apprehended by KGB."

I leaned back. "The Cold War is over, Dmitri, and there's no more KGB. We don't hand out suicide pills anymore. Those days are gone."

He laughed. "Foolish American. There is no more sign hanging over Yasenevo saying 'Welcome to KGB,' but no matter initials— SVR, FSB, GRU—is still KGB in sheep's clothing."

Clark's voice cut through the looming cloud. "We'll provide the suicide pill. Keep talking."

I wasn't sure which of us Clark wanted to keep talking, but I was in way over my head, so I held my tongue, hoping Dmitri would start gushing.

My silence was in vain. Barkov and I stared at each other as if neither knew what to do next, so I broke the second layer of ice. "I've got an idea, Dmitri. How do you feel about us trying a little honesty? I'll go first."

He nodded, and I said, "This is my first time."

He frowned. "You're first time for what?"

"Putting a spy into harness for the U.S. I'm not a CIA case officer. I've never been trained for this. I mean, I had the initial overview orientation, but that was meant to teach me what one of your comrades would do to try and recruit me."

Horizontal lines formed on his forehead. "You are not CIA?"

"No. Did you think I was?"

He squeezed his eyes closed as if trying to keep his brain from leaking out of his head. "If you are not CIA, then what?"

"Let's change gears. Tell me why you wanted me to believe you were SVR."

"Is simple. I was testing loyalty for you."

I palmed my chest. "You were testing my loyalty? To whom or what?"

"To America," he said as if it were obvious. "If you had agreed to spy for me to stay out of prison, you would not be loyal, patriotic American. You would be coward, and I have no time for cowards."

"What was your next step if I had agreed to spy for you?"

"I would listen and use information you gave to me to further my purpose until you were no longer valuable to me. Then, maybe I would kill you, or maybe I would tell to American FBI you are spy."

"To further your purpose. What purpose is that?"

He grumbled. "I have already told to you this. Is my purpose to see Vladimir Putin become same as Nikolai Alexandrovich Romanov."

"Tsar Nicholas?"

"Yes. Just as he and his family were slaughtered by Bolsheviks, this is what I want for Tsar Vladimir Putin."

"He's not really a tsar, you know."

Barkov laughed again as if he were hysterical. "You do not think so? Then, perhaps you should ask him if he is tsar next time you have conversation with him. He is tsar for same reason any Russian leader is ever tsar . . . Because he says it is so."

"We're getting off track. Let's focus. You want to dethrone Putin."

He grinned. "Not only dethrone him, but also humiliate him and take from him everything he believes is his."

"Why?"

"Again, I have already told to you all of this. He stole what was rightfully mine when he claimed my father's fortune for his own. He left me better than peasant, but only slightly better."

"So, it's all about the money?"

"No, of course not. Money is only beginning of revolution."

"Oh, so, you're a revolutionary?"

He held out an open hand. "Now you are beginning to understand. Revolution like Bolshevik is no longer possible. Kremlin and military are too strong. An uprising of peasants will be squashed like cockroach beneath heel of boot, but if I can give to Putin what he wants and then yank this thing from beneath his feet at last moment, he will be humiliated, and he will lose standing. First step in bringing down mighty building is to crack foundation."

The wheels inside my head spun in wild rotation as I tried to piece together the insanity falling from Barkov's lips. As it began to come together for me, I asked, "Why me?"

He smiled as if indulging a child. "Is not you, Chase Fulton. It is America. Only mighty country like America can do this thing. I will give to you everything your country wants in Eastern Europe, and you will give this thing to your masters. You will be celebrated hero. America will be strong again, like when it was Cold War. And Russia will no longer live beneath heavy KGB thumb of Putin."

"I think you're leaving out what you stand to gain in all of this. Is it the prime minister's seat you're after, or does your butt lust for Putin's chair?"

He relaxed. "This is for people of Russia to decide. I am merely one man giving my people choices they do not have under Tsar Vladimir's rule."

I leaned forward. "You're a madman, Dmitri."

He grinned. "Show to me one revolutionary who was not."

I stood and lifted my sat-phone from the table. "Excuse me for a moment, won't you?"

Before he could say a word, I left the room, pressed the speaker button, and stuck the phone to my ear. "What are we doing here, Clark?"

My handler said, "We're putting a spy in harness. Welcome to the espionage big leagues. You're about to hit a grand slam."

"I'm not so sure. Barkov is clearly insane. He's full of grandiose ideas, and I don't know if we're the right conduit for him. Can't we pass him off to the CIA or somebody? We kill people and break things. We don't run spies."

"We do now. Go back in there and find out what's in his pear tree."

"What?"

"It's a 'Twelve Days of Christmas' reference. Try to keep up. He's going to hand us a bunch of gifts, so I want to know if the first one is a partridge or some of those maids a-milking."

"I'm starting to believe I'm the only sane person in this whole operation."

Clark said, "Sanity is boring and highly overrated. Now, get back in there, and take your patient's straitjacket off, Mr. Psychiatrist."

"I'm a psychologist."

"Yeah, whatever."

Back in my seat across from the man I was quickly coming to believe was a modern-day Rasputin, I said, "Okay, let's have it. If you believe you've got something the U.S. wants, spit it out. I'm not carrying an empty bucket of promises to my superiors. Give me something that'll blow their skirts up at Langley."

Barkov cocked his head like a confused puppy. "Blow their skirts up? I do not know what this means."

"I'll keep it simple for you. Prove to me and the American Intelligence Community that you have something we want."

He said, "If you are not recording this, you must write it down."

Skipper's voice came through the sat-phone's speaker. "Just keep talking. We'll take care of the clerical requirements."

Barkov leaned forward and inspected his fingernails. "There are eight thousand three hundred twenty-one American military personnel at Guantanamo Bay. This number was correct ten days ago. It has likely changed, but only by a few. You can check this number if you would like."

I gave him a look. "You're going to have to give us something we don't already know. Counting heads at a Navy base doesn't impress anybody."

He narrowed his gaze. "How many of those are you willing to lose to defend the unlawful prison?"

It was my turn to lean forward. "What are you saying, Dmitri?"

He licked his lips exactly like his father had done at the Belmont Stakes over a decade before. "One of assets I was allowed to keep when you murdered my father was small transportation company with eleven ships, six thousand shipping containers, and two hundred trucks."

"What does that have to do with Gitmo?"

"My company was hired to deliver two hundred containers of military hardware to Cuba. The containers were sealed and guarded, but Russian soldiers are, at times, easily distracted by beautiful women, American dollars, and gallons of vodka. We opened few containers and found Russian infantry equipment such as weapons, armored personnel carriers, explosives, body armor, and food rations."

"Are you telling me that Putin is planning to assault Guantanamo Bay?"

"I am suggesting nothing of the sort. Putin would be a fool to try such a thing."

"Then what are you saying?"

"Also inside containers was . . . I do not know English word, but in Russian is *svyazki*."

I dug deep into my Russian vocabulary. "Bales? Or maybe bundles?"

"Okay, if you say this is word. I do not know. But was *svyazki* of Cuban national pesos, *moneda nacional*. I think this is phrase in Spanish."

"Bundles of Cuban money?"

He nodded. "Is counterfeit, of course, but no one cares. Cuban pesos have no value outside of Cuba, so it doesn't matter."

I said, "I have two questions. First, why did you open the containers, and second, where did you deliver them?"

"Some to Santiago, some to Puerto Tarafa, and Matanzas."

"Hold on," Skipper said. "Give me just a minute."

Dmitri looked at me as if he were waiting for me to scold the woman who dared to interrupt him, and I held up one finger. He huffed, and Skipper said, "Matanzas is a petroleum port, not a container port. You're lying."

Barkov barked. "Lying to you will accomplish nothing. You are correct. Matanzas is petroleum port, but my ships have cranes to off-load anywhere there is water deep enough. I do not have exact numbers, but I am certain we took many containers to this port."

I said, "Okay, for now, let's assume you're telling the truth. How about Havana?"

"Yes," he said. "Also to Havana, but only eighty containers between Matanzas and Havana. I do not know what was inside."

"Is that it?" I asked.

"Yes, this is all ports we delivered containers, but your other question was why I opened. I did not open. I was not there. I have many men who work for me in many companies. This is only one, but is same in all companies in Russia. Maybe somebody else will pay more for what is inside containers."

"But when you found out what these containers held, you decided not to double-cross the tsar?"

His shoulders and eyebrows raised simultaneously, and his wordless reply spoke volumes.

"When?" I asked.

"I have no way to know when they plan to strike."

"I mean, when did you deliver the containers?"

"Beginning sixty-five or seventy days ago and ending maybe thirty days ago."

"Are you the only shipping company who delivered military hardware to Cuba?"

He shook his head. "How could I know this?"

"Is your contract with the Russian government complete?"

He smiled. "There is no contract. Someone pays for me to deliver containers, and I deliver containers. This is how is done."

Clark said, "I've got a question. Where did you pick up these containers of military hardware?"

Barkov said, "St. Petersburg."

"Do you have pictures of the contents?" Clark asked.

"This is ridiculous question. Do you know what would happen to me if I am caught with such pictures?"

Clark said, "Fair enough. Give us the names and registrations of the ships you used for this job."

He rattled off the names of three ships and claimed they were under Greek registrations.

Ten seconds later, Skipper said, "That checks out."

I said, "We're off to a good start, but there are two things you and I have to work out, man-to-man."

He focused intently on my eyes, and I continued. "First, hands off my family. If I even dream that you're threatening my wife or any member of my team, I'll find you, and I'll feed you a full magazine of nine-millimeter. You got me?"

He nodded once. "Understood. I am sorry it had to come to threats, but—"

"Saying your sorry doesn't buy you any ground with me, Dmitri. You made it personal when you sent a man inside my wife's house in California. Trust me, you do not want to learn how I make things personal."

"What is thing two?"

"Anya Burinkova. Where is she?"

He cast his eyes to the floor. "I do not know."

I sprang from my seat and loaded a massive right fist, but Hunter grabbed my arm. "Easy, Chase. Let's find out what he does know about her before you take his head off."

He spoke barely above a whisper. "I hired seven former Spetsnaz to capture and photograph her after interrogation. Pictures were taken in Copenhagen and sent to me electronically. Bodies of five men were found in Malmö, Sweden, just across Øresund Bridge. Other two men have not been found, and they have not asked for final payment. After this, I have no more use for her, so I do not care where she is, but I believe maybe I hit nerve of you by taking her, yes?"

"You hit a nerve the instant you showed up in my life, Dmitri. Get this through your head, and don't forget it. You and I may temporarily have a common enemy, but we'll never be allies. The only excuse I need to cut your head off is the fact that you're still breathing."

Chapter 16
As We Know It

Before we cut Dmitri Barkov loose, we fingerprinted him, recorded a pair of retinal scans, and compiled a list of his commercial assets other than the shipping company. We equipped him with a pair of satellite phones, an encryption key for secure email, and one more reminder that he wouldn't survive our interaction if he made any effort to mislead me, my team, or the United States.

The flight back to St. Marys and the op center was uneventful and devoid of hijacking intervention work. What it did include, however, was my plummet into a cerebral black hole.

Singer pulled me from the depths. "Chase, wherever you are, come back."

I shook off my stupor. "Sorry. I was thinking about all of this, and I'm in way over my head."

He put on his reassuring smile that always makes the world a better place. "When was the last time you *weren't* in over your head? This is where we do our best work."

"It's just that I've never run a spy. I've never even been trained to run a spy. That's the meat and potatoes for the boys out of Langley, but I'm lost."

Singer reclined his seat ever so slightly. "Don't worry. There's a first time for everything. We'll get through it together, but it's not like this is going to be a long-term assignment. If it turns into a circus train, we'll hand it off to the Agency, but that's not our big concern at the moment."

I followed suit and leaned back in my seat. "You're right . . . as always. What do you think we'll do with the information on Cuba?"

He yawned. "We'll brief Clark, he'll brief the Board, and we'll do whatever they tell us to do. Until then, don't hurt your brain worrying about things that may not be ours to worry about."

"How do you always know how to deal with whatever comes up?"

"I live my life in two places, Chase. The first is in the loving arms of my God. There's nothing this world can serve up that He can't handle. And the second place I live is behind a large-bore rifle with my window on the world being a ten-thousand-dollar scope. From that spot, there's not much the world can serve up that I can't handle. Anything that falls outside those two places is somebody else's to worry about."

His breathing fell into a deep, peaceful rhythm as sleep took him, and he left me to be somebody else worrying about everything.

* * *

It was no surprise to find Skipper immersed inside her computers when we reached the op center. Without looking up, she said, "He's telling the truth, mostly. Check out these satellite shots."

Several high-altitude shots appeared on the upper monitors, and the team and I examined them closely.

Skipper zoomed in to show us two transport ships, a thousand feet in length. "Those are two of the culprits. It took a lot of work, but I dug through the old shots, and look what I found."

The screens flashed, and a pair of higher-resolution shots appeared, showing the same two ships unloading in two different ports. "Monitor number one shows the port of Santiago, about fifty miles west of Gitmo. Number two is Puerto Tarafa on the northeastern coast of Cuba, about a hundred seventy-five overland miles away."

"And you're sure those are Barkov's ships?" I asked.

"I'm certain about those two, but take a look at monitor number one again."

The screenshot changed to a third port and a view of a smaller cargo ship.

She said, "That's Matanzas, and I'm about ninety percent confident that's one of Barkov's boats. This one and Havana are the two I don't really understand. Matanzas is over four hundred fifty miles away, and Havana is another fifty miles west. It doesn't make sense to deliver military cargo that far away from your target. Moving that much equipment over the already terrible roads in Cuba is a herculean task, to say the least."

Mongo said, "Not if they're Silkworms."

Skipper flushed pale and spun in her seat. "I can't believe I didn't think of that. If you're right, this is going to make the Bay of Pigs look like a day at the park."

I stuck a finger in the air. "Could somebody brief me up on a Silkworm? I assume you're talking about the missile."

Skipper said, "Uh, guys . . . This just got real. Take a look at the main overhead monitor."

A crystal-clear satellite image of a highly industrial port with one cargo ship alongside filled the screen.

"What are we looking at?" Hunter asked.

Skipper leaned back in her chair and quivered. "That's Barkov's ship in Kangwon, North Korea."

Clark said, "Don't put the apple cart before the upset horse. Barkov's boats sail under the Greek flag. There's nothing necessarily sinister about one of them being at a dock in North Korea—or even China, for that matter."

I wasn't certain if my chuckle came from nerves or in response to Clark's dependable torture of the common phrase, but either way, it came.

Before I had to defend the involuntary sound, Skipper said. "Look at monitor two."

The same ship with the same cargo containers on her deck lay alongside a port I immediately recognized. "That's Havana."

I settled into my chair and closed my eyes as the possibilities poured over me. When I finally opened my eyes, every eye in the room was on me, and I said, "Somebody give me worst case."

Skipper spoke up. "Worst case is easy. Those containers are loaded to the gills with cruise missiles capable of carrying nuclear warheads to mainland U.S."

Clark's apple cart wasn't funny anymore. "Give me best case."

Skipper huffed. "Best case is even easier than worst case. Best case is *absolutely* anything else other than cruise missiles."

Clark laid a hand on Skipper's shoulder. "Get the Board on the phone."

As if programmed to do so, the team assumed their usual positions around the table, and the doors were sealed. When the monitors came to life, only two Board members were on the screen.

The first said, "The remaining members are en route and should be online in minutes."

Clark said, "We should wait. This is far too big to brief twice."

"As you wish. Elizabeth, silence our feeds, please, and we'll advise you when we have a quorum."

Skipper said, "Yes, sir, but you probably want more than a quorum for this one."

"Very well," the man said. "We'll advise when we're one hundred percent."

Hunter and I locked eyes across the table, and he mouthed, "What's about to happen?"

"The end of the world as we know it."

Even Singer wore a look of anxious concern that was well outside his typical countenance. The thought of cruise missiles in Cuba worried me, but not as much as seeing our sniper uncomfortable.

As we waited for the Board to assemble, the questions in my head expanded exponentially with every passing minute, but one question, above all others, kept bouncing off the front of my skull. So, I set it free. "Clark, what do you expect the Board to do?"

He pulled off his cap and tossed it onto the table. "We'll know soon, but until then, your guess is as good as mine. I've never been in a situation like this before."

Singer spoke up. "I'm not sure anybody has ever been in a situation like this before."

Clark chewed on his toothpick that was little more than a soggy splinter. "Of course I'm not, but if I were making the decisions on this one, I'd send you into Cuba to get a look inside some of those containers in Havana and Matanzas. The simple answer is to park an aircraft carrier battle group off the coast of Cuba and dare them to start throwing rocks at Guantanamo Bay, but the president would never authorize anything like that. Whatever happens will be done in the shadows by people like us."

Singer sighed. "People the federal government will say never existed. I'm pretty sure they call that plausible deniability."

Skipper perked up. "They're ready."

Clark stuck his cap back on. "Put 'em on the screen."

The overhead monitors filled with the faces of seven of the most powerful people in the country, and Rawlings spoke for the

Board. "We're all secure and ready, Mr. Johnson. Let's hear what this is about."

Clark cleared his throat. "Thank you, Mr. Rawlings. You're fully aware of the initial situation with Dmitri Barkov, but his opening revelation is something none of us could've expected. He stated—and we've verified through satellite imagery—that his shipping company, at the behest of President Putin, delivered four hundred land/sea containers to the island of Cuba under military guards. Barkov stated that some of his men were curious enough about the containers to lure the soldiers away from their posts to get a look inside a few of the containers. He states that the containers were full of military hardware, likely intended to be used in an attack on Guantanamo Bay."

Rawlings straightened his tie. "What would lead Barkov to that conclusion?"

Clark said, "In addition to the hardware, there were bales of counterfeit Cuban pesos in the containers. That can only mean the cash is intended to be used to hire Cuban nationals to assault the base."

Rawlings lowered an eyebrow. "Isn't that a bit of a stretch, Mr. Johnson?"

"I don't think so, sir. Cuban pesos have no value outside of Cuba, so the only logical use of the cash would be to hire locals for some nefarious task. The cash, combined with the military hardware, make up a convincing argument for exactly what Barkov suggests. As damning as that is, there's more."

Rawlings held up a hand. "Just a moment. Does anyone have questions about what we know so far?" Heads shook, and he said, "Okay, keep going."

Clark said, "Skipper—I mean, Elizabeth—acquired some satellite photography footage of one of Barkov's ships at the port of Kangwon, North Korea."

Rawlings seemed to relax. "That's not surprising. Barkov is the owner of a Russian shipping company. Russia does business with North Korea."

Clark said, "Of course, you're right, but the problem is, that same ship appeared in Havana Harbor, where it off-loaded the same containers it appeared to pick up in Kangwon."

Rawlings said, "What are you suggesting, Mr. Johnson?"

"I'm not suggesting anything. I'm simply reporting intel we gathered in the field, but if I were a betting man, I'd put money on a large-scale jailbreak."

"A jailbreak," Rawlings said. "So, that's what you think this is. The Russians are planning to empty the detention center at Gitmo?"

"It's one of the possibilities," Clark said. "But there are others. If the containers that went to Havana and Matanzas contained something more alarming than AK-forty-sevens, RPGs, and counterfeit pesos, we could be looking at the early stages of a missile attack on the U.S. mainland."

Rawlings ran his fingers through his thousand-dollar haircut. "I need to have a talk with the president, and we need to get a look inside those containers."

Clark stared into the camera. "Is that a tasking, sir?"

"No, Mr. Johnson, infiltrating a sovereign foreign nation and gathering intelligence on imported military hardware is not a tasking, but if it were, what would you need from us to make it happen?"

Instead of giving Clark time to answer, I said, "We'd need our ship back, sir."

Rawlings almost smiled. "In that case, Dr. Fulton, I'll call the National Science Foundation and tell them you want *your* ship back."

Chapter 17
That Was a Tasking

When the monitors fell dark, I turned to my handler. "That was a tasking, wasn't it?"

"You better believe it was, College Boy."

Singer slid his palms across the smooth surface of the table. "How many people do you think know about this?"

"Too many," Clark said. "That's why it's crucial that we get in there, ASAP, and find out what's inside those containers."

"How do we find them?" our sniper asked.

Skipper said, "Don't worry. I'll find them for you. You boys just worry about getting in and back out of there before World War Three breaks out."

I turned to Clark, and he threw up his hands. "Don't look at me. You heard Rawlings. This is your non-assignment, not mine. Besides, you're the only one of us who's ever broken into Cuba."

"That's not true. You and I stole—well, we *appropriated*—a minisub from Havana Harbor ten years ago."

Clark stared at the ceiling. "Oh, yeah, that's right. That was fun, wasn't it?"

Skipper clapped her hands. "Boys! Focus! If you keep this up, it's not going to be the Bay of Pigs all over again. It's going to be the Bay of Jackasses. Now, will one of you please tell me what you need from your beloved analyst?"

In perfect stereo, Clark and I said, "Our ship."

Skipper spun to her console. "I'm on it."

Seconds later, the main monitor came to life with Captain Barry Sprayberry's face the size of a small planet. "Hey, Chase. What's going on? I didn't expect to hear from you."

I felt the urge to retreat. "Hey, Barry. Could you back away from the camera a little? You're enormous in here."

He chuckled. "Oh, sorry. They'll let me run a half-a-billion-dollar ship, but I can't operate a webcam. Please tell me you have something for us to do. I'm freezing to death and losing my mind hovering over a tiny spot in the Southern Ocean while a bunch of scientists study something I'm not smart enough to spell."

"Funny you should bring that up," I said. "That's exactly why I'm calling. Where are you?"

"Have you ever heard of a place called the Machu Picchu Scientific Base?"

"No, but I've heard of Machu Picchu, and I can't wait to hear how you got that ship into the middle of the Peruvian rain forest."

"Oh, to be so lucky," he said. "The Machu Picchu Base is a frozen outcropping of hell they call a research station, about six hundred miles south of Tierra del Fuego, on the beautiful and picturesque continent of Antarctica."

"Sounds lovely. I think you'll be glad you took my call. The NSF is being notified as we speak that your services, and that of your vessel, are needed in the Caribbean."

Captain Sprayberry turned his attention skyward. "Thank you, God! If I have to hear about one more amoeba, I'm likely to drown somebody. How soon do you need us? We're not exactly in the neighborhood."

"It's not me who needs you. It's your country. And you're late."

He grinned from ear to ear. "In that case, I'll tell the geeks downstairs to strap down their microscopes. We're on our way, baby. I'm sure Skipper will keep you posted on our ETA. Oh, and there's one more thing . . ."

"Sure, what is it?"

"Please tell me Disco is coming aboard."

I cocked my head. "Uh, why? Is everything okay with the helicopter?"

"Oh, aside from being frozen to the deck, the chopper is fine. It's our financial officer. She's moping around like a teenager with a broken heart."

I relaxed in my seat. "I think we can arrange a reunion and fix that broken heart of hers. We'll see you soon."

He gave me a mock salute. "Research Vessel *Lori Danielle*, out."

I dug my heels into the carpeting and rolled myself beside Skipper at her console. "How long?"

"It depends on their route. If Captain Sprayberry takes the eastern route around the tip of Brazil, that's around eight thousand miles. Depending on his willingness to burn fuel, it could take anywhere from four or five days to three weeks. On the other hand, if he goes west and through the canal—"

I laid a hand on her shoulder. "I meant, how long will it take you to find the containers? I doubt Captain Sprayberry is concerned about fuel burn. He'll be here as quickly as he can."

"Maybe seventy-two hours, since you let me build the computers we needed. Before that, it would've taken weeks."

"Weeks? What's so hard about tracking down two hundred containers?"

She rolled her eyes and tapped the keyboard. A satellite picture of a massive collection of containers filled the screen. "They all look pretty much the same, don't they?"

I studied the picture and had to agree.

She said, "The only way to track them is to command the computer to find uniquely qualifying elements of each of the containers we believe to be sinister, and then search tens of thousands of satellite shots looking for exactly those same elements."

"What kinds of elements?"

She zoomed in and pointed toward the container. "Look closely at that one. You can see how it's been painted recently, but not the top. The overspray from the careless work makes this container unique. That's an obvious one, but it could be something as simple as damage to a corner that isn't common, or rust patterns, and things like that. There's no way I'll ever find them all once they leave the port and head inland, but I'm confident the computer and I can find most of them."

"I don't know how you do it."

She grinned. "I don't really do it. Thanks to the processing power we have here, coupled with a few thousand other machines I happen to be tapped into, all of this is possible through a process known as deep learning. It's even more advanced than artificial intelligence, but you'd never understand it."

I threw my arms around her. "How does the rest of the world function without a Skipper of their own?"

"I have no idea. Now, get out of here and let me get to work."

I spun and rolled myself back to the table. "How's everyone's immunization? We're headed for a Third World country where some nasty things crawl around."

Heads bowed, and murmurs wafted, so I said, "Singer, it's on you to get us up to date. Call that nurse who makes those pound cakes I love. I can never remember her name."

He said, "It's Cindy, and if she finds out you forgot her name again, there won't be any cake for you."

"Yep, that's it. Cindy. I was just testing you. Let us eat cake." I waved a hand toward Hunter. "You've got loadout. It'll be scuba insertion and multiple days in the bush. Keep it light, but don't skimp."

He asked, "Who's going?"

I checked Clark, and he said, "It's your op. You call it."

I ran the mental inventory. "Full complement. Everybody's going on the boat, and we'll pick the landing party from there."

Singer raised a finger. "I've got a thought. If this goes bad and we get shot up, we could really use a good medic who's not afraid of incoming fire."

"Do you have anybody in mind?" I asked.

"There's that eighteen-Delta from Captain Stinnett's crew. He's no spring chicken, but he knows his stuff."

Mongo said, "He's younger than Disco, and he can still hang."

Hunter chimed in. "Everybody's younger than Disco."

Our chief pilot grabbed his chest. "Thanks, Hunter. I thought I could depend on an Air Force brother not to throw me under the bus, but I see how it is."

Hunter threw up his hands. "It was a hanging curveball, and I had to swing on it. It was just too easy."

I knuckle-knocked the table. "That's enough, guys. Get to work. We'll plan a dress rehearsal when the *Lori Danielle* gets here. A little ten-mile swim in the North Atlantic to assault Cumberland Island ought to be a fair warm-up for our Cuban field trip."

Singer pushed himself from his chair and belted out, "Make it hurt, drill sergeant! Make it hurt!"

"Get out of here," I said. "I'll be down to help with the loadout in a few minutes. Remember, you have to carry everything you pack, so make it smart."

The op center emptied except for Clark, Skipper, and me.

Clark said, "Singer's right. If we get hit down there, it'd sure be nice to know we've got a medic who'll stick his hand in our chest and pinch off a bleeder."

I chewed my bottom lip. "I may live to regret this, but I'm not taking a man I don't know into that jungle with me, and we don't have time to get Fingers up to speed."

Clark said, "That's his name. I knew it was something crazy."

"Yeah, the story I heard was that he lost his fingers when he grabbed the muzzle of an AK that was on full auto and sweeping toward his A-team."

Clark sighed. "SF is full of guys like that. Are you sure you don't want him in the mud with you?"

I leaned back in my chair and pondered the question. "Would you take him if you were running the op?"

He didn't hesitate. "Damn right I'd take him. In a heartbeat. He wore the same beret I wore. The man's an operator, and operators don't stay alive as long as he has without knowing how to fit into a team. We're going to make contact on the ground. You can count on that. Maybe they'll be Cuban peasants with holes in their shoes, but I wouldn't be surprised if there were enough Russian regular army down there to give us a good kick in the teeth."

"You think the Russians are that careless?"

"No, they're that calculated. Somebody has to teach the Cuban rent-a-soldiers how to set up a mortar and fire an RPG. You can bet your fake foot that place is crawling with red-commie commandos who don't speak a word of Spanish."

The printer beside Skipper's workstation began regurgitating sheets of paper, and she motioned toward the machine. "That's Bobby 'Fingers' McGee's service record, including four Purple Hearts, a Silver Star, and Distinguished Service Cross."

Clark pulled the stack of papers from the printer and leafed through them. "Sure enough. He got the DSC when his Medal of Honor was denied."

He slid the stack toward me. "You're in charge, but I'd hate to see your guts spread all over that jungle and nobody there to shove them back inside you."

"That's the thing I like most about you, Clark. Your subtlety."

He dusted off his shoulder. "That's me . . . The most subtle freight train in town."

Chapter 18
What Could Possibly Go Wrong?

Days passed like millennia, and we pulled out every training trick we could remember to prepare for the Cuban mission. It all started with underwater refreshers, with Hunter leading the way.

We dusted off our diver propulsion vehicles, the torpedo-shaped machines designed to pull us through the water for our twelve-mile trek beneath the waves and onto Cuban soil.

Mongo inspected every inch of each machine, replaced seals, charged batteries, and repaired any damage he discovered. He held up a splintered propeller. "You boys are tough on dive gear."

Hunter said, "I don't weigh enough to break a prop, but you, on the other hand . . ."

"I guess you're right," Mongo said. "A brain this big is certainly heavy to carry around, but you wouldn't know anything about that."

Hunter surrendered and pitched in to help with repairs. When Mongo declared the rigs to be seaworthy, we donned our wetsuits and headed for the black water of the North River.

Hunter passed out laminated charts of the river. "We'll start with a simple navigation refresher. I'll lead the first leg to show you how it's done. After that, you'll take turns leading the team." He pointed to his chart. "Our goal is the shallow water buoy, here.

If we do it right, it'll be just under four miles and should take us about ninety minutes. Any questions?"

Clark groaned. "Let's get in the water already. I'm roasting in this rubber suit."

Hunter clipped his DPV to his vest and slipped beneath the inky surface of the river. We followed and gathered as close together as possible as our teacher set the initial heading for the first leg. The DPVs purred their comforting tone, and we set out for our first dive together in over two years.

Twenty minutes later, Hunter drifted to a stop and spoke into his comms. "We're right here." He pointed to a spot on his waterproof chart. "It's your turn, Chase. Take us to the open water."

I moved into the lead position, set my compass, and squeezed the trigger of my DPV. We continued down the river and into Cumberland Sound, taking turns at the helm.

Concern set in at the two-hour mark when we hadn't reached the buoy yet.

Clark was leading the pack when the realization set in. He released his trigger and sank to the muddy bottom. "I hate to admit it, but I'm lost."

I said, "I'm glad I'm not the only one. I've been lost for the past hour."

Hunter said, "We've got a lot of work to do, but thankfully, the swim into Cuba will be a straight line, adjusted for current. Would anyone like to take a guess where we are?"

Mongo said, "I think we're probably on the south end of the sound, somewhere around Tiger Creek."

Hunter sighed. "There's hope for at least one of us. Hit the surface, and take a look around."

We ascended to the surface and found ourselves across the mouth of the Amelia River from Fort Clinch.

I couldn't believe it. "We only missed it by a mile or so."

Clark slapped the water. "If we miss Cuba by a mile, we'll swim to Brazil."

"Take it easy," I said. "It's been a long time since we've been in the water, and we've got at least three more days before Captain Sprayberry shows up with the *Lori Danielle*."

He pulled off his mask. "I'm not mad at you guys. I'm mad at myself. I shouldn't let myself get this rusty."

"Don't beat yourself up," Singer said. "We're all guilty. We can't undo it, but we can make sure it never happens again. How about this? Let's break up into two-man teams and make our way back to Bonaventure."

Hunter agreed. "I like it. I'll take Clark. Chase and Disco can follow a few minutes behind. And Singer and Mongo can bring up the rear in case the rest of us get lost along the way. Also, I rec-ommend taking turns leading for twenty minutes each and surfac-ing every forty minutes to double-check your navigation. Compare your charted position with your actual position, and make adjustments on the next two legs. Got it?"

We agreed, and Clark took a compass bearing then disappeared with Hunter at his side. We gave them a few minutes to create some distance before Disco and I headed northwest. I could only assume Singer and Mongo would do the same.

Disco led the first leg across the sound, and I took over after twenty minutes. Then, we surfaced to check our position.

Disco scanned the area and grimaced. "We should be a lot far-ther up the river by now."

I motioned toward the swaying sawgrass. "The tide is running out. We didn't take that into consideration."

He palmed his forehead. "We're idiots."

"No, we're just out of practice. Let's go."

All three teams surfaced at the Bonaventure dock within fifteen minutes of each other.

Mongo shucked off his gear and pulled the water hose from the boat house. "Did anybody else forget about the tide?" Everyone raised a hand, and the big man laughed. "Let's rinse off the gear, and I'll clean it up before I put it away for the night."

None of us was willing to let Mongo do all the work, so we cleaned our gear and hung it up to dry in the boathouse.

I said, "I'm still a little chilly. How about you guys?"

Clark said, "Me too, but we've been in the water a long time. It'll be warmer in Cuba. The water temp should be in the low eighties, and we'll be in dry suits, so we'll be fine."

We showered and headed to the op center for an update, and Skipper didn't disappoint. "The computer found seventy-four possibles, and I've been going through each one to manually match them. So far, the computer is batting around five hundred. About half of the seventy-four containers are definite matches, and I'm running the others back through with tighter parameters."

I said, "Thirty-seven containers out of two hundred doesn't sound so good. Don't get me wrong . . . It's a big job, but are you happy with those numbers?"

"Oh, no. Definitely not. But we're not searching for two hundred containers. We're searching for eighty. The other hundred and twenty went to Santiago and Puerto Tarafa. It's likely those are small arms and platoon-level gear. The scary stuff is likely in the missing eighty containers. And I said the computer was batting about five hundred. I've actually found forty-one definitive matches."

"I get it. Let's see where they are."

She brought up a map of the north-central Cuban coastline. "This is where I expected to find them, but I was way wrong." She zoomed out and back in on the south-central coast and pointed toward a spot on the map. "This is the town of Trinidad. It's a medium-sized town with about forty thousand residents. Twenty-nine of the containers showed up at a spot of nothingness twenty-five miles northeast of the town."

"Nothingness?" I asked. "What do you mean?"

"I mean a place where there's nothing except trees."

I stared at the map. "Show me."

She pointed to a heavily wooded area, and I leaned in.

"Bring up the satellite shots of this area." In seconds, the image changed to a photograph showing dense vegetation, and I said, "A topo map would be nice."

She struck the keys, and the image populated with topographical lines ringing the area.

The pain in my gut was visceral when Skipper said, "That's high ground, eighteen hundred feet above sea level, to be precise."

Mongo sighed. "The perfect location for a missile-launch site—desolate and elevated."

My mouth felt like the Sahara. "Show me the highest elevation on the island."

"Give me a minute," Skipper said. "I'm not a Cuban geography expert yet." She zoomed in closer to the naval base. "It's Pico Turquino, sixty-five hundred feet above sea level in the Sierra Maestra mountain range, a hundred miles west of Gitmo."

I dropped onto my chair. "Look there for the rest of your containers."

As if a limitless wall had appeared between Skipper and the rest of the world, she poured herself into her computers and showed no signs of coming up for air.

Rather than wasting my breath pretending Skipper could hear me, I turned to the team. "Am I looking at this wrong? Are you seeing what I see?"

Clark was first. "As much as I want you to be wrong, if I were planning to hit Gitmo, I'd do it from the high ground, too."

Heads nodded in agreement, and the sickening feeling in my gut turned even more bitter. "We have to brief the Board."

Clark said, "I agree, but we need to know where our ship is first."

I dialed the ship's satellite phone and waited. The connection finally happened, and the voice of a young officer poured from the speaker.

"Bridge, officer of the watch."

"This is Chase Fulton. I need your ETA to Key West and your alternate ETA to St. Marys."

"Stand by, sir." A few seconds later, he said, "We're steaming for St. Marys at forty-eight knots. That puts us alongside in three days. We can make Key West six hours earlier."

I closed my eyes and drew a map of the Caribbean. "How about Santo Domingo in the Dominican Republic?"

"A full day earlier, sir."

"Continue for St. Marys, but stand by to reroute to Santo Domingo."

"Yes, sir. I'll brief the captain. Is there anything else?"

"Just one more thing. Are you making forty-eight knots because of the sea state or for some other reason?"

"It's the most efficient speed on foils, sir. Faster burns fuel at a much higher rate."

I said, "Don't worry about the fuel. I need you to make maximum safe speed."

"I'm not authorized to give that order, sir. I'll have to brief the captain."

"Where is the captain?"

"He's sleeping, sir."

"Then the choice is yours. Give the order on my authorization or wake up Captain Sprayberry."

I didn't wait to hear his decision. Either answer would result in max speed, but I admired the officer's adherence to protocol.

Mongo slid a legal pad toward me with two columns of calculations.

I ran my finger down the page. "Are you sure these are accurate?"

Mongo nodded. "If the seas are less than ten feet, they are. At max cruise, they can make the DR in thirty-five hours."

I leaned back in my seat. "That means we're wheels up for the Dominican Republic tomorrow morning. We don't have any time to waste."

I pieced the plan together in my mind. "Clark, you brief the Board. Disco, rig the *Ghost* for two pallets. And everybody else, pack the gear. We're out of time."

Singer steepled his hands. "Let's see. We've done exactly two underwater training events in the past thirty months, and we failed miserably at both attempts. We've not spent a single day in a jungle for the same length of time. We've fired maybe ten thousand rounds when we should've run through at least a million to stay proficient. Now we're throwing everything we own into an airplane we *just* bought, to hop on a ship we haven't seen in two years, so we can start a war in a Third World communist country. Hmm . . . What could possibly go wrong?"

Chapter 19
Saving the Planet

As I sat alone at the table in the op center pondering Singer's admonition, Skipper took a call at her console.

"Op Center . . . Sure. In fact, he's right here. I'll put you on the overhead. Stand by."

She spun to face me. "It's Captain Sprayberry."

I nodded and looked up at the overhead speaker as if I could see his voice leaving the black box. "Good afternoon, Captain Sprayberry. How are things aboard the *Lori Danielle*?"

"We're shipshape here, Chase. I've just taken over as officer of the watch, and I have some conflicting instructions. You want me to dump the scientists and meet you in the Dominican Republic. Is that right?"

"Not exactly," I said. "To be honest, I forgot about the research team. How many of them are there, and where do they want to be?"

"There are eighteen of them, and if I were guessing, I'd say they want to be back in Antarctica to finish their study, but that's not really what you're asking, is it?"

"No, it wasn't. I really want to know where you can put them ashore that won't ruin your shot at getting another research grant from the National Science Foundation."

"Don't worry about the grants. They'll come without any problem. This is the most high-tech research vessel afloat. Nobody else can compete with our capabilities. I could drop the scientists off in a life raft and still be flooded with funding."

"In that case, put them ashore in Santo Domingo, and take on fuel and supplies. I'll pay the airfare to get the scientific team home, wherever that is."

"Home is the Rosenstiel School of Marine, Atmospheric, and Earth Science in Miami."

I said, "Something sounds familiar about that school, but I can't quite remember why. Have you and I discussed it before today?"

The captain said, "Not that I know of. I've not seen you in a couple of years, so I was afraid we might never get to do anything exciting again."

"Don't worry, Captain. The next couple weeks of your life are going to be more than enough excitement to make up for two years of peacetime."

"I can't wait to have you brief me in."

Skipper snapped her fingers. "Masha!"

I cocked my head. "Masha?"

"Yeah, Masha. Hank's granddaughter from the Ocean Reef Club Airport. She was going to the Rosenstiel School for her PhD. We wrote a check to help cover her tuition."

"That's right," I said. "Did you hear that, Captain?"

"I did, and you won't believe it, but we've got a Hungarian researcher named Masha on the boat. What are the chances? Maybe you can see her when we make the transition in the DR."

"I'm glad to hear she's still with the program. We'll see you tomorrow morning. Let Skipper know if you're going to be delayed."

The captain chuckled. "We're the fastest thing on the water. Nobody can catch us to delay us, so we'll be there."

Skipper cut the connection and raised an eyebrow. "You may not want to exchange pleasantries with Masha tomorrow. If she's one of the researchers, she's going to want some answers to why her project got delayed, and you probably don't want to try explaining it to her."

"Excellent point," I said. "I've got enough to worry about without dealing with a ticked-off Hungarian oceanographer."

* * *

I spent an hour with Penny and a pot of coffee before heading for the airport.

"Chase, please promise me you'll be careful. This thing sounds more dangerous than anything you've ever done."

I took her hand in mine. "We'll be careful, I promise. We're back in shape, our equipment is solid, and the team is ready."

She stared down at our interlocked fingers. "It's just that whole ordeal with bringing the medic along. I guess that's what scares me."

"Bringing him along dramatically improves our chances of getting out of there alive, even if something bad happens."

"I don't like the way that sounds, but I think I understand. I'm glad he's going, but I hope he's not necessary."

I gave her a smile. "I hope for exactly the same thing. You know what we do is dangerous, but there's a lot at stake, so this mission is likely the most important deployment I'll ever make."

She squeezed my hand. "Just make sure that mission includes coming home safely."

I gave her a kiss and an extended bear hug. "I'll see you soon. I love you, and I promise to be careful."

She didn't cry while I was watching, but my gut told me the

tears came as soon as I turned my back. That moment of walking away never got easier. In fact, it got a little harder every time.

When I pulled onto the airport, the *Grey Ghost* rested peacefully on the tarmac in front of the main hangar as if she were anxious to go anywhere.

"You guys were up early," I said.

Hunter wiped a bead of sweat from his brow. "Yeah, we're ready to go. She's loaded, weighed, and balanced. That thing is so much more airplane than the Citation."

Minutes after I'd parked the microbus inside the hangar and closed the massive door, we were airborne and climbing to the southeast with Disco and Clark at the controls. Skipper busied herself with whatever she does while I played the mission through my head.

I'd been taught to envision my performance on the baseball field by a sports psychologist at the University of Georgia, and I'd learned that doing the same with battlefield performance typically increased my ability to stay calm and fight smart when the bullets began flying. There was sure to be no shortage of lead in the air in the coming days.

We landed at Santo Domingo and taxied to the transient ramp. Immigration and Customs in the Dominican Republic were notoriously anxious for a few American dollars to pave the way, but someone obviously made some calls and kept our time with the uniformed officers to a minimum.

I slid beside Clark and whispered, "Did you do that?"

He shook me off. "It wasn't me. It must've been the Board."

"Whoever it was, I like it."

He agreed, and we found the rental truck Skipper arranged exactly where they said it would be. Handing every piece of gear off the plane and loading it in the truck was no picnic, but we made short work of the task. Clark was noticeably missing during the manual labor, and I thought that odd.

After closing the door on the truck, I found him beneath a palm tree with his sat-phone pressed to his face. He held up the universal gesture for "give me a minute," and I nestled beneath a neighboring palm.

When the call was over, I asked, "Are you all right? It's not like you to bug out when the heavy lifting starts."

"I was doing a little heavy lifting of my own, and I scored you a surprise you're going to love. It's going to solve a huge problem for us."

"Do tell."

He dropped his chin. "If I told you, it wouldn't be a surprise. You'll just have to wait . . . but not long. I promise."

It took two vans, plus the moving truck, to get all of us and our gear to the port where the *Lori Danielle* was lying alongside the pier with sailors scrubbing every exterior surface.

Captain Sprayberry met us at the foot of the gangway. "Well, aren't you guys a sight for sore eyes? How was the flight?"

I pumped his hand. "It's good to see you, and the ship as well. What's with all the cleaning?"

He glanced across his shoulder at the progress. "We've been iced up for two months, and ice is filthy. The ship looked like a tramp steamer, so I thought she could use a good bath while we're up here in more pleasant climes."

"Are the scientists gone?"

He checked his watch. "Most of them. In fact, you probably passed them going the other way while you were descending onto the island. We got them on the nine o'clock outbound to Miami."

"What do you mean, most of them?"

He cast a thumb over his shoulder. "There's a handful of them left to off-load, and protect their specimens and samples, and God knows what else. We'll off-load the refrigerator units as soon as they double-check all the cataloging. I'm learning there's a lot of recordkeeping when you're digging up morsels from the bottom of the world."

As if on cue, the deck crane came alive and hoisted a massive stainless-steel unit from within the bowels of the ship. The crane operator set the unit on the back of a flatbed truck as if he were tucking in his baby girl. Four twenty-somethings came bounding down the gangway, and the only Hungarian I knew locked eyes with me, but the look on her face said recognition wasn't coming.

She stepped beside the captain and continued staring at me. "Have we met? You look quite familiar."

Her English had improved in the years since I'd seen her at the Ocean Reef Club Airport on Key Largo, but she still looked the same. My first inclination was to lie and blow her off, but part of me knew she'd wake up at two a.m. and remember my name, so I went with the truth.

"Yes, we have. I'm friends with your grandfather, Hank."

She threw her arms around me and hugged me as if we were twins separated at birth. "I thought that was you, Chase. I cannot tell you how much the scholarship means for me. I thought I was going to have to work my way through grad school, but thanks to you, I'll defend my doctoral thesis in the spring."

"That's fantastic," I said. "We were happy to help. Your grandfather has been a great friend to us for a long time. He and my— well, my mentor, I guess—flew together during the war, and friendships like that never die."

She grinned up into the bright morning sun. "Anyway, thanks again. I mean it. But what are you doing here? We're getting kicked off the research ship we thought we had secured for another four months, and they won't tell us what's going on."

Captain Sprayberry came to my rescue. "It's a vitally important political issue that requires our assistance. I'm sorry for the displacement, but we're not kicking you off. You're welcome back aboard as soon as we complete this mission."

She rolled her eyes. "No surprise there. We're out here trying to save the planet, and some politician *needs* our ship for some publicity stunt, probably. It's like they haven't got a clue what's happening to the world's oceans. What could possibly be so special about our ship that they have to have this specific ship right now? I don't get it."

I gave the captain a wink. "Whatever it is, I'm sure it'll be over quickly, and you'll be able to get back to your research."

"I'm not holding my breath, but you didn't answer my question. What are you doing in the Dominican Republic?"

"I was, uh . . . just sort of in the neighborhood, and Captain Sprayberry is an old friend. We don't get to see each other very often, so I wanted to take advantage of the opportunity."

She closed one eye, tilted her head, and looked up at me. "Okay, if you say so, but I'm not sure I'm buying that story."

I motioned toward the flatbed truck. "Good luck with your specimens, and I'll make sure Captain Sprayberry gets *your* ship back to you in no time."

She grimaced. "Yeah, right. I appreciate the thought, but I doubt you have any say in when we'll get it back. It's okay, though. The planet might be able to last another few years before we destroy it."

"There's all kinds of ways to save the planet," I said. "Some of them probably even include politicians. It's good to see you, Masha. Good luck on your thesis."

"Thanks, Chase. Maybe I'll see you again soon."

As she walked away, the captain gave me a look. "Really? There's all kinds of ways to save the planet? That's what you're going with?"

Chapter 20
Rendezvous with Darkness

With fuel bunkering complete and supplies aboard, Captain Sprayberry ordered the cleaning operation secured, and he motored us away from the pier without the assistance of a tug or even a pilot on board.

The captain met my team in the wardroom. "Okay, we're underway, and for the moment, I'm in command. How about briefing me up?"

I patted a chair beside me. "Have a seat, and I'll fill you in." He obeyed, and I spilled my guts. "The Russians are planning to start a war, and they're kicking it off by blowing Guantanamo Bay off the map. We're here to put eyes on a selection of shipping containers that likely contain enough Russian, Chinese, and North Korean military equipment to light up the Western Hemisphere."

He shook his head. "So, you weren't lying to Masha when you told her there was more than one way to save the planet."

"I'm a lot of things," I said, "but a liar isn't one of them. She's young and idealistic, and she probably thinks that cooler full of deep-sea specimens is more important than stopping a shooting war ninety miles from Key West."

He said, "We and she will have to disagree on that, but how do you propose I put you ashore in Cuba? We're an American-flagged vessel."

Clark answered before I could. He slid a slip of paper from his pocket and passed it to the captain. "That's where these come in."

The captain unfolded the slip of paper and read it carefully. "It's a set of coordinates. Do you want me to drop you off in the middle of the Caribbean?"

Clark put on the grin that always means something cool is about to happen. "No, Captain. We'll be picking up a little something that'll make our lives a lot easier. Oh, and is it okay if we just call you Barry instead of all this formality?"

The captain laughed. "Call me whatever you want. Just don't make me go back to the bottom of the world, where the sun doesn't seem to exist."

I chuckled. "You'll have to take that up with the save-the-world crowd, but as long as I'm on board, I can promise we won't go anywhere without sunshine."

"That's good enough for me. Now, I should get these coordinates up to the bridge. What's the T-O-T?"

Clark checked his watch. "Time on target is twenty-three hundred, Eastern Standard Time."

I pounded the table. "It's time to come clean, old man. What's happening at those coordinates?"

Clark leaned his chair back against the bulkhead and crossed his ankles as he propped his boots on the wardroom table. "I'll put it this way. You'll want to be down at the moon pool at ten forty-five tonight."

* * *

The time passed without Clark divulging another word about the mysterious rendezvous in the dark.

At 10:40, the captain came over the ship's PA system. "Attention on deck. Mr. Fulton and Mr. Clark, report to the bridge, ASAP."

I chased my handler up the ladder. "Are you going to tell me now? Barry doesn't sound like he's in a very good mood."

Clark just kept climbing until we reached the hatch to the navigation bridge, then he leaned through the opening. "Permission to come aboard the bridge?"

"Get in here," Captain Sprayberry ordered. "We're parked on your coordinates, and sonar reports an Ohio-class nuclear ballistic missile sub hovering at a hundred fifty feet. Care to explain that?"

"Imagine that," Clark said. "The good ol' U.S. Navy being on time. If you'll open the moon pool, they've got a present for us."

The captain snarled. "You're going to have to do better than that, Mr. Johnson. You parked my boat on top of a ballistic missile sub in the middle of the night. You Green Berets may get to play cowboy, but this is serious."

Clark turned to me and said, "Head down to the moon pool while I brief the skipper."

I followed his order and descended to the belly of the ship with the rest of the team. Four seamen in harnesses clipped to overhead securing points waited by the edge of the bay as the doors retracted, giving us a view of the sea beneath us.

One of the crewmen flipped a panel of switches, and the water turned brilliant blue and crystal clear beneath the subsurface floodlights. Seconds later, a sleek black form appeared at the extent of the light's reach.

"What is that?" Hunter asked.

Mongo grinned. "That's the reason we don't have to worry about underwater navigation on this little field trip."

With every inch that the black form rose closer to the surface of the moon pool, the more I became displeased with having been kept in the dark about whatever the object was. I practiced the conversation I'd have with Clark in my head and kept my eyes trained on the object until I was finally able to identify the SEAL Delivery Vehicle. A broad smile replaced my rising anger as the twenty-two-foot-long SDV nestled itself into the belly of the *Lori Danielle*.

Clark came down the ladder and onto the deck of the moon pool. He gave me that patented crooked grin. "Still mad at me, College Boy?"

"Yes, but your bribery is doing a nice job of quenching that anger. How did you score an SDV?"

He gave the device a glance. "Oh, I just pulled up rent-a-sub-dot-com and typed in your credit card information."

"Seriously. How'd you pull this off?"

A pair of SEALs climbed from the vehicle. "Permission to come aboard?"

Clark offered a hand. "Come on up, guys. Thanks for the front-door delivery."

The first SEAL said, "It was more of a bottom-door delivery, but you're welcome. Are you Mr. Fulton?"

Clark staggered backward. "Lord, no! Don't put that evil on me. I'm Johnson. That motley character over there is Fulton."

The SEAL pulled off his gloves and offered a hand. I shook it, and he said, "Try not to break or lose our SDV. We'll be needing it back when you guys are finished doing whatever it is you're doing."

"We'll take very good care of her, I assure you. But are you two not coming with us?"

"No, sir. We're under orders to drop off the SDV and not ask any questions."

"Are we at least getting a little training on the thing before you duck out?"

Clark stepped in. "Don't worry. Hunter and I are qualified."

I threw up my hands. "Now I get it. That's what this is all about. You didn't want to get left behind on this one, so you brought a piece of equipment into the mission that only you and one other team member can operate."

The second SEAL pointed back at the SDV. "It's pretty simple. We can give you a quick rundown if you want."

Clark spoke up. "No! That's not necessary. We've got it from here. Thanks, guys."

The SEALs stuck their regulators into their mouths and stepped from the deck, disappearing into the depths beneath our ship.

"All right. Let's have it," I said. "How did you and Hunter get qualified on a piece of SEAL hardware?"

Hunter was first to speak up. "We didn't do it together. Clark's really old. He got checked out in these things when you still had to pedal them. I got involved with a bunch of Dev-Group guys when they were doing some testing up at the Navy base. Once they figured out I was a former special ops guy, they let me inside the circle, so to speak. I never technically qualified in the SDV, but I've got at least a hundred hours at the controls from both the nav and the pilot's seat."

The four-man crew in the moon pool connected the crane to the lifting eyes on top of the SDV and hoisted it from the water. With a little wrangling, they situated the vessel on a pair of makeshift cradles and lashed it to the deck. Connecting the charging harness took a few minutes, but soon, the moon pool doors came closed, and we were back underway in no time.

Hunter and I climbed into the front of the SDV, and he went through the controls and navigation panel with me. "It sounds simple, but it takes a while to get used to. It's no sports car, but it's not exactly slow. We'll hit the beach in record time, and we'll be wet, but we won't be tired from the swim."

The seamen broke out squeegees and soon had the deck dry of the water the SDV expelled.

The 1MC intercom crackled to life with the bos'n pipe call. "Mr. Johnson and Mr. Fulton to the bridge, ASAP."

Clark and I ascended the ladder from the moon pool and reported to the captain on the bridge. Barry rolled out a chart on the table. "This would be a great time to tell me where we're going."

I stepped around the table and studied the nautical chart of Cuba. Motioning toward the south coast, I said, "Somewhere east of Trinidad with nobody on the beach would be ideal. The fewer eyes there are on the shoreline, the better our chances are of getting ashore undetected."

The captain rolled the chart and slid it into a tube. As he did, the chart table lit up, depicting the south-central coast of Cuba. He said, "Show me your objective, and we'll find a cozy little spot to put you on dry ground."

I pointed toward the high ground twenty-five miles from Trinidad. "The top of this hill."

Barry propped his elbows on the chart table and studied the coast. "How about here?"

Clark and I followed his finger as he traced a small river from the delta toward the high ground where we wanted to be.

I said, "Looks good to me. How about you?"

Clark leaned in a little closer as if he were memorizing the chart. "Yeah, I like it. The Rio Higuanojo will give us a reference line for the land nav just in case our GPS wets the bed."

After concentrating on the chart a few more minutes, Barry said, "I can get you in there, but not close. That's shallow water, and we need some depth to get your new toy out of the belly of the ship. It's going to be a ten- to twelve-mile trip once you're clear of the ship. Is that close enough?"

I eyed Clark. "Does the SDV have the range for that?"

"We can't run at full speed and still have enough juice to get back to the ship, but we can still make good time and have enough life left in the batteries to run home to mother."

"Then it's agreed," I said. "The mouth of the river will be our primary, but we need to pick an alternate in case something goes wrong."

Clark let out a groan. "I think you mean, for *when* something goes wrong."

I turned back to the chart and pointed to a small bay. "How about here, four miles west of our primary?"

Clark gave it a look. "I can dig it. Let's brief the team."

Captain Sprayberry said, "Good. Now, get off my bridge. I've got a ship to fly. I can have you on the spot by noon if you want."

I played out the timeline in my head. "No, let's wait for sunset. We need every advantage we can manufacture on this one."

The captain said, "I'll lay in a course and speed that will put us on target an hour after sunset. Now, seriously, get off my bridge."

Back in the wardroom, Skipper brought up the map of our intended landing site, and I began the briefing.

"Here's the plan. Captain Sprayberry will park the *Lori Danielle* about twelve miles offshore an hour after sunset tonight. We'll take the SEAL Delivery Vehicle as close as possible to the mouth of the Rio Higuanojo. We'll park the sub and swim ashore with everything we can carry. If the primary landing site is compromised, we'll move four miles west to our alternate. Any questions so far?"

Skipper said, "I don't have a question, but I've got something to add. If the weather is good, I'll fly the reconnaissance drone ten minutes ahead of your landing. Does that new toy of yours have a periscope?"

"It has a makeshift periscope that's essentially a pair of mirrors in a tube," Clark said. "But it's a shallow-water tool. It's only about six feet tall, so we have to practically be on the surface to use it. If there's surf, it'll get touchy."

Skipper said, "How about a commo buoy?"

"Yeah, we've got a buoy and internal comms on the SDV."

She said, "Okay, great. Sorry for interrupting."

"Don't be sorry," I said. "You're at the heart of this thing. Interrupt anytime you want."

No one else spoke up, so I continued the briefing. "Once we're feet dry, we'll go to ground and make our way up the rising terrain to this point." I stuck a finger on the projected map. "This is the high ground where most of the containers seem to have shown up. It's six and a half miles from feet dry to the objective, so keep that in mind while you're selecting what gear you'll carry."

Hunter raised a finger. "Are we strictly look-see, report, or are we prepared to intervene if we find something we don't like?"

"That's an excellent question," I said.

Hunter huffed. "I try not to ask stupid ones."

I ignored his jab and continued. "At the moment, we're strictly reconnaissance and report. If the Board makes the call for us to crash the party, we'll start some fires, but not without somebody else making the call."

"Sounds simple enough," Mongo said. "But I've got what you might call a *big* question. Will I fit in the SEAL Delivery Vehicle?"

I grimaced. "I wish I'd thought of that. The only way to know for sure is for you to go below, grease yourself up, and try to slither inside. Any other questions?" Nobody spoke up, so I said, "All right. That's all for now. Get some rest, and be ready for showtime when the sun disappears."

The team rose, and I took Disco by the arm. "Stick around for a minute."

He nodded and stepped aside to let the rest of the team hit the corridor. Once he and I were alone in the wardroom, I said, "I need to talk with you about something serious. Have you got a minute?"

"I work for you. I've always got a minute for the boss."

I took a seat on the corner of a table. "Listen, don't take this as a reflection of your tactical ability on the ground. Every member of the team would gladly take you into the foxhole with us any day of the week against any foe, but for this one, you're more valuable in the chopper in case we get pinned down and shot up."

He cracked a smile. "I thought that's what this was about. Whatever you need, whenever you need it, I'm here. I don't have an ego when it comes to crawling around in the jungle, so I'm happy to leave that to you and the Green Berets."

I gave him a slap on the arm. "I'm going to tell Hunter you called him a Green Beret. You might want to sleep with one eye open for a while."

"I just happen to know that Air Force combat controllers spend a lot more time with SF guys than they do with their comrades in blue, so he'll probably consider it a promotion."

"You may be right," I said. "Stay with Skipper in the CIC tonight, but keep the chopper warmed up. If we need you, we'll need you quick."

"I can't fly the Loach and fire the Minigun, so I'll need a door gunner."

"Get with Mr. LaGrange. He's the ship's weapons officer. He'll assign you a door gunner. He may even volunteer himself."

"You got it," he said. "Anything else?"

I checked my watch. "You must have a date."

He blushed. "It's not a date. I was just going to have lunch with Ronda. It's been a while."

"Go enjoy your lunch . . . and Ronda No-H."

He turned on a heel and left me alone in the wardroom with my thoughts. I was on the verge of invading a sovereign nation, with six commandos, without the official sanction of any government. I would likely encounter armed combatants willing to do us harm, and there was a better-than-good chance that we draw and return fire. If we were captured, the U.S. government would deny any knowledge of our operation. I was about to hang five good men way out on a limb, and if that limb cracked, I'd pull two more warriors into the fight in a million-dollar airborne dragon capable of breathing fire and lead into the jungle at six thousand rounds per minute. To call our operation the lynchpin on an international incident was a terrible understatement. If the Russians were planning an attack on Guantanamo Bay—a piece of U.S. real estate—my team and I were the only thing standing between them and World War III.

Chapter 21

Our Last Sunset

No one could sleep, so we gathered in the moon pool two hours before sunset.

"I can't fit," Mongo said. "But depending on how fast this thing will go, I may have a solution."

I turned to Clark. "How fast?"

His eyes searched the overhead. "I'm ashamed to admit I don't remember. It's been a long time since I've been in an SDV."

Hunter came to his rescue. "It's classified."

"Classified? I'll classify you upside the head if you don't tell me how fast this thing will go."

He laughed. "I've seen you fight, and I'm not scared."

"Have you seen me shoot?"

"Point taken. It'll go a lot faster than we're going to ask it to go. We'll run between five and six knots, and I think I know what Mongo has in mind."

The big man said, "I thought you might. And six knots will be just fine. I plan to clip into one of those pad eyes on top of the SDV and hang on for the ride."

"Will that work?" I asked.

Hunter said, "We strapped some gear on the outside of one of these in the sound, but I've never heard of anyone riding on the outside."

"There's only one way to find out. Gear up, guys. I'll get the captain to stop the ship, and we'll take her for a joyride." I made my way to the bridge and briefed Captain Sprayberry on our plan.

He said, "Sure, we can stop right here, but we're in about twelve hundred feet of water. If something goes wrong and you have to scuttle that thing, it'll be gone forever."

I scratched my beard. "I didn't think of that. Is there any shallow water about?"

He motioned toward the chart table and pointed to the southeastern end of Cuba. "There's an underwater ridge that runs from Cabo Cruz to the Cayman Islands. There are places on that ridge where the water is less than a hundred feet deep."

"How long will it take to find us one of those spots?"

"Give me twenty minutes, and I'll have you parked over a nice shallow peak."

"Thanks, Captain. We'll be in the moon pool. Let us know when it's safe to launch."

By the time I made it back to the moon pool, a forty-something man with only seven fingers stuck out his hand. "I'm sure you don't remember me, but I'm Fingers, the medic. It's nice to see you again, Chase."

"I remember you," I said. "Thanks for volunteering."

He laughed. "Are you kidding me? I wouldn't miss it for the world. I've been treating frostbite on snotty-nosed scientists for six months. I jumped at the chance to throw a rifle over my back and hit the jungle."

"Have you ever been in an SDV?"

He examined the black tube. "Not yet, but it's just a school bus underwater, right?"

We donned dry suits and rebreathers as the crew lifted the SDV with the overhead crane. By the time we were suited up, Captain Sprayberry called down from the bridge and gave us permission to open the doors.

We climbed aboard the SEAL Delivery Vehicle and forced ourselves into the cramped space. I found the least uncomfortable spot I could and plugged into the onboard oxygen and commo systems. "There's no way we'd ever get Mongo in here, even if he were by himself. This is tight."

Hunter said, "I'm the little guy, and I feel like a sardine."

When Singer, Clark, and Fingers pressed themselves into the machine, Mongo crawled on top and clipped himself to the forward lifting ring. Then, he carefully rigged a second tether through the front eye and all the way to the aft ring. We checked our comms built into our full facemasks, and everyone was loud and clear.

I signaled the crewman to lower away, and the SEAL Delivery Vehicle was, once again, back where it felt most at home—beneath the waves. Hunter flew the SDV clear of the keel of the *Lori Danielle* and rose to ten feet beneath the surface beside our ship. Clark gave the hand signal for Mongo to raise the mast on top of the craft. The long antenna extended above the surface of the Caribbean and allowed the Doppler inertial navigation system to align itself. The process took a couple of minutes, giving us time to squirm, wiggle, and try to find a position that didn't break our spines. I didn't like anything about the confines of the SDV.

Hunter's tinny voice came through our comms. "Alignment complete. Are you ready to have some fun?"

No one sounded excited about the adventure, but no one complained, so Hunter flooded the ballast tanks and dived the machine to twenty-five feet. Coming to a hover, he looked up. "Tell me when it gets uncomfortable out there, Mongo."

Our external passenger gave the okay sign, and we accelerated through the water.

As the digital display passed 8.5 knots, Mongo grunted. "It's getting pretty windy out here."

"Are you okay?" Hunter asked.

"Yeah. Just give me a minute to find a position that doesn't feel like I'm caught in a tornado."

Hunter held the craft at 8.5 knots and performed some climbing and descending turns. The SDV didn't do anything violently. It was smooth and docile but the absolute antithesis of comfortable.

After Hunter had spent twenty minutes in the driver's seat, Clark said, "Let me have a little stick time. It's been too long."

We hovered, and they traded seats. Clark wasn't as confident on the controls as Hunter, but after a few minutes at the helm, all the old skills came flooding back and he was flying the craft like an old pro.

Hunter checked on our giant one more time.

Mongo said, "I found a position that works pretty well. I don't think I'll be sleeping up here, but it's not bad."

Clark said, "Let's trade seats again. I don't want to play patty-cake with the *Lori Danielle*."

They swapped positions again, and Hunter flew the SDV into the moon pool as if he'd done it a thousand times. The crewmen raised us from the water, and Mongo dismounted his trusty steed while the rest of us pulled and pawed our way out of the nautical coffin.

Mongo pulled off his mask. "That wasn't as much fun as I wanted it to be."

I slithered out of my dry suit and helped the big man out of his. "I'll be glad to trade places with you if you want to compress yourself inside that thing."

"I think I'll stick with my first-class seat on top, if it's all the same to you. It's not so bad as long as you don't turn your head. The current likes to grab face masks turned sideways in the slipstream."

"Can you do it for two hours?" I asked.

"I wouldn't do it for two hours for sport, but I can hang on for something as important as what we're doing. Don't you worry about me. I wouldn't miss this, even if it meant I had to walk on the bottom to get on dry land. You can count me in."

With our dry suits hanging on pegs and dripping salt water, we headed topside to get our last taste of fresh, free air for a while. The confines of the SDV, coupled with the strangling taste of communism ashore, wasn't our preferred breathing gas. Perhaps we'd take one small step toward freeing the island nation of the oppression it had endured for over half a century.

Disco unchained the chopper and took it for a little joyride of his own. Well, it wasn't exactly on his own. He somehow managed to talk Ronda No-H into taking the ride with him. When they returned, she looked even more smitten with her fly-boy.

He had the crew top off the fuel and came bounding down the ladder. "She's in great shape."

Hunter gave him a playful shove. "Who? No-H or the helo?"

"Don't make me throw you overboard, Staff Sergeant Hunter."

My partner snapped to attention and whipped out the best left-handed salute I'd ever seen. "Yes, sir, Colonel Disco, sir."

Disco returned the salute with a jab to Hunter's ribs. "Give me a break, would you?"

Hunter shook his head. "Nope. Not now. Not tomorrow. Come to think of it, tomorrow I'll be busting my hump in that rainforest over there, and you'll be here in your nice, cushy, air-conditioned ready room. That's all the break you're going to get."

Disco threw an arm around him. "Just don't make me leave my nice, cushy, air-conditioned ready room to come rescue your butt."

It was a lighthearted comment, never meant to dampen the mood, but the reality of what we were about to do rained down on us like a wet blanket.

Hunter seemed to feel it first. "I know you're just messing around, but if we get in a pinch on that island, I can't think of anybody I'd rather have come pull me out of there than you."

Fingers pulled his cigar from his mouth and hooked it with what was left of his hand. "I've been knee-deep in the mud and blood and beer with a lot of teams in my day, but I've never seen one like you guys. I know I'm the FNG here, but I want every one of you to know that if there's any life left in you when you go down, I'll plug the holes in you, keep your heart beating, and shoot back just like you were my own brothers."

"We know that, Fingers, and we appreciate it"—I sniffed at the air—"but you need to get rid of those nasty-smelling cigars. We're headed for a little vacation where they grow and roll the best smokes on Earth. Maybe you can pick up a box or two while we're touring the riviera."

He examined his stogie and flipped it overboard. "I can't afford good smokes. I'm just a medical corpsman on a working boat."

I said, "You *were* just a corpsman on a working boat, but for the next few days, you're the corpsman on an action team, and *that* pays well."

He spat a piece of tobacco from his lips. "That sounds like good work if you can get it."

"It sure beats treating frostbite on scientists."

The western sky turned to brilliant orange and purple as the burning orb sank into the sea, and we watched as if it might be the last sunset we'd ever see.

Chapter 22
All Aboard Who're Going Aboard

The chef aboard the *Lori Danielle* fed us as if we were a whole platoon of hungry soldiers. None of us slowed down long enough to count the calories, but even Disco, who wouldn't deploy with us, poured at least three thousand calories down his goozle.

I pulled the cook from the galley. "I don't know what your goal was tonight, but I fear you may be on the verge of putting the whole team into a food coma. That was spectacular."

He took an abbreviated bow. "Thank you, sir. I'm glad you approve. The captain told me I'd be keelhauled if any of you left the ship hungry, and I need this job."

I slapped him on the back. "I'll pass it along to the captain that you deserve a raise and six weeks off."

"From your lips to God's ears, Mr. Chase."

We ran through our loadout one final time and fine-tuned our weight distribution and efficiency.

I said, "We're in for a six-mile, uphill move, so we won't make it before sunup. Make sure your gear will support you for at least four days. I've packed for five. We'll make all movement under the cover of darkness and go to ground when the sun comes up."

Hunter hefted his ruck across his shoulder. "What about ammo? I've got a thousand rounds."

I tied my watertight bag inside my rucksack. "I hope we don't need any, but I'm a thousand-rounder with you."

Mongo said, "I'll carry plenty of extra five-five-six for you little boys who can't haul a man-size pack."

The ship came to a gentle stop, and I said, "Here we are, boys. It's showtime."

Singer perked up. "I didn't hear the anchor deploy."

"It didn't," I said. "That's one of the *Lori Danielle*'s tricks she keeps up her sleeve. The captain can hover the boat using the Azipods and bow thrusters to hold the ship in a precise GPS position. They use it when they need to sit still in water that's too deep to anchor for the research stuff."

Our sniper nodded. "I like it. I guess that makes the ship less of a sitting duck if she needs to fly away in a hurry."

I said, "Speaking of flying away . . . Let's do a little of that ourselves."

When we reached the moon pool, the SEAL Delivery Vehicle was already in the water but still connected to the crane for stability.

Hunter inspected the onboard oxygen supply, the battery state, and the general seaworthiness of the craft. "I think she'll get us there and back. All aboard who are going aboard."

We wedged ourselves into the SDV, and Mongo strapped himself to the top. Before we submerged, we conducted comms checks, including a call to Skipper in the combat information center.

"CIC, Alpha One, comms check."

She said, "Alpha One, CIC, loud and clear. How me?"

"I have you the same, Skipper. We're sixty seconds from splashing. Has anything changed?"

"Negative, Alpha One. Proceed at will. Godspeed, boys."

"I don't know what that means," I said, "but it sounds fast."

"You're starting to sound like Clark."

"Heaven forbid. Bombs away. We'll be in the dark for the next two hours, but we'll check in as soon as we reach the objective."

I gave the thumbs-up to the deck crew, and they pulled the pins, severing our only physical connection to the *Lori Danielle*.

In an instant, we were submerged, and Hunter maneuvered us alongside our support ship for our alignment process. He'd programmed the waypoints and our destination into the vessel's navigation system before splashing, so two minutes with our mast raised above the surface was all the sub needed to be ready to take us to the beach.

With the masthead antenna still in the air and the initialization complete, I signed off for the long, dark ride. "Start the clock."

Mongo folded the mast, and we dived away from the ship and into the inky depths of the Caribbean Sea. With no moon overhead, the celestial forces granted us the priceless gift of darkness for the operation.

In seconds, Hunter established our cruising depth of twenty feet and set us on course for the southern coast of Cuba. Fifteen minutes into the ride, my legs began their protest. Although not as big as Mongo, my body was not the body they had in mind when someone decided the SDV could transport six SEALs. I fell well outside the physical boundaries of the typical Naval Special Warfare operator.

The psychological toll the mind endures when engulfed by total darkness is enough to challenge a man's sanity, but coupled with cramped confines, the darkness was far more brutal. I knew my team was in the cauldron with me, and I trusted Hunter and Clark to put us on the beach, but that trust didn't relieve the terror my amygdala was trying to process.

Everyone experiences fear. The difference between the average nine-to-five clock-puncher and warriors inside the special operations community boils down to the ability to suppress that fear and command our bodies to perform at the extreme limits of our capabilities while that fear is still churning deep inside our caveman brain.

For reasons I'll never understand, closing my eyes made everything better, and focused breathing gave my body the ability to relax and stop the fast-approaching cramps. The last thing I needed was for the muscles in my legs to be useless when I needed them to swim ashore and hike through the jungle until the break of dawn.

Hunter's voice came through the comms. "Checkpoint Alpha, one fourth of the way to the beach."

Except for Clark and Hunter at the console in our underwater bullet, the passage of time was impossible to gauge, so his checkpoint calls gave my head something to do other than think about the discomfort of my position. When we passed checkpoint Charlie, three quarters of the way to our waterborne objective, Fingers was the first to break. "I've got to get out of this thing."

Holding the positions of team commander, as well as team psychologist, the response fell solidly on my shoulders. "Hold on, Fingers. It's almost over."

"I can't," he groaned. "I'm cramped up, and if I don't get some relief, I won't be able to walk when we hit the beach."

"Listen to my voice," I said. "Focus on your toes. Give them a wiggle, and feel them press into the soles of your boots. Picture their movement, and keep wiggling them."

"I've been doing that for an hour. I'm telling you, I've got to straighten my legs, or you'll have to carry me ashore."

"Twelve minutes to objective," Hunter said.

I continued in my measured, reassuring tone. "Close your eyes, and take nice long breaths. We'll stretch you out when we make our objective. Just breathe and think about those toes."

He almost growled. "I'm telling you . . ."

Green Beret Master Sergeant Clark Johnson made his appearance. "Embrace the suck, and soldier on, Ranger! You're not in pain. You're just temporarily uncomfortable. You better pull that beret down tight and pretend like you deserve to wear it. You got me, soldier?"

I'd stood beside Clark on more occasions than I can count when he put the fear of God into a bad guy, but I'd never heard him climb that deep into anyone's butt who was on our team. Silence claimed the darkness, and our SF medic apparently embraced the suck.

A few thousand hours later, Hunter spoke the words we'd all been praying to hear. "Objective made. Rising to periscope depth."

A collective sigh of relief rose from our capsule as, one by one, we disconnected our breathing apparatus from the SDV's oxygen system and took our first breaths through our Draeger rebreathers.

As Hunter hovered the vessel six feet beneath the waves, Mongo raised the mast, and Clark deployed the makeshift periscope.

Clark said, "It looks like the coast is clear, but let's take a naked-eye look before we breach like a humpback."

Mongo volunteered. "I'll take a look."

Seconds later, he said, "There's not a soul in sight. I don't even see any ground lights."

Hunter asked, "Is everyone clear of the vessel and on rebreathers?"

We all reported clear and breathing, so Hunter took the SDV to the sandy floor in twenty-five feet of water. We anchored our trusty steed with screw anchors and a pair of lines to a couple of boulders.

"I sure hope she's here when we get back," Hunter said.

I laughed. "If it's not, I hope I'm not the one who has to tell the SEALs we lost it."

We formed up into a wedge at ten feet deep, and I noticed our medic twisting in the water and massaging his hip. "Are you all right, Fingers?"

"Negative," he said.

Clark took the man by the vest and shook him like a rag doll. "What's wrong with you?"

"Are you in command?" Fingers asked with pain echoing through his voice.

Clark called, "Chase, get over here."

I swam beside Fingers and held a D-ring on his vest. "What's going on?"

He groaned. "My hip's out of place. I thought it was just cramps, but it's definitely out. I can't swim."

I tugged on Mongo's fin. "Come with us."

He followed Clark, Fingers, and me to the bottom beside the SDV. I swam inside the vessel and braced against the framing. Fingers backed himself against me, and I cradled him beneath his arms.

"This is going to hurt, but we don't have any other options."

"Just do it," the medic said.

Mongo wrapped his arm around Fingers's leg and hooked his elbow behind his knee. "On three. Ready?"

"Do it," Fingers growled.

Mongo dug his heels in against the side of the SDV. "One . . . two . . ." He yanked the medic's leg as if he were trying to tear it from his body. Fingers roared in pain, and Mongo grabbed him by the vest. "Don't pass out, man. Stay with us."

He breathed in heaving gasps, and his voice broke with every word. "It . . . didn't . . . go. Do it . . . again."

Clark drove a thundering fist into the side of the SDV. "Dammit! How did you dislocate your hip riding a bus?"

I laid a hand in the center of Clark's chest and gave him the signal to surface. He followed me twenty-five feet to the first sight of
the sky we'd seen in two hours.

"What's going on with you? Are you all right?"

He wiped his hair from his forehead. "I'm fine, but we don't
have time to deal with that!"

"We don't have any choice other than dealing with that. He's
hurt, and it doesn't matter how it happened. If Mongo can't set
that hip and get him back in the game, we have to consider
aborting."

He glared at me. "We're not aborting the one mission that
stands between the Russians and a missile attack on Gitmo—and
probably Miami."

"What other option do we have?"

He shook his head and tried to calm down. "If I have to swim
him back out of here, I'll do it, and you can take the rest of the
team inland."

"That's not an option. We need both of you on this thing. Let's
get back down there and try one more time. Have you ever seen
this actually work?"

He sighed. "Once, but I've seen it tried a dozen times or more.
Even if we get his hip back in place, he's not going to have the
stomach to hike twelve miles with a hundred pounds of gear on
his back."

"We'll deal with that when it happens. For now, let's get him
back in the game the best we can."

We dived back to the bottom, where the rest of the team had
assembled.

Singer was probing Fingers's hip and shaking his head. He said,
"It's definitely out of place. Are we trying again?"

Fingers said, "Yeah, we're trying again right now."

Mongo gave me a look, and I nodded.

We assumed the position again, and Fingers said, "Don't count. Just do it this time."

Singer said, "Pull some pressure, and let me help position it."

Mongo leaned back, and Fingers grunted.

Singer manipulated the joint. "Okay, Mongo. Relax."

Fingers sighed as if the weight of the world had been lifted from his shoulders. When he caught his breath, he said, "I've been on the other end of that procedure a dozen times or more, but I've never been the patient until tonight. I'm sorry for slowing you down, but I was out of the fight."

Clark swam to within inches of Fingers's face mask. "I shouldn't have given you a hard time. I didn't know you were injured."

Fingers slapped Clark on the shoulder. "Apology accepted."

Clark brushed his hand away. "It wasn't an apology. I was simply admitting I was wrong. Your hip may be back in place, but we can't carry you up that hill. You're still out of the fight, Ranger."

"You're not sidelining me yet. When we get to the beach, I'll put some weight on it, and I'll make the decision."

If I could've seen Clark's face, I'm certain I would've seen pride. His brother-in-arms was still embracing the suck.

We double-checked our gear and the anchoring of the SDV, and for the second time, we headed for the beach with Mongo on point.

Chapter 23
All Ashore Who're Going Ashore

We swam at a comfortable pace, just far enough beneath the surface to avoid being shot at should an errant tobacco farmer stumble onto our beach. Mongo drifted to a stop and signaled for us to hold position, so we let ourselves sink to the sandy bottom while our point man broke the surface for our first up-close look at our landing site.

Seconds later, Mongo landed on the sand in front of us and gave the all-clear sign, so we continued our swim into the shallows until we were in waist-deep water. One by one, we removed our fins and slowly rose from the black ocean with the gentle waves lapping at our dry suits.

Singer placed himself behind Fingers in case the hip wouldn't carry his weight. Every cell in my brain said we had a lame medic who'd have to be returned to the ship, and I scoured the contents of my skull for a solution to accomplish that foul necessity without delaying the mission that demanded our vigilance. To my surprise, Fingers climbed the gentle slope into ankle-deep water, finally putting his full weight on his leg. He winced, but he didn't go down.

I laid a hand on Singer's shoulder. "He's yours until we clear the beach."

He nodded, and I joined the rest of the team covering Fingers and our sniper as they carefully made their way across the beach and into the tree line. My night vision made it impossible to interpret the look on the medic's face, but I couldn't imagine the pain he must have been enduring.

Safely beneath the concealment of the trees, we shucked off our dry suits and rebreathers and shoved them into waterproof bags, being careful to squeeze out every breath of air from each bag. Hunter gathered the bags and waited for orders.

I held up a fist, instructing him to hold, and I turned to Fingers. "How bad?"

Instead of an answer, Fingers said, "I need my pack."

Singer slipped the bag from his shoulder and silently laid it on the ground. Fingers unzipped a side pouch and withdrew a syringe and a small vial. He drew out a carefully measured dose of whatever was inside the vial and injected it into his thigh. He capped the syringe and replaced both it and the vial back into the pack. "Give me two minutes. How steep is the climb?"

I checked my watch and turned to see the rising terrain in front of us. "It's not steep, but it's rocky. What are you thinking?"

The determination inside Fingers's chest radiated from him. There was little doubt what he would say next.

He whispered, "I need another minute, and then we can move. I probably can't carry the pack all night, but I'll carry it as long as I can."

Clark stared across the medic and directly at me. I shrugged, and Clark said, "He's a Green Beret. I'll carry his pack."

Mongo reached down and grabbed the rucksack before Clark could claim it. The big man extended the straps to their full length and threaded his arms through them, situating the medical kit on his chest with his own ruck perched on his back.

Fingers said, "There's the morphine . . . That's nice . . . Okay, let's move out."

Clark returned to his familiar spot—in the medic's face. "If you go down, I have to leave a man with you and soldier on. This is too important to call off halfway up that hill. You're going all the way, or you're going to die trying, capisce?"

Fingers pulled his nods into place. "Move out, Sergeant."

I gave Hunter a nod, and he hefted the gear bags over his shoulders and moved back to the water. He dragged the gear down and anchored it to the bottom, well offshore, with the confidence we'd complete our mission and need those tools again in the coming days. Adding the weight and bulk of the gear to our packs was a wasted effort. Rebreathers are worthless on mountaintops, and we'd either make it back to the beach or we'd never leave the island of Cuba alive. Either way, none of us wanted to carry the dive gear through the jungle.

While waiting for my partner to return, I took a knee and fired up my comms. "CIC, Alpha One."

Skipper's voice always made me feel a little safer, no matter how many communists were about. "Alpha One, CIC, go ahead."

"We are feet dry with no contact. Is your drone airborne?"

"Affirmative, Alpha One. I'm in high orbit, and the closest signs of life are just over two miles west. IR isn't picking up anything between you and the objective."

"Roger. Alpha Six suffered an injury to his hip on the infiltration, but he's still operational, and we're moving inland. Advise if you detect any movement that isn't ours."

"Roger. How long will you stay on open-channel comms?"

Using the option on our radios to always keep the channel open for every team member ate battery power at an alarming rate, even when no one was talking. With our loadout for the mission, carrying extra batteries for our comms wasn't practical, so we'd be reduced to push-to-talk comms unless we encountered resistance requiring us to switch back to open channel.

I said, "We're coming off open-channel now, but we'll be listening for anything you think we need to know. Alpha One, out."

"CIC, out."

Once our team was whole again, Hunter moved to the front, and we moved through the trees at a snail's pace, making our way up the gentle slope.

Fingers moved gingerly but with dogged determination. I still questioned my decision to press on with him in so much pain, but Clark was right: the mission was far too important to scrap at the last minute. Delaying even twenty-four hours could mean the difference between American peacetime and missiles landing in the chow hall at Guantanamo Bay.

We moved through the darkness with sweat pouring from our bodies and the weight of our gear growing more oppressive with every step.

As we approached a clearing in the trees, Hunter held up a fist and whispered, "Contact, ten o'clock."

We froze where we stood until he gave the hand signal to take cover. We spread out, making every move intentional and silent until we became part of the environment.

I ordered, "Open comms."

We thumbed the safeties on our rifles, and every eye focused on the western edge of the clearing. A soft, mechanical hum resonated through the night air.

I spoke as softly as I could and hopefully loud enough for Skipper to hear in the combat information center aboard the *Lori Danielle*. "CIC, Alpha One."

"Go for CIC," she said.

"Contact two thousand yards west of our position. Does your drone see it?"

"Negative, Alpha One. Nothing. Not even a heat signature."

I turned back and stared across the clearing through my night vision. "There's definitely something mechanical out there. It could be a small engine of some kind."

She said, "If it were an engine, it would show up on the infrared. Are you seeing a heat signature through your nods?"

"Negative. But I hear it running, whatever it is."

She said, "Stand by, Alpha One. I'll take a closer look."

I rolled onto my back and stared into the star-speckled sky in search of Skipper's drone, but I never saw it.

As we lay, staring toward the sound to our left, our sniper whispered, "Contact, right, movement at two hundred yards, right to left."

Have we wandered into an ambush? Is the sound designed to catch our attention while a squad attacks from our right flank? What's happening?

Hunter whispered, "Somebody check our six. This is starting to feel organized."

"I got you," Clark said as he turned to check for movement behind us. "Clear to the rear."

Running was out of the question. We'd lose Fingers in the first thirty seconds, and I wasn't willing to leave a man behind.

Skipper said, "Tallyho! I've got a minor heat signature to the west, and an even smaller signature to the east, about two hundred fifty yards."

Almost before Skipper finished, Singer said, "Incoming. I've got two inbound from the east."

I could hear the blood coursing through my skull as I played out the coming minutes in my mind. The best possible outcome of the contact would keep my team well camouflaged while whoever was out there on the edge of the clearing walked right past us without noticing a thing. But that was unlikely.

My concern was that the two incomers Singer spotted on our eastern flank were just the tip of the iceberg, and that there were two dozen men trailing behind them. A full-blown gunfight less than two miles from the beach would spell certain disaster for us.

I whispered into my comms. "Are they armed?"

Singer breathed, "Unknown."

I sent up a silent prayer that I'd made the right decision and whispered, "Singer, move to cover. Everyone else, dig in, and save your bullets."

Singer clicked his tongue against his teeth to acknowledge my order, then he slinked through the trees to a position from which he could not only watch the action but also halt it with a few well-placed rounds from his muzzle.

The rest of us pinned ourselves against the earth behind what little cover and concealment the trees offered, and the minutes ticked off like eons. Finally, the pair moving into the clearing from our right appeared in the green glow of our nods, but the pair wasn't what I expected to see. Instead of two Cuban farmers on an early-morning trudge to their tobacco field, I saw two men who weren't bent by decades of topping and harvesting long green tobacco leaves. They walked erect with the confident stride of soldiers instead of the lumbering gait of downtrodden peasant farmers.

I slowly lifted my night-vision devices from in front of my eyes and peered beneath the electronic wonders to take my first naked-eye look at the clearing. Two unwanted characters were wandering onto our playing field. The Cuban night refused to give up her candy, so down the nods came, back into place, and my eyes danced as they readjusted to the grainy, green world inside the glass. The closer the men came, the clearer the image painted itself on my wall of fear.

Singer was first to announce the discovery I'd made seconds before. "Two military-aged males, sidearms and rifles. I have the angle."

"Hold," I said. "It's not worth the noise so far."

The noise wasn't my only concern, though. I wouldn't be the first to fire on the ground of a sovereign nation in which we'd not been invited. Nothing good could come of putting the two men down. Instead, I needed to know where they were going and why their heat signatures weren't visible to the IR camera on Skipper's drone.

As if on cue, our analyst's voice echoed through my earpiece. "Are they Cuban or Russian?"

The piercing volume of her voice felt like an icepick in my ear, but the weight of her question felt like the crushing weight of the world landing on my shoulders.

Singer whispered, "The rifles are AKs, and they don't walk like Cubans."

It was time for my question. "Can you see them, Skipper?"

"Yeah, but just barely. It's like they're under a shroud or something."

"Can you see us on IR?"

"You're glowing like lightbulbs, but the two guys in the clearing are not."

Singer's harsh whisper interrupted. "Freeze."

Both Skipper and I turned silent, and I slowly rotated my head to watch our intruders. Singer's warning was well-warranted. The two men changed their course and headed directly toward our position. As they came, the first man drew a flashlight and thumbed the switch. I slammed my eyelids closed and lowered my head to protect my night vision. The flashlight's beam would explode like a flare inside the nods, and the last thing I needed when we were seconds away from being discovered was a case of battlefield blindness.

The crunch of the brittle twigs and grass of the clearing echoed through the darkness like the sound of galloping hoofbeats.

"I still have the angle," Singer's comforting voice declared.

I swallowed the lump in my throat. "If they draw on us, put them down."

Singer clicked again but didn't say a word.

I slowly lifted my nods and raised my eyes to see the oncoming flashlight. The beam swept the ground ten feet in front of the men, but the poor quality of the light, or perhaps dying batteries, made the light less than usable beyond that range. That was the first stroke of good luck we'd encountered since leaving the safety of the *Lori Danielle*.

The two men crept toward our position, continuously sweeping the failing light. Their steps reminded me of Elmer Fudd hunting that wascally wabbit, and I almost let myself call out, "Eh, what's up, doc?" But I held my tongue and tried to suppress the Looney Tunes lobe of my brain.

"There they are!" the second man yelled in undeniable Spanish.

The flashlight wielder thrust the light outward and shone its yellowing beam into a stand of bushes to our right as his partner hooked a thumb beneath the leather sling of his rifle and pulled it from his shoulder. In subdued Spanish, he said, "I don't see them. Where are they?"

Please don't shoulder that rifle. If you do, Singer will cut you down before you can draw a breath.

Clark dug the toes of his boots into the soft ground like a cat ready to pounce. I couldn't think of a single scenario in the coming seconds that would leave the two soldiers alive. All that remained for me was to come up with a plan to mitigate the disastrous fallout that would inevitably follow.

It may have been my imagination, but I could have sworn our sniper was singing "Meeting in the Air" in the softest whisper he could produce. Traditional Baptist hymns from Singer's mouth when he was peering through a scope meant only one thing: At least one soul was only seconds away from departing its earthly body. And I believed that day would be no exception.

"*Allí!, Allí!*" the man with the flashlight yelled.

Without shouldering his AK, the second man buried the trigger, and 7.62 mm rounds and orange flames exploded from the muzzle. Fingers shoved his palms into the ground to thrust himself to his feet, but I chopped the inside of his left elbow, sending him thudding back to the ground.

Through the echoing reports of the AK, Singer's voice rang loud and clear through our earpieces. "Hold! Hold! Hold!"

As confusion engulfed my mind, tunnel vision set in and sent the whole world out of focus except for the muzzle of the belching rifle. The gunman spun, sending full-auto fire into the ground only feet from our position. When the magazine was finally empty and the bolt locked open on his Kalashnikov rifle, the man cursed and stomped like a spoiled child.

The flashlight wielder laughed until he couldn't catch his breath. When he finally gathered himself, he said, "Hutia are safe, and you must now buy more ammunition, you fool."

The gunman ejected the spent magazine and slammed another in its place. "It was your fault, Hector. That light is like you, getting more useless every day."

As the pair walked away, the first man still laughing at his partner, Singer asked, "Is anyone hit?"

"Negative," I said. "They were shooting a few feet to our left, but I still don't know why."

Skipper spoke up. "I can tell you why. There were three or four warm-blooded animals over there, but they're scattered to the wind now."

"Animals?" I said. "What kind?"

Skipper huffed. "I told you, they were warm-blooded. That's all I know. They showed up on the infrared."

I scowled. "Animals showed up, but two armed gunmen didn't?"

"I can't explain it. The rifle glowed like a torch, but the soldiers were barely more than a slight warm spot on the ground."

Clark said, "Come on, College Boy. I thought you spoke pretty good Spanish. Did you hear the guy calling the gunman a hutia killer?"

"What on Earth is a hutia?"

Clark chuckled. "You've never spent much time in Cuba, have you? It's the national animal down here. It's a twenty-pound rat about the size of a beaver."

"A rat the size of a beaver? You've got to be messing with me."

He said, "Nope, they're real, and they're nasty little jokers, too. I'll catch one for you."

"That's okay. I'll pass."

Singer slithered back into our hiding hole without a sound, and Mongo asked, "Were you singing 'Meeting in the Air'?"

The sniper said, "I don't know. Maybe. That just happens. I can't really control it."

"Never mind the singing," I said. "Why didn't you cut that guy in half when he opened fire?"

Singer said, "He obviously wasn't shooting at you, and I didn't want us to have to deal with two dead Cuban soldiers on our first night in the country."

"Nerves of steel," I said.

He gave Fingers's boot a tap. "Where were you going in the middle of the melee?"

The medic said, "I was going to do what I expected you to do. Turn those guys inside out. But I guess I'm glad Chase stopped me."

The sniper gave him a smile. "Welcome to the team that rarely shoots. Pressing the trigger is always the last resort. Now we just have to follow those guys and see where they're going. Are you coming, Hop Along?"

Chapter 24

Shots Fired

"We may not need to follow those guys," I said. "If they're headed to whatever that is at the western end of the clearing, you should be able to make it out with your scope as soon as the sun offers a little light."

Singer cocked his head. "You want me to stay here until the sun comes up?"

I checked my watch. "We've got ninety minutes. We can spend it digging in here for the day and get your eyes on that site, or we can move west to get a good look before those ninety minutes are up."

"You're the boss," Singer said. "But I've got a suggestion if you want to hear it."

"I always want to hear your suggestions."

"You guys stay here and babysit our crippled medic. Hunter and I will track those guys. We've got good comms, and Skipper can keep an eye on us."

I gave his idea some thought. "I like it. If you get pinned down, we'll be close enough to shoot you out of there."

While Singer and Hunter made their way to the west, staying well inside the tree line, the rest of us watched the clearing carefully and shoved some calories down our throats.

Thirty minutes after creeping away, Singer said, "Alpha One, Alpha Five."

"Go, Alpha Five."

"I found them, but you're not going to believe it. This is some sort of listening post. It's a little shack with a pair of directional antennae on top. It was shift change. The two guys who got our blood pressure up relieved another pair, and the off-duty team is headed your way. I recommend not shooting them, but I'd love to grab them and ask what they're listening for."

I asked, "How are they powering the thing?"

"You won't believe this, either. They've got at least three hundred square feet of solar panels. The humming we heard is a fan, probably more for keeping bugs away than for climate control."

"Get some pictures, and meet us on the north side of the clearing."

"Will do. And I think I figured out why Skipper can't see these guys on the infrared."

Our analyst burst into the conversation. "What is it?"

Singer almost chuckled. "Keep your pants on. It's just a hunch for now, but I think they're wearing some kind of material that blocks the IR spectrum."

Skipper said, "Get me a sample of that material."

"I'll do what I can, but no promises. Alpha Five, out."

We skirted the clearing to the east, making our way through the brush and staying clear of open ground. It took forty-five minutes to circumnavigate the clearing, and we rendezvoused with Singer and Hunter only minutes before the morning's light flipped its switch and changed everything.

We found a spiderweb of fallen trees that were likely the result of some passing hurricane, and we used nature's gift as a Motel 6.

Singer said, "I'll take first watch. You guys get all the sleep you can. At this rate, it's going to take us a week to get to the objective."

Mercifully, sleep came in minutes, and I slumbered like a baby, knowing Singer wouldn't let anything or anyone get near us. As the day wore on, the sun warmed the sky until our comfortable little hole became a sauna.

By midafternoon, sleep was impossible, so we crawled from our den like a gang of thieves begging for nightfall. My watch said it was almost four o'clock, and I studied the sky for confirmation. As I sat on a log, pondering the merits of movement in the daylight, Singer made a kissing sound with his lips and whispered, "It's shift change again."

Every eye turned back for the clearing to see four men crossing the space.

I leaned toward our sniper, "Why do you think there's four of them today?"

He shrugged and tracked the men's movement like a predatory cat. "Two of them aren't armed."

We watched in silence until the four new men replaced the two who'd been the day watch.

I keyed my mic. "CIC, Alpha One."

"Go for CIC," came Skipper's voice.

"Put your drone back in the air. I've got a mission for you."

"Way ahead of you, Kemosabe. I launched tonight's drone five minutes ago. It'll be overhead in high orbit when you're ready to move out."

I said, "That's not the mission. I want you to get a good look at the shed at the west end of our clearing, and then I want you to go hunting for more of them. Whatever that place is, it can't be the only one. I have a theory that they've established some sort of electronic perimeter—"

"Uh, Chase. We've got a problem. Somebody just shot down my drone."

"What?"

The stress in her voice sent my heart rate pulsing. "Are you certain it didn't malfunction on its own?"

"Yeah, Chase. I'm pretty sure I know what it means when the software I designed reports inbound fire, followed immediately by an explosion."

"Where did it happen?"

"Five hundred yards after crossing the beach inbound to your location."

"Do we need to recover the remains?"

She groaned. "No, if the initial explosion didn't demolish it, the crash would've. There's nothing proprietary about the hardware. It's the software that's valuable."

I considered the implications. "Are you launching another one?"

"It's already airborne, but it'll be half an hour before it's overhead. I'm flying a long, arcing route to the west."

"Did you get any origin data on the incoming fire?"

"A little," she said. "Whoever did the shooting was an excellent shot. They put at least two rounds in the drone from about forty-five degrees off the nose. That's all I really know. The camera survived the first shot, but not the second. That's why I said at least two rounds. Who knows how many more landed after the camera was dead."

I scratched my chin. "I don't like it. First, we find some sort of manned listening post, and then our drone gets shot down. Is there any chance it was friendly fire?"

Skipper hesitated. "I don't think so. Gitmo is too far to the east, and I don't think any friends of ours would be sending smalls-arms fire into the sky on the southern coast of Cuba."

"I just don't like it. Let us know when drone number two is overhead, and we'll move to contact."

I caught a flash of movement to my left and spun to see Clark sprinting from our position without his rifle. The conversation with Skipper suddenly became meaningless.

I stuck a finger in the air. "Where's he going?"

Hunter raised his rifle to the low-ready position and moved in the direction Clark ran. Singer broke into the trees ahead of us and into an arcing flank maneuver with his M4 at the ready.

Mongo looked at me as if the world was coming to an end, and we joined the pursuit of whatever Clark was pursuing.

Seconds later, Clark appeared behind a clump of low vegetation with victory in his eyes. "I got him."

"You got who?" I asked.

He glanced down at his captured victim, then back at me. "You can put your gun away and come see for yourself."

Based on the grunting and squirming, whoever Clark had pinned to the ground was still conscious and willing to fight, so I closed on his position, but I did not put my weapon away.

Singer appeared in my peripheral vision with his rifle pressed into his shoulder and his focus locked on Clark's position. Hunter stepped over the clump of undergrowth and shook his head in what appeared to be utter disbelief. Because of Hunter's reaction, I lowered my rifle and rounded the edge of the vegetation. The instant I was clear of the bushes, Clark lunged upward and launched a mass through the air and directly toward me. Shocked by the move, I sidestepped the flying object and threw up a pair of fists to block whatever it was.

It didn't hit me, but when the creature landed with a thud only inches from my feet, I stared down in shocked amazement. The animal shook off the landing, looked up at me, and scampered away.

"What is that thing?"

Clark laughed and dusted his hands against his pants. "That's the Cuban national animal, College Boy. The hutia. That one wasn't fully grown yet. They get a lot bigger."

"You're a sick, twisted man. You realize that, right?"

He shrugged. "You said you wanted to see one, so now you've seen a banana rat up close."

"Is that really what they're called?"

"It depends on who you ask. Over at Gitmo, the place is overrun with them, and that's what they call them."

"Do they eat bananas?" I asked.

"I guess they'll eat anything, but that's not why they call them banana rats. That beloved pet name for the adorable little creatures came from the other end of the thing. What they leave behind resembles a rotten banana."

"Thanks for the insight, but I could've gone the rest of my life without knowing that."

"Look at it like this. It's a cultural experience, and I'm broadening your horizons."

"I think my horizons are the perfect width, so let's lay off the broadening effort for a while. I'll let you know when I'm ready for another Clark Johnson wildlife adventure."

Skipper's voice crackled in my earpiece. "I don't know what's going on down there, boys, but drone two is overhead and ready to rock and roll."

Chapter 25

Release the Kraken

As the evening shadows stretched longer and the cloud-dotted sky surrendered her throne on which she'd sat, ruling over her half of the world's daily pirouette, distant flickering evidence of creation freckled the depths of the heavens, reminding me I was but an instant in a limitless eternity. Nothing I achieved would endure. Nothing I would accomplish would leave a lasting mark on time. But every pulsing ribbon of my soul burned to protect elusive peace and make the lives of those I love temporarily warmer and quieter and safer.

I pulled on my ruck, slung my weapon, and turned to face the five men who'd follow me onto a mountain peak in Cuba—or into the depths of a brimstone pit in Hell. "We're pushing to contact. What's behind us stays behind us. Whatever that listening post is doesn't matter now. Our objective is to put eyes on the contents of as many containers as possible, and that happens before the sun comes up. I'm on point, and I intend to put us on those boxes before midnight."

Without a word, every man donned his gear and fell in line with the same fire in his gut that I felt burning in mine. Too many American lives lay in the balance for us to let another day pass without sticking our thumb in the hole of the dam of communism and treachery.

The first hour passed with the world around us transitioning from day to night. The sun-loving creatures put themselves to bed while we animals who thrive in the night came alive to impose our will on the forces who'd never see us coming.

Ninety minutes into the march, I took a knee. "Huddle up."

We formed a semicircle, and I set my eyes on our medic. "Can you keep this pace?"

He wiped the wall of sweat from his face and pressed his lips into a tight, thin line. "Not much longer."

I flipped the nipple of my camelback into my mouth and downed two swallows of warm water. "We're making good time, but the terrain gets a little steeper for the next couple of miles. You set the pace, Fingers. Even if we cut our speed in half, we'll easily make the objective by midnight."

He dropped his pack from his shoulder and helped himself to another dose of the morphine that had given him the stomach to overcome the agony of his hip. "We don't have to cut it in half, but ten percent would be nice."

When the narcotics were back in the pack, Mongo snatched the forty-pound med kit and slung it across his chest. "I've got this. You just focus on walking. I pray we're not going to need you and your little bag of tricks, but if we do, I want you as close to rested as possible."

The look on his face said he was ashamed to let another man bear his load, but sincerity dripped like honey from his words as he exhaled, "Thank you."

"Is everybody good?" I asked.

Answers came in the form of five men hitting their feet.

Our pace slowed, but not much. Every time Fingers's stride hit the ground, his body exhaled an involuntary sigh of pain, but he never complained.

With the steepest portion of our climb complete, I grounded my pack and took a seat beside it. The sixty-pound ruck made a nice backrest as I caught my breath and poured more water into my body. Fingers first took a knee, then gingerly lowered himself to the ground. He massaged his thigh and hip with both hands as he tried to find a comfortable position.

I leaned into the huddle my team had created from sheer habit. "We're a thousand yards from the clearing where the containers should be, so here's the plan. We'll move to within a hundred yards of the clearing and build a nest for Fingers. I hope that nest doesn't become a surgical ward, but I want you rested, hydrated, and prepared to put us back together if this thing goes south. Depending on the configuration, we'll work from the perimeter of the clearing and hit individual containers as covertly as possible. There will be guards, but they won't be expecting us."

I turned to Singer. "I want you to run scout and position us where we need to be. Take Hunter with you, but don't let him start killing people. You know how he gets."

Hunter stuck out his lip. "I never get to have any fun."

Ignoring the quip, I said, "Here's the one thing that scares me. If we have to beat a hasty retreat, Fingers will be the weak link. Running is out of the question for him, so make every move as if your lives depend on it. We don't want to be discovered, and we absolutely don't want to get into a gunfight with a superior force."

Mongo said, "If it hits the fan and we have to run, I'll carry Fingers as far as I can."

Fingers bowed his head. "I'm sorry I put you guys in this position."

In unison, five voices whispered, "Don't be sorry. Be better."

That almost got a chuckle from the old Special Forces medic, but Skipper came alive in our earpieces before we could continue the good-natured jab. "I'm feeding live infrared video to your sat-phones. Those guys don't look like a welcoming party to me."

We fired up our sat-phones and watched the screens come alive with white heat sources that looked a lot like human bodies.

Singer asked, "Do you still want me and Hunter on overwatch? It looks like Skipper's got it covered."

I considered our options. "No, let's modify that plan. We'll cut up into two teams. Mongo, you're with Clark, and I'll take Hunter. We'll start at the eastern end of the clearing and work our way west with your team on the south and mine on the north. If we can pull it off, I want Singer on top of the highest thing we can find."

Singer nodded. "Sounds good. How hard do we fight back if they start throwing punches?"

I said, "If we can escape without shooting back, that's our plan. We don't need to get caught up in a gunfight on top of a mountain in Cuba. International incidents aren't good for our careers."

"Run, but don't gun," Singer said.

"That's right. But don't run back here to Fingers. If it falls apart, move southeast, if you can. The closer we get to Gitmo, the better chance we have of running into the good guys."

"Speaking of the good guys," Skipper said. "The staff duty officer at Gitmo has been partially briefed, so the Marines know you're out there. They just don't know exactly what you're doing out there."

Consulting my sat-phone and Skipper's IR video, I said, "I count fifteen."

Singer said, "Don't forget about the heat-shielding material from the listening post. They were able to hide humans and machinery from the infrared cam on Skipper's drone. If they did it back there, it's likely they're doing it here."

"Good point," I said. "Skipper, keep us updated on the head count. We're moving north."

"Will do."

We slung our rucks and moved through the trees like prowling cats until we were within a hundred yards of the southeast corner of the clearing. We found a collection of fallen trees and dug in a cozy spot for our medic.

I said, "Keep your head down, but stay in the fight. You'll be able to see us on the sat-phone screen. If you think you see something that Skipper doesn't catch, I want to hear your voice in my earpiece. We're outnumbered at least three to one, so we need every pair of eyes we can get on this thing."

Fingers gave me a nod, and we stashed our gear in his lair. With everyone relieved of their burdensome rucks, our movement was quieter, cleaner, and a lot more comfortable.

We crept within ten yards of the clearing and were rewarded with our first sighting of the reasons we were in the Cuban rain forest in the middle of the night.

"There's more than I expected," I whispered.

Hunter said, "Yep, me too. But that's not the bad news. It looks like every container is facing the center of the clearing. We'll never get inside them without being seen, especially if they've got night vision."

"Let's hope they don't," I said.

Hunter and I advanced in silence along the northern limit of the clearing and counted containers as we moved.

Singer said, "I found a tree I like, and I've got about ninety-percent visibility of the clearing."

I stared across the open space to the southwest and toward my brother-in-arms perched atop some tropical tree. Knowing one of the world's deadliest snipers had an eye and a rifle scope trained on the battlefield I was about to enter gave me reassurance as if God Himself were looking over my shoulder.

In his soft baritone, Singer said, "There are four containers about three hundred yards west of you, Chase. They're in a blind spot for everyone I see moving around. I think you can get to those without being detected."

Hunter and I increased our pace to the west until Singer said, "Right there. See those four containers by themselves just ahead and left?"

"Got 'em," I said.

"You're in the blind spot. I'll report any approaches."

Hunter and I moved as if speed were our mortal enemy, keeping one eye on the western end of the clearing and one eye on the four accessible containers. Every step I took sounded like a potato chip bag in my head, but I chalked that up to hypersensitivity and continued toward the first container.

When we reached the doors, we found a crimped metal band securing the latch. Hunter made quick work of the band with his Leatherman, and I lifted the handle. The squeak of the hinge might as well have been the scream of a hyena. No matter how slowly I pulled the door, the protesting hinge refused to be silenced.

"Give me a leg up," Hunter whispered.

I assumed the position with my right foot eighteen inches in front of my hips and my knee bent at forty-five degrees.

Hunter planted his left boot on my knee, and I cupped his heel. In one swift and silent motion, he propelled himself upward, landing his right foot on my shoulder. I scanned the clearing with sweeping glances, praying no one heard our acrobatics.

My partner leaned toward the upper hinge and spat on the mechanism until his mouth could make no more makeshift WD-40. Combining our strength to preserve our silence, we pulled against each other in a slow, steady motion to bring Hunter back to the ground. It was my turn to treat the lower hinge, so I followed my partner's example and doused it until I was dry.

I gently pulled the door, and the hinges protested again, but only for an instant. As soon as the pins turned inside the barrels, our combined saliva worked its magic, and the door swung silently, giving us our first look inside the container that had last seen the light of day in St. Petersburg.

Hunter gave a nod, and I stepped inside while he stood watch. Our night-vision nods, though remarkable devices, weren't magic. They couldn't create light where none existed. They could only magnify what light was already present. The interior of the container offered nothing for the nods to work with, so I was forced to produce my own illumination.

The IR light mounted on my rifle offered the best option, so I raised the weapon and activated the beam. The pitch-black pit exploded to life through my goggles, and I was overcome with disbelief. Everything was crated, but the Cyrillic markings told a story my mind wasn't willing to process.

After snapping a dozen pictures with my IR camera, I planted a toe on the first row of crates and propelled myself atop the stack. What I discovered deeper inside the container made the crates of Russian Army AK-47s look like a child's toys.

If my understanding of the Cyrillic was correct, the four containers I could see held Russian Sprut-B Kraken artillery pieces. With my eyes closed, I pored through the thousands of pages of data I'd studied in an effort to remember the range and payload of the Kraken, but it wasn't coming.

Skipper's voice pulled me from my concentration. "We've got a problem, Chase."

Chapter 26
Blinded by the Light

I slithered across the crates of AK-47s and back onto the deck of the container. "What's the problem?"

Skipper said, "Somebody just lased my drone, and I'm blind."

I forced the Kraken to the back of my mind. "What do you mean, somebody lased you?"

"I meant just what I said. "Somebody on the ground just destroyed the camera on my drone with a laser. Now, I'm completely blind, and somebody knows we're here."

"How?" I asked.

She growled. "I don't know, but I don't like it. First, they shot down number one, and now they've blinded number two. I thought I was too high to see, especially in the dark, but somehow, they found me and hit me with a laser strong enough to eat my camera. And that's no Walmart laser. Most civilians will never see a laser that powerful. Only the military and NASA have easy access to them."

"All right," I said. "Let's walk through this. I found a stash of at least five hundred rifles, enough ammo to start a war, and four Kraken one-hundred-twenty-five-millimeter guns."

Skipper said, "Those are ten-mile tank killers."

"They sure are, and that's just the first container."

Clark's voice broke in. "Singer, are you still in your nest? Skipper's drone is blind."

"I'm still on overwatch, but I didn't see the laser. Is the bird still flying?"

Skipper said, "Yes, but it's useless—"

Singer cut her off. "Get out of there, Chase! Four tangos are headed your way. Move!"

Hunter wasted no time closing the container door and winding the now-snipped metal band back through the lock hole. At a glance, it would appear undisturbed, but it would never stand close scrutiny. We rounded the container and headed for the tree line, making as little noise as possible, but moving quickly and moving quietly are mutually exclusive.

As we drew ever closer to the trees, I believed we'd made it, but Singer told a different story. "You're busted. Turn on the speed!"

There was no time to question the man with the best eyes in the business, so Hunter and I pinned our rifles to our bodies to avoid them bouncing on their slings, and we opened the throttles. We made the tree line before anyone cracked off a rifle shot, but with four armed men giving chase, the trees offered little assurance of safety.

Just as Lot's wife experienced in Genesis when Sodom and Gomorrah were tasting the wrath of God, I couldn't resist looking back. Fortunately, I didn't turn into a pillar of salt, but I did taste a little of the brimstone burning metaphorically in my gut as we ran for our lives.

To my horror, the area around the container I'd just invaded lit up like high noon. It looked like every handheld light in Cuba was full of fresh batteries and trained on the huge metal box.

As I turned back to scan our avenue of escape, my partner vanished before my eyes, only a few strides ahead. He didn't stumble or turn. He simply vanished as if abducted by some unseen force.

A thousand terrifying thoughts hit me as I tried to make sense of his disappearance. My brain was in ultra-fast-forward, but nothing about the scenario made sense. If he'd been shot, I would've heard the rifle. If he'd fallen, I would've heard the contact with the ground and the breath leaving his throat. But none of those things happened. The only remaining option nearly stopped my heart, though it came to me an instant too late. Hunter hadn't disappeared. The earth beneath our feet had vanished.

I took a running stride, expecting my heel to strike terra firma, but instead, I found myself plummeting through space with no way to estimate how far I'd fall or what I'd hit on the way down. Cascading through space and time, I tried to focus my night vision on the waiting ground, but I couldn't make it happen. Just like inside the container, there wasn't enough natural light below me to feed my nods the information they needed.

As my falling speed increased, branches of a tree brushed against my face, and I threw both arms forward in a desperate effort to grab anything that might slow me down.

My disorientation grew with every swipe of a branch or thud of a limb. Just as I thought I'd strike a limb and be left tumbling downward into the abyss, the world beneath me turned into a chasm of green light. In that moment, the source of the light didn't matter. Every action and every thought had to be laser-focused to slow my descent. I'd worry about the light if I survived the fall.

The tree limbs grew more substantial with every new brush and bounce, slowing my descent until I could finally get both arms wrapped around one of the protruding branches. Ultimately, it broke, but not before almost slowing my fall to a full stop. The tree couldn't support my weight multiplied by the momentum of my fall, but it held on just long enough to grant me a clear vision of the rocky, sharp field of protruding stones waiting to slice my body into bite-sized pieces.

Taking advantage of my reduced speed, I pawed at the branches, gripping with all my strength, hopefully pulling myself toward the trunk of the tree and not into open space. Finally, my boots impacted something substantial enough to stop my fall, but transferring the kinetic energy I'd amassed in the fall to a solid object sent my torso crashing against my thighs and knees. The collision knocked the breath from my lungs, just like so many runners from third base had done when we collided over home plate.

That old familiar feeling of believing I'd never breathe again came rushing back, but unlike the boy who'd crouched behind home plate in thousands of games, I wasn't that eighteen-year-old kid any longer, and my situation wasn't a game. There would be no athletic trainer who'd rush from the dugout with his med bag in hand and kneel by my side with one hand on my chest while offering encouragement to breathe. If anyone came for me, it would be the heavily armed Cubans, and in that instant, the horrific truth of the situation flooded my senses.

Where's Hunter? Is he alive? Is he lying on those rocks with his life's blood filling the crevasses of stone? If he is alive, can he walk? Can he run? Can he shoot back if the incoming fire begins?

As my breath returned in fits and starts, I took a self-inventory of my situation. Everything worked: my arms, legs, eyes, ears. I forced my mind to push through the adrenaline to feel the pain, to search for the unseen trauma, to feel the blood oozing from some open wound in my abdomen, but there was no serious blood loss. I was scratched up, bruised, and disoriented, but I was alive, and no one was shooting at me . . . yet.

With my senses gathered, it was time to make my way to the ground. If I were fifty feet above the earth in an age-old oak, it may be thirty feet or more to the ground from the lowest limb. I may be trapped in the most vulnerable position of my life. But the light . . . What was the source of the infrared light? It could only be Hunter. There was no other answer.

I reached the base of the limb that had saved my life, then turned my attention to the ground below. If Hunter was down there and capable of shining his light into the tree, he was at least alive and conscious.

I stuck a finger into my right ear, reseating the earpiece. "Hunter, are you there?"

Nothing.

"Hunter, Hunter, do you read?"

Nothing.

"Any station, this is Chase. Can anybody hear me?"

Nothing.

Work the problem, Chase. One thing at a time. Just work the problem.

I braced myself against the trunk of the tree and raised my rifle to my shoulder. I could flood the area with my IR light and hopefully find my partner. I reached for the switch to bring my light online, but it wasn't there. My thumb found only the aluminum forearm of my rifle where my light should've been. I was alone, with no working comms and no sources of infrared light. I was, most assuredly, up a tree without a paddle.

The human brain tries to make sense of what it experiences. When a person hears hoofbeats, he thinks horses and not zebras . . . unless, of course, he's in the plains of Africa. My brain was working overtime to explain my situation to itself. The light below had to be the IR light that had once been firmly attached to my rifle. The collision with the ground turned it on instead of pulverizing the piece of hardware. The silence of my teammates had to be a radio failure. I'd probably lost my transmitter in the fall. I had survived by sheer luck and determination, and I prayed my partner had done the same. Finding him was important, but first, I had to get my boots back on the ground.

As I descended the tree, I was grateful to find a second tree that had fallen against mine. The sloping trunk gave me a steep but survivable avenue back to the rocky earth. I hit the ground harder and faster than I wanted, but I stayed on my feet and didn't break the one remaining ankle I owned. Feeling for my transmitter that should've been tucked into my shirt pocket, I discovered nothing but torn fabric where the credit-card-size radio should've been.

Keep it together, Chase. Find Hunter, and stay alive.

I made my way toward the source of the IR light and discovered my hypothesis was correct. It was the formerly weapon-mounted light that should've been on the forearm of my M4, but the bracket was twisted and snapped. I took a knee and scanned the rainforest around me through my grainy green window on the world, shining the broken light ahead and methodically searching for my partner.

When I was convinced he wasn't within twenty yards of me, I moved down the slope and started the scan again. After fifteen minutes of increasing fear that Hunter had met his fate, I repositioned one last time and found myself on a small outcropping of stone that gave me a vantage point that was only slightly less advantageous than my favorite tree limb.

I scanned inch by inch and foot by foot until I saw what I had most feared—what I had most dreaded finding. My partner's body lay across a protruding rock about thirty yards beneath me with his left leg bent unnaturally underneath and behind him. From my position, there was no movement, no sound, and no sign of life.

I sent up a silent prayer and scampered down the slope toward Hunter's body with my rifle in one hand and the IR light in the other. A few feet from him, I dropped my rifle, letting it dangle across my chest on its sling, and I lunged for my partner and brother.

There was no question his leg was broken. It looked worse than mine had after the accident that cost me my right foot and ankle. With any luck, he was just unconscious from the pain and shock of the badly broken limb.

I slid to a stop beside him and immediately thrust a pair of fingers onto the side of his neck, desperately searching for a pulse. I could feel a faint, rapid pumping, but was that Hunter's pulse or mine? I leaned down with my cheek against his nose and mouth, begging all of Heaven to let me feel his breath.

Heaven answered, and a raspy, gurgling exhalation came. The armed Cubans a hundred feet overhead were the last thing on my mind. I ran my fingertips up the back of my partner's neck, feeling for anything that might be broken. I had to get him on his side, if I could do it without killing him. The gurgling sound coming from his lungs was only slightly better than the absence of any breathing. If I didn't roll him over, he'd drown in whatever bodily fluid was filling his lungs. In that moment, I would've given my own life to have Fingers, the SF medic, by my side, but he wasn't coming, and no amount of money could buy Hunter's and my way out of the trainwreck we'd fallen into.

Chapter 27
Burning Bridges

I wish I could say I instantly knew what to do and how to deal with the situation in which I was absorbed, but that wasn't the case. Not even a little bit. I kept my cool and suppressed the panic rising in my chest. Nothing kills more warriors than panic. I wasn't going to die at the base of that rocky cliff I should've known was there, and more importantly, I wasn't going to let Hunter die so far from home.

Convinced his spine wasn't broken, I cradled his broken leg in my right arm and grabbed a fistful of his collar just beneath his chin. I lifted his hundred eighty pounds as if he were a newborn baby and positioned him on the flattest, least rocky patch of earth I could find. I hadn't been through the Special Forces 18-Delta Combat Medic training Singer and Fingers had, but I knew enough from my training and experience to move Hunter's leg only once before splinting it. So, with that knowledge in place, I took his foot in one hand and his shin in the other and pulled and twisted until his foot was at least facing the correct direction. I expected him to wake up and bellow like a trapped bear when I moved his leg, but he never made a sound.

With his leg unwound from the horrifically unnatural position, I scanned the area for anything I could use as a long, immovable splint. As my search continued, my M4 bounced against my chest, and I couldn't resist smiling. Kneeling back beside my partner, I pressed the quick disconnect at the end of his rifle sling and slid the webbing from around his shoulder. I unloaded his rifle and stuffed his ammo in my pouch. The rifle fit nicely against the outside of his leg, and the sling made a decent binding. A roll of duct tape would've been priceless in that moment, but the sling would have to do.

Every thirty seconds—or what felt like thirty seconds—I looked up, expecting the muzzles of a hundred Russian AK-47s to belch orange fire, sending a ton of lead raining down on us, but the top of the cliff remained empty of riflemen.

A-B-C. Airway, breathing, circulation.

His airway was relatively clear—at least clear enough to let breaths in and out. I had calmed down enough to recheck for a pulse, and that time, I found an unquestionable, rhythmic thud in both his neck and wrist.

MARCH. Come on, Chase. What is MARCH? You've got to remember.

M . . . Oh, yeah. Massive hemorrhage.

Finding blood through my night-vision nods would be like playing pin the tail on the donkey with a live donkey. It wouldn't happen, but I had to determine if Hunter was losing blood with every beat of his heart. Everything in combat is a tradeoff. I needed to remain concealed beneath the blanket of darkness the moonless sky provided, but if I wanted to keep Hunter alive, I had to look for massive blood loss.

I pulled my penlight from my pocket and slid the barrel into my curled palm. When I pushed the switch, it felt like the sun itself was shining down on us, but in reality, it was a beam of white light that was barely big enough to discern. When my heart rate slowed, I panned the light across Hunter's body in search of anything that looked like blood. He was beaten up, and there were some abrasions and cuts from which small amounts of blood were oozing, but there was nothing life-threatening about any of those. As Clark would say, I should rub some dirt on it and tell my partner to embrace the suck.

In that moment, he was embracing unconsciousness, and I was thankful for that. If he were awake, the pain from the broken leg would've been too much to quash.

A . . . Airway. I've got that one covered.

R . . . What's the R? Come on, Chase. Remember!

I decided it didn't matter, and I had to move on.

C . . . Is C circulation? Maybe. If so, we've got that one figured out.

H . . . Ah! I remember this one. Head injury. Or is it hypothermia? Who cares? Check for both.

Hypothermia wasn't a serious issue. The air was warm, and the sun would soon be up.

Oh, crap. The sun. That's the last thing I need. What time is it? Focus! The other H. Head injury.

I ran my hands through his hair, beard, and beneath his jawline. Nothing felt broken, and my hands came away wet with sweat but devoid of blood.

I remember now. R is respiratory support. But there's nothing I can do. He's breathing, so that has to be enough.

I shoved my sleeve above my watch and checked the time. In thirty-five minutes, the eastern sky would turn purple and gradually become orange within ten minutes after that. I had forty-five minutes to carry my partner a mile back to our medic in his den.

If only I could get somebody on the radio . . . Hunter has a radio!

I shoved my hand into his shirt pocket and yanked the transmitter from inside. It came clear of the fabric in three pieces, and my momentary elation melted back into grim reality.

I stuck the mouthpiece of my camelback between my teeth, press-checked my rifle for a round in the chamber, and took a full breath. There's something about an unconscious victim that makes them heavier than a wide-awake passenger. Even though Hunter weighed forty pounds less than me, he felt like Mongo when I hefted him over my shoulders.

My first few steps looked like the first strides of a baby giraffe minutes after it falls six feet from its mother's womb, but I adjusted and repositioned Hunter's limp form in preparation for the longest mile I'd ever walk.

Looking at my watch would do little more than add pressure I didn't need. Every stride was punctuated with arguments for and against continuing my trek after the sun made her appearance.

Is Hunter critical? Will he die if I don't get him to Fingers in the next hour? Can he survive a day if I decide to go to ground and wait for nightfall to shroud us once again? Just keep moving, Chase. We'll burn those bridges when we come to them. For now, just keep moving.

Silence was out the window. I would be just one of the many creatures who'd come alive with this rising sun, so being quiet wasn't a priority. Covering more ground was the only thing that mattered.

I'd seen Penny do it. I'd seen her find her stride when she rode her horses as if they were one. She bounced in the saddle, balancing her weight between the seat and the stirrups. She made it look easy, but it wasn't. Nothing about riding those beasts from the pits of Hell was easy. To me, they were all possessed and impossible to tame.

But it happened. I found a speed and stride at which Hunter's body would rise and fall on my shoulders in perfect time with my boots striking the ground. I wasn't going to break any land-speed records, but if I could keep that pace for fifteen or twenty more minutes, I would deposit my unconscious partner at the feet of a seasoned medic who'd keep him alive. Getting him off the island and back aboard the *Lori Danielle* would be another bridge I'd torch if we found our way across it.

My lungs and legs held out, thanks to the efforts of the unconscious man on my shoulders. The physical training he put us through in preparation for this mission paid off in spades, and Fingers's trauma center came into sight the same instant the highest arch of the golden sun shone above the horizon.

The sun wasn't the only thing that shone. The muzzle of Fingers's M4 rifle got my attention, and I galloped toward his nest. He quickly realized I wasn't an invader, and he lowered the weapon. He shoved himself to his feet and moved toward me, but amid panting breaths, I said, "Get out your kit!"

He spun and stepped back beneath the fallen tree where we'd put him six hours before. I eased Hunter to the ground and rolled back onto my haunches, my breath coming hard and my back aching from the fall and the mile of ground I'd put behind me. I didn't know exactly where San Juan Hill was, but I suddenly felt like one of Teddy Roosevelt's Rough Riders.

Before going to work on Hunter, Fingers tossed me his satphone. "There's going to be a few people who are extremely happy to hear your voice. Give that analyst of yours a call. My comms are almost dead, but there's still some life left in that thing."

Skipper answered on the second ring. "Yeah, Fingers, what have you got?"

"It's not Fingers."

She almost squealed into the phone. "Chase! You're alive? What happened to you? Where are you? Where's Hunter?"

"You're starting to sound like Penny. How about letting the rest of the team know we're alive, and then I'll answer all your questions."

She made the radio call and returned to the phone. "Okay, so tell me what happened."

I took a long breath and leaned forward to drink from Hunter's camelback. "Singer gave the order to get out of Dodge, so Hunter and I took off. What neither of us remembered is that there's a nice little cliff in an extremely inconvenient place on the other side of this mountain. We ran right off the cliff in the dark. I wound up in a tree, but Hunter wasn't so lucky. He's got a broken leg, at least, and maybe more. Fingers is checking him out right now, but he's still unconscious."

"You carried him all the way back? Are you serious?"

"What else was I supposed to do? I'm no medic, and our comms were gone. I had no choice."

"I guess you're right. How do we get Hunter out of there?"

"I'm still working on that, but I'd appreciate any ideas."

"I'm thinking," she said. "In the meantime, everybody's out looking for you, but they'll make their way back to your position when they can. This thing has turned into a cluster—"

I didn't let her finish. "It's not over yet. We still have a lot of recon to do."

Skipper said, "Oh, it's over, and you'll understand why as soon as you hear what Clark found."

Her ominous tone sent a chill through my very soul. "What did Clark find?"

"Have you ever heard of a Russian Klub-K?"

I closed my eyes and ran through the Russian arsenal. "Maybe, but it's not coming to me. What is it?"

She said, "It looks just like a shipping container, but it's a bit of a transformer. Push a few buttons, and it turns itself into a launch platform for the Three-M Fifty-Four cruise missile. NATO calls it the SS-N-Twenty-Seven Sizzler."

The realization of the discovery of the Klub-K package washed over me. "Have you briefed the Pentagon yet?"

"Negative. I briefed the Board. That's our chain of command."

"You're right, but this thing just turned into a hurricane in the making. How many of the Klub-K packages do they have?"

"There's no way to know unless we find and open every container."

I took a long, somber breath in preparation for the answer to my next question. "Are the cruise missiles capable of delivering a nuclear payload?"

Skipper's voice cracked as she said, "Yes, Chase. They're capable."

I tried not to react, but my gut was churning. "Has anyone briefed Guantanamo?"

Skipper cleared her throat. "I asked the same question, and the answer I got is going to drive a spike through your heart."

"Give it to me."

"I was told there's no one on the ground at Guantanamo who's qualified to respond to a nuclear threat."

"What? What do you mean, no one is qualified? They've got at least two companies of Marines down there. Every one of those guys from the lowest-ranking private to the colonel himself is qualified to overrun this place and drive bullets through the eye sockets of every communist on this island."

"It's more complicated than that, Chase. We can't invade a sovereign country before we exhaust diplomatic channels."

"The hell we can't! If those missiles are carrying nuclear warheads, they've got the range to hit central Florida, and maybe even farther than that."

She said, "We don't think that's what's going on. We think it's posturing to put political pressure on the American government to close Gitmo."

"Who is *we*? Who thinks it's posturing? Two hundred containers of military artillery, small arms, and especially cruise missiles—some of which might have nuclear capability—isn't posturing. It's a direct threat to the United States."

"Take a breath, Chase. You're preaching to the choir. Let's focus on the priorities right now."

I turned to Fingers. "How's Hunter?"

The medic shook his head. "He's in bad shape, and there's nothing I can do for him here. Look at his gut."

He pulled up my partner's shirt to expose his bulging belly that was already turning black. "He's bleeding into his abdomen. I can't cut him open and find the bleeders. He needs a surgeon if he's got any chance of living through this."

"Are you sure that's not just bruising from bouncing on my shoulders for a mile?"

Fingers shook his head, and the look on his war-hardened face punctuated the severity of the moment. "If we don't get him back to the ship, he won't ever see another sunset."

Chapter 28
Who's That Gunner?

I pulled my ruck from the stack and plucked a new set of comms from a pocket. I tossed a new transmitter to Fingers, and he flipped his spent set toward me. Spending the night with our radios on open-channel comms had sucked the life from the batteries, and somewhere across a field dotted with the seedlings of World War III, my radio lay at the base of what I'd begun to call my tree of life. Without that deciduous monster, my body would be lying on the rocky ground beside Hunter, both of us well on our way to the Promised Land.

I keyed up. "Alpha Two, Alpha One."

Clark replied, "It's good to hear your voice, One. Are you all right?"

"I'm good, but Hunter's not. We have to get him back to the ship, now."

He said, "I didn't hear any shots. What happened?"

"When we were exfilling in the dark, we found a handy little cliff in a not-so-convenient place. He took a bad fall—broken leg, internal bleeding, unconscious. Fingers says we've got to get him to the doc, double-quick."

Clark's tone sounded like I felt. "We'll be back at the nest in ten minutes. Get Hunter packaged up, and we'll haul him out of here."

When I turned back to Fingers, he was already way ahead of me. The improvised splint I'd built from Hunter's rifle had been replaced by an inflatable cast, and a bag of fluid was flowing through a catheter in the back of my partner's hand.

Fingers looked up. "I can keep him out with morphine and keep pushing fluids, but it's a long way to a real doctor."

Clark, Singer, and Mongo crept back into the den, and I stepped out to check for any tails they may have picked up along the way.

Singer grabbed my boot. "It's okay, Chase. Nobody's behind us."

I trusted the sniper with my life, but too many things had already gone wrong for me to relax. My team was dropping like flies, and our mission was exploding into far more than I ever imagined. I was supposed to sneak into the country, verify the presence of enough hardware to kick Gitmo around for a couple of days, and spoil the bad guys' party, but that had turned into a drop in the ocean compared to what we discovered.

When I'd convinced myself there were no trackers, I slinked back into the subtropical igloo beneath the fallen trees. When I met Clark's gaze, every reality floating through my head exploded with impossibility.

"He's not going to make it, Chase."

I swallowed hard and stared down at my fallen partner. Maybe the words left my mouth, or maybe they only thundered inside my head. "I'll be damned if I'm going to let my brother die on a mountain in communist Cuba."

I thumbed my radio. "CIC, Alpha One."

"Go for CIC," Skipper said.

"Find Disco, and get him on the radio."

"Stand by."

Seconds later, our chief pilot said, "Go for Disco."

"Did Skipper brief you on Hunter?"

"Affirmative, and I'm working options. We can put a high-speed boat in the water and hit the beach in twenty minutes."

I said, "He can't survive the six miles back to the beach, and we'll get busted moving in the daylight."

I could almost hear Disco sigh. "Can you get him to a clearing big enough for me to put the Little Bird on deck?"

The battle raging inside of me made the proposition of putting a civilian helicopter in the air over Cuban water and jungle almost unbearable, but sacrificing Stone W. Hunter wasn't a price I was willing to pay. "Spool up the chopper, and get a door gunner who can shoot the wings off a gnat. I'll call you with coordinates in three minutes."

By the time I turned back to my team, Clark had a chart spread open on the ground beside Hunter. A few seconds later, he stabbed a finger onto a spot on the chart. "Right there. It's the eastern edge of the tree line with a village about two clicks northeast. Disco can get in, we can load Hunter and Fingers, and hopefully, they can fly away before we get anybody's attention. But I sure wish we could wait for the sun to set."

Fingers huffed. "I don't think I can keep him alive another twelve hours. His abdomen is filling with blood faster than I can get fluid into him."

"Plot the coordinates," I said. "We're moving now."

Clark ran a finger across the page and then up from the scale at the bottom. "I get twenty-one degrees, forty-five point eight minutes by seventy-nine degrees, forty point nine minutes west. Somebody double-check my plot."

Mongo leaned across Clark's shoulder and recomputed the coordinates. "That's it. Let's move."

I relayed the lat and long to Disco, while Clark and Fingers built a makeshift litter from a pair of rain ponchos and two poles.

Disco said, "Copy the coordinates. Give me a second."

I waited as he entered the coordinates into the chopper's GPS. A few seconds later, he said, "Call me when you're ten minutes from the clearing, and I'll jump off the deck. I can be there in eight minutes."

"Did you find a gunner?" I asked.

"Sure did. I just hope we don't have to pull any triggers."

Skipper's voice joined the conversation. "Keep in mind that somebody shot down my first drone over the coastline and blinded my second one from the ground. There's more going on out there than just a bunch of tobacco farmers turned soldiers."

With Hunter strapped to the litter, Singer walked point while Mongo and I carried our combat controller and Clark covered our rear. Fingers limped beside Hunter as we moved over the rainforest floor as quickly as possible. The litter and our crippled medic limited our speed, but nothing could douse our determination to get our brother back aboard the *Lori Danielle* and under Dr. Shadrack's scalpel.

The higher the sun rose, the hotter the air became and the heavier Hunter felt. We'd practiced this scenario hundreds of times, but I'd never done it on the ground of a foreign, unfriendly nation with a real casualty on the litter. My heart pounded, and my lungs toiled to provide enough oxygen to the muscles in my legs and back to continue the mission. No matter what it cost, I wouldn't be the reason my partner died in the jungle.

With every stride, Fingers limped more painfully. His gait was agonizing to watch, and I could only imagine how badly he must've been hurting, but his only concern seemed to be for his patient. He changed IV bags twice while never slowing down and monitored Hunter's pulse and breathing every few minutes. The determination and grit inside a man who should've turned in his jungle boots a decade before was both humbling and impressive. I hoped I had a man of Fingers's caliber next time I found myself under fire in some godforsaken corner of the globe.

I heard the pounding footfalls of Clark running from the rear, and I turned to make sure he wasn't reporting contact. When he caught up with me, he spoke through heaving breaths. "Launch Disco. We're almost there."

I keyed my mic. "Little Bird, Alpha One."

"Go for Little Bird."

"Come get our men, Disco."

"I'm airborne."

I listened intently as we approached the clearing, but the design of the chopper left most of its noise to the rear. The idea was to never hear it coming.

The clearing came into sight, and I gave the order to stop. "Put him down, and let's clear the landing zone."

We placed Hunter on the ground and spread out to approach the opening. Fingers stayed with his patient while the rest of us hoped we wouldn't encounter any resistance.

When we reached the clearing, there was no question what it had been. The ground was plowed in meandering rows with the rich, dark soil exposed to the sun. Tobacco had undoubtedly been grown in that field for perhaps hundreds of years.

Scanning the horizon, I heard and saw no one, so I keyed my mic. "Does anyone see anything they don't like?"

Clark said, "It's clear on my end."

"Clear here," Mongo said.

Singer didn't report, so I said, "Do you see anything, Singer?"

"Give me just a minute. I'm not quite high enough yet."

To my left were the branches of the heftiest tree in the area waving as our sniper propelled himself ever higher. A few seconds later, he said, "Looks good from up here, and Disco is screaming up the valley as fast as that thing will fly."

"Stay where you are," I ordered. "If this thing turns ugly, we'll need you up there."

"Holding position."

Those words were some of the most comforting sounds I'd ever heard. Knowing Singer was watching everything in the environment was the best insurance I could buy.

Mongo and I sprinted back through the trees and retrieved the litter. We hefted it from the ground and sprinted for the clearing. Fingers ran as fast as his damaged hip would carry him, but by the time he made the clearing, we'd already slid Hunter onto the deck of the Little Bird.

Disco shot a look over his shoulder, and I gave him a nod.

The sound of the rotors pitching to lift the chopper from the ground sent me beating on the back of his seat. "Wait! We're sending Fingers with you."

He lowered the collective, and the chopper settled back to the earth just as Fingers hobbled in beside me.

I took him by the collar and stared into his skull. "You're going back to the ship."

He yanked away from me. "I'm not leaving you without a medic."

"We're keeping your kit, and Singer's a medic. If the chopper takes fire and goes down on the way out, you're their only hope for survival."

He sighed and glared down at Hunter's form on the litter.

I gave him a shove toward the door of the helicopter. "Don't let him die! You got me, Ranger?"

Fingers shook his head. "Clark's wearing off on you, and that's not necessarily a good thing. I'll see you back on the ship."

With pain radiating from his face, he pulled himself aboard the chopper, and I glanced up to see who Disco had chosen to run the M134 Minigun. The warrior manning the devastating weapon stood stoically behind General Electric's ultra-modern version of the Old West Gatling gun capable of firing up to six thousand rounds per minute. The gunner's face was shielded behind a black glass mask built into the helmet.

I admired Disco's choice immediately. The gunner was small, adding little weight to the chopper, and obviously diligent in target acquisition. The helmeted head never stopped scanning the area until I got caught staring up. The gunner glanced down and raised the face shield back into the helmet. To my utter disbelief, the *Lori Danielle*'s purser and chief financial officer, Ronda No-H, gave me a wink and a mock salute. The look on my face must've been a window directly into my disbelieving mind.

She leaned down and yelled, "You better catch your chin before your jaw drops any further, Chase. I guess you didn't know I was an Air Force door gunner before I was a CPA. Somebody had to pay for college, and Heaven knows I couldn't afford it."

I returned Ronda's salute and slapped the back of Disco's seat. "Get out of here."

Almost before I could step clear of the landing skid, the Hughes 500 Little Bird leapt skyward and banked away to the southeast with the muzzle of the Minigun sweeping the tree line for potential targets.

I scampered back to the tree line just in time to watch Singer leap to the ground from his new favorite tree.

He asked, "Was that No-H on the Minigun?"

"No . . . What gave you that crazy idea?"

As the sound of the chopper faded into the southern sky, we moved deeper into the trees and took a knee near a clump of dense bushes.

I said, "It looks like it's just the four of us now."

Mongo said, "I sure hope they make it back over water before anybody else sees 'em."

"They're probably already over the water. Dr. Shadrack will have Hunter patched up before lunch."

Clark said, "We can't let ourselves think about that. We've still got a mission here on the ground. I expect orders to turn those containers into bonfires tonight."

I keyed my mic. "CIC, Alpha One. Any word from the Board?"

Skipper said, "Not yet, but I'm anticipating new orders any minute now. I'm tracking Disco on radar, and he's less than a minute out. It looks like they made it."

"Finally," I said. "We needed something to go our way."

She said, "Oh, I have a little good news. Even though we're out of drones, I've tasked a pair of NSA satellites. They're worthless in the dark, but I'll have decent eyes as long as there's light."

"That's better than nothing," I said. "We're moving back to the ridge to await orders, but I'm not waiting long. If you've not heard from the Board in an hour, I need you to rattle their cage. The longer we spend out here in the jungle, the better chance we have of getting caught."

Chapter 29
Yes, Sir

Singer, Mongo, Clark, and I moved through the trees like snakes, twisting and turning to find the path of least resistance until we made our way back to the den we'd made for Fingers.

Singer opened the med kit and inventoried the contents. "What are we going to do if we get shot up without a medic?"

"You're our medic," I said. "So, you'll have to make sure you're not the one who gets shot."

"I always do my best to be the one who doesn't get shot, but I don't want any of you to take a bullet, either."

Clark said, "It was a good move sending Fingers back to the ship. He would've been a liability if this thing turned into a footrace."

I nodded. "It was a calculated gamble, but I think I made the right decision."

Mongo said, "We'll see."

"Alpha One, CIC."

I answered Skipper's call. "Go, CIC."

"Alpha Three is in surgery, but I don't have any further info. I'll pass along anything they tell me from sick bay."

"Did they make it across the shoreline without being engaged?"

Disco answered, "Somebody locked us up with ground radar, but they didn't fire on us. I made the call to continue to the ship instead of taking out the radar sight. I put the skids in the tops of the ocean waves so they couldn't keep us locked up. They lost us about a mile offshore."

"Good call," I said. "We can always take out the radar sight with an artillery round from the *L.D.* if it becomes necessary."

Skipper broke in. "Hey, the Board is calling. Stand by." Everyone waited impatiently as she fielded the call. When she came back on the radio, she said, "I'm patching through to your sat-phones."

We pulled out our phones and stuck them to our ears. Playing the conversation on speaker would risk having prying ears from the clearing picking up the sound.

I said, "Alpha elements One, Two, Four, and Five are on."

A man's commanding voice filled our ears. "Gentlemen, first things first. We've been briefed on your casualties, and we're pleased to hear you got them back to the ship."

"Thank you, sir."

He continued. "We've also been briefed on your findings on the mountaintop. Obviously, we can't let those Klub-K Containers exist. Do you have sufficient ordnance to take them out?"

I said, "No, sir, but we can cycle back to the ship and resupply."

"Keep that in your back pocket for now. We may have another option. Do you have accurate grid coordinates on the mountaintop clearing?"

It sounded like there was a naval artillery option waiting in the wings.

Singer said, "Yes, sir. We have solid coordinates for the clearing."

"Good," the man said. "Pass those through your CIC, and we need you to return to your ship."

"Return to the ship?" I said. "There are possible nuclear weapons less than half a klick from where we're sitting, and they very well may have the cruise missiles to carry those warheads to the continental U.S. And you're telling us to retreat?"

"What are you going to do, Alpha One? Take on a platoon of Cuban regulars and destroy an unknown number of cruise missiles with just four men?"

"I don't know," I said. "But running away isn't in the cards."

"You're not running away," he said. "You've completed your mission. You found and identified the cargo. That was your mission. Now, get out of there and make your way back to your ship. This thing just turned into the only Cuban missile crisis the world will remember."

I huffed. "I don't like it, sir."

"I don't like it, either, Chase, but you've done all you can do."

"That's not true. We have enough explosives to disable a significant number of the Klub-K Containers. Let us go back in there tonight and wire them up. We can set delayed timers and give ourselves plenty of time to get back to the water before that mountain turns into a fireball. With any luck, there are enough explosives in the containers to do the job for us if we can just start the fire."

The line was silent for a long moment, and I covered my mouthpiece with my hand. I eyed Clark. "Are they thinking?"

He shrugged and held up a palm.

The voice came back on the line. "Alpha Two, what's your assessment?"

I raised an eyebrow toward my handler, and he said, "Chase has a good point, sir. It's likely we could start a big enough fire to cook the top off that mountain, but this isn't the only site with containers. There are two more sites on the north shore of the island."

"We're aware of the other sites, and we've got other assets working that problem."

Disbelief dripped from Clark's words. "There's another team on the island?"

"Not exactly," the man said. "We have assets already on the island who are dealing with the other sites."

"Other assets already on the island? And why didn't you brief me on these other assets?"

"There's no chance of you crossing paths with them. They're a hundred miles away. Come on, Mr. Johnson. You know more than most about the necessity of compartmentalization. You know . . . the whole left hand not knowing what the right hand is doing philosophy."

Clark cast his eyes toward the sky and took a long breath. "Okay. I get it. My assessment is that we have the best chance of eliminating the threat here with a carefully orchestrated detonation."

"In that case," the man said, "the Board approves the action, but we want you in the water when those explosions cook off. Regardless of the safeguards, there are nuclear warheads in those containers, the possibility of turning them into a dirty bomb when you light the fires is too great to leave you in the kill zone. Set the explosives, and get your butts back to the boat."

Clark said, "Consider it done, sir."

Skipper killed the connections, and her voice reappeared in our earpieces. "Nice negotiations, boys."

I said, "What else do you have for us?"

Her voice softened. "Just be careful, all right? We've been hurt enough already."

"Let us know when you hear anything from Dr. Shadrack."

With the decision made, it was time to inventory our explosive stores and create a detonation plan. Every eye, naturally, turned to Mongo.

The big man and keeper of the big brain said, "I can do it, but I need an overhead."

Singer pulled out his pad and drew a sketch of the clearing with locations of containers placed with precision on the page. "There. That's a pretty fair mark-up of the site. The boxes with Ks in them are suspected Klub-K Containers."

I pulled out everything we owned that would create a bang and spread it on the ground. "We've got twenty pounds of C-4, two dozen grenades, and about a thousand feet of det cord."

"Sounds like a party," Mongo said. "That'll start a nice little fire. Too bad we don't have any marshmallows to roast."

Singer closed his eyes and bowed his head.

That caught my attention. "What's wrong, Singer?"

"We're going to kill a lot of people tonight. A lot of people who probably don't understand what's going on."

I laid a hand on his forearm. "If one of those cruise missiles lands at the Magic Kingdom in Orlando, how many of those people will understand what's going on?"

He raised his head. "This is a role-reversal, huh?"

I squeezed his arm. "Yeah, it sure is. You're usually the one making sense of what we have to do, and I'm the one wishing there was another way."

Mongo said, "I may have an idea that'll keep most of those guys alive."

Suddenly, he had our attention, and the big man leaned back against his pack and scratched his chin. "We first need to know what kind of men they are. Are they the kind who run toward a gunfight, or the kind who run away from one?"

Clark kicked my boot. "Come on, College Boy. You're the shrink. What do you think?"

I didn't hesitate. "Neither. I think they're honorable, loyal men who'll likely do what they've been paid to do, and unless I have the wrong picture of all of this, they've been paid to protect those containers. I think I know where you're going with this, and I like it, but put it on the table, and let's talk it out."

Mongo said, "If we set a charge about a quarter mile to the west and touch it off a few minutes before the main charges on the containers, those guys might see that initial blast as an attack and position themselves to deal with it if it comes up the mountain. If they're not in the clearing when we blow the boxes, they'll likely survive."

Clark chewed on his bottom lip. "I like it, but it's a gamble to burn up what little C-4 we have on a chance at keeping those guys alive."

Singer pulled off his hat and ran his hands through his hair. "I could always stay behind and pepper them with a little love from the muzzle of my three-oh-eight. That might run them out of town."

"Yeah, and it might get you killed," I said. "I'm not taking that chance. We've put too many men in sick bay already, and you're too valuable to join that list."

He shrugged. "It was just a thought."

Clark gave me a look and said, "What's cooking in that head of yours? I see the wheels turning."

I grimaced. "It's not a complete plan yet, but I do have an idea, and part of it involves Mongo's idea. What if we simply tell them to run for their lives?"

Mongo leaned in. "You heard what Barkov said his men saw in those containers. There were billions of pesos in there. These guys are peasants, at best. When you put that kind of money in those kinds of hands, you buy a lot of loyalty. I don't think we can ex-pect them to run just because we say boo!"

"Here's what I'm thinking," I began. "We can set a small time-delayed charge a few hundred yards west of the clearing, like

Mongo suggested, but instead of gambling on how they'll react, we can play into what we know any soldier would do."

Clark said, "Keep talking."

"When we set off that charge, any reasonable person would immediately turn toward the blast. It's just a natural human reaction. But phase two of my plan is where it gets interesting."

I paused to swallow a drink of water. "Somebody on this island already knows we're flying drones around. They've made that crystal clear. What they don't know is what we're doing with those drones. I suggest crashing one right in the middle of the lion's den. While those soldiers are staring at the initial explosion, Skipper can fly one of her drones right down their throat with a love note suggesting, in no uncertain terms, that if they want to live, they need to run . . . and run fast. That solves Singer's morality conflict and gives the rest of us one fewer thing to lay awake regretting."

Clark said, "I like it, but those guys knew what they were signing up for. If this little diversion tactic doesn't work, we still did all we could to protect them. If they don't heed our warning, that's not on us."

Singer offered part of a smile. "I'm proud to be part of this little squad. You guys are better men than you'll ever let yourselves admit."

I checked my watch. "We've got a lot of work to do if we're going to get this done and off this mountain by midnight."

Clark scowled. "Who said anything about midnight?"

"I did," I said. "I figure we can make the coast in two hours since we're not dragging a crippled medic around with us. If the SDV is still where we left it, we can squeeze Mongo inside since we're down two bodies and run that thing as hard as she'll go. With any luck, we'll be having steak and eggs on the *Lori Danielle* when the sun comes up."

Mongo grabbed his stomach. "I could really go for some steak and eggs. I've been hungry for two days."

Singer gave him a shove. "Stop lying. You've been hungry for thirty years. You're not fooling anybody."

We needed the levity, but it was time to go to work. "Clark, I want you and Singer to set the charge to the west while Mongo and I put together the demolition plan for the containers."

Our handler and our sniper hopped to their feet, and Clark asked, "What time do you want to kick off the festivities?"

I closed my eyes and tried to picture the timeline, but it wasn't coming together for me.

Fortunately, the big brain rescued me. Mongo said, "Don't rig it on a timer. Rig it on a sat-phone. That way, Skipper can light the candles whenever she wants."

Clark said, "I like it," and Singer selected the gear for their diversion mission.

By the time Clark and Singer were clear of our nest, Mongo had a sketch of the clearing with container counts and positions. It took a little over an hour for the smartest man I know to come up with the most efficient and destructive plan for destruction of as many containers as possible with our limited explosive inventory. The other hour we spent bent over the plan was my formal academic training to learn the basics of the complex plan Mongo created. What I knew about explosives before the class would fit inside a thimble, and what I knew after the class was enough to blow that thimble to the moon.

We wrapped up planning and learning simultaneously, with Clark and Singer returning.

"It's going to be quite the fireworks show tonight." Clark grounded his gear and shucked off his shirt. "Have you heard any news from the doc?"

I thumbed my mic. "CIC, Alpha One."

Skipper answered almost immediately. "I was just about to call you."

"I hope it's good news."

She hesitated. "Well, it's not necessarily bad news. It's progress, at least. Alpha Three is stable but critical. Dr. Shadrack did what he could, but Hunter needs a thoracic surgeon and a real operating room—neither of which we have on the *Lori Danielle*."

"He's going to live, right?"

Another pause came, and I felt like I'd been kicked in the gut.

Skipper finally said, "Dr. Shadrack says that depends on how long it takes us to get him on a good surgeon's table in a good hospital."

Chills ran down my spine. "So, what's the plan?"

"That's why I was about to call you. Disco can fly him to the Dominican Republic in the Little Bird and then back to Miami in the *Ghost*, but that creates a problem for us."

I lay my head back and sighed. "We'd lose our pilot and our helicopter."

"Exactly, but there's more. Dr. Shadrack says he needs to go with his patient, regardless of how we get him back to the States."

Clark keyed up. "How about the hospital at Gitmo?"

Skipper said, "No dice. They've got a general surgeon and a podiatrist."

Clark shook his head. "I didn't mean Gitmo for their hospital. I meant Gitmo for their airport and airplanes with American flags painted on them."

"Way ahead of you," Skipper said. "They've got five King Airs on deck. Two have never run, one is flyable, and the other two have been on fire recently. But that's not the problem. The problem is that they don't have a flight crew."

Clark exploded. "Flight crew? Kiss my butt, a flight crew. I'll fly the damned thing."

Skipper stood her ground. "Take it easy. Disco already made the plea, and it was denied. The Pentagon isn't exactly in the loop on this thing, so they're not willing to hang anybody in uniform out to dry."

Clark wasn't finished with his private explosion. "Out to dry? What do you call us? We're up here hanging off this mountain without any support from anyone, and our people are dropping like flies. I think we're the epitome of 'out to dry.' Somebody give me a sat-phone!"

It was time for my psychologist's therapeutic tone, so I turned it on. "We're wasting time, Clark. The Pentagon said no. The Board will come up with some Coast Guard Dolphin and maybe a naval surgeon on a ship somewhere, but if that was you lying in that bed on the *L.D.*, I'd put you, Disco, and the doctor on our Little Bird to the Dominican Republic, and you'd be in an OR in Miami before the Coast Guard could get their rotors turning. I appreciate your passion, I do, but I'm making the call."

I keyed up. "Skipper, put him on the Little Bird, and make sure there's a surgical team waiting for him in Miami."

I expected her to pound me with logic about having no air support and chain of command, but instead, she said the last two words I ever expected to hear from her mouth. "Yes, sir."

Chapter 30
Cigars and Sweet Tea

Singer prayed, and that surprised no one, but what did surprise me was that while he was talking with God, he never mentioned the four of us still on the mountain. He only asked for protection for Hunter, and I made a mental note to discuss that with him over cigars and sweet tea when all of the Cuban madness was over and we were safely back in Georgia on the banks of the river.

Our sniper made another move that pleased me beyond description. He took Clark for a walk, and as I'd learned in the decade I'd had the Southern Baptist sniper by my side, his walks were never about the walk. They were all about a greater understanding of our responsibilities to ourselves and those around us. I understood Clark's fury, but what I needed from him in the coming hours was the soldier inside the man. I needed him focused, determined, and unstoppable, just like he'd been since the day I met him.

As the sun descended the western slope of the sky, we re-inventoried our explosives, det cord, and grenades, and divided them equally between the two teams.

I said, "I'll take Mongo, and I want Clark to take Singer. We'll start as far apart as possible and work toward the eastern end of the clearing. My theory there is pretty simple. I figure the likelihood of us getting caught goes up with every minute we spend on-site. So, if we're going to get busted, I want to be as close together as possible when it happens. We're outnumbered about a dozen to one. I'm not saying we can't overcome those odds. I'm just saying I'd rather fight together than separately. If they stick with their previous schedule, they'll walk a patrol just before sunset, then have evening chow. When they get their bellies full and fire up the Cohibas, I think we'll have free run of that mountaintop—as long as we don't get careless."

Clark said, "I like the way you're thinking, but we need a contingency plan if we do get busted."

"I've been thinking about that all afternoon, and in my mind, there's only one option. If either team gets confronted, we run downhill like our feet are on fire and blow the top of that mountain all the way to Mexico. After that, it's just a six-mile run for our lives."

My three soldiers each gave a nod, and Clark said, "Great minds, like the same kind of bird feathers."

In that moment, I hoped I would never be crazy enough to understand what happens inside that man's skull.

Darkness consumed the Cuban wilderness, and Skipper chirped in my ear. "Alpha One, CIC."

Once we established two-way comms, she said, "I have some news. Hunter's in surgery, and Penny and Irina are on their way to Miami so he won't be alone when he wakes up."

"What about Disco?" I asked.

"He's already airborne and headed for Montego Bay. I begged him to stay in Miami overnight, but he wouldn't have it. He's determined to be here in time to cover your exfil."

"Montego Bay?" I said. "I thought he flew out of the DR."

"He did, originally, but he had Gun Bunny fly the Little Bird to Montego Bay so he'd be closer to the ship when he came back."

"Gun Bunny? Who's that?"

"You remember her. She was with us on the job in St. Barts."

"I guess I never knew her name . . . or call sign."

"Whatever. Anyway, she's on the job and waiting on the ramp in Jamaica."

I tried to imagine how tired Disco would be by the time he made it back to the ship, and it occurred to me that he'd likely be almost as exhausted as the four of us would be in a few hours.

Evening chow came, and the beautiful smell of Cuban tobacco burning wafted on the breeze. "That's our cue, gentlemen. Let's blow up a few shipping containers."

We shouldered our gear and headed for the ridge. The last time Clark and I played with explosives was underwater, beneath the Bridge of the Americas connecting North and South America near the Miraflores Locks of the Panama Canal. I got blown out of the water because I didn't know what I was doing, and I would've died had it not been for the efforts of the same doctor who cut Hunter open a few hours earlier. With any luck, there wouldn't be a repeat performance.

I became little more than a mule with eyes while Mongo placed and wired the charges on every container we encountered. He worked, and I bore the weight of our gear and watched for approaching guards. As my pack grew lighter, we distanced ourselves farther from the guards who seemed to have settled into their cigars and revelry.

As I considered their positions, their lighthearted approach to guarding a mountaintop full of shipping containers nobody was supposed to know about became more logical. After all, who'd be crazy enough to sneak into Cuba, climb a mountain, and molest containers full of military hardware provided by the Russians?

Reaching the eastern end of the clearing, Mongo and Clark connected their two webs of explosive mayhem to one trigger.

We took a knee in the tree line, and Clark said, "That went way too smoothly. It freaks me out when things go that well."

I rolled my eyes. "Now you've done it. You just had to say that out loud, didn't you?"

"Sorry, but it's true."

"I'll tell you what's true," I said. "It's time for us to get our butts off this mountain and back on anything with an American flag on it."

Singer said, "I couldn't agree more. Let's move."

We made our way back toward the nest we'd built for Fingers to reclaim our gear before making our run for the beach. We were careful to stay well into the trees to avoid detection by ear or sight, but we had no way to anticipate what we'd find back at the nest . . . or rather, what would find us.

As we drew closer to what had been our hidey hole, voices—English-speaking voices—rose on the wind.

I threw up a fist and motioned for my team to hit the deck. In an instant, we were prone, with our rifles trained on the darkness ahead of us. What starlight there was gave our nods enough ambient light to feed a terrifying sight into our pupils.

"Are those dogs?" Mongo whispered.

At that, the animals' ears perked up and their tails stiffened, and we were thoroughly and completely treed.

We froze in place, hoping in vain that the dogs would be more interested in the stash of food we had in the nest than they were with the four commandos pinned down on the side of a Cuban mountain.

I whispered, "Two by two," and as slowly as possible, Singer and Clark crawled backward. The saddle in the terrain just behind us was our only hope of escape. If one of the dogs caught a glimpse of movement, they'd be on us almost before we could react. Killing a pair of military working dogs wasn't in my plan for the night, but neither was a team of English-speaking dog handlers.

Who are those guys? What are they doing here? Could they be the other team the Board dispatched?

When Clark made it to the saddle, he called the ship. "CIC, Alpha Two."

"Go Alpha Two."

"We've encountered an English-speaking team with working dogs. Who else is on this mountain?"

I was relieved to know Clark had the same questions as the ones bouncing around in my head.

"Stand by, Alpha Two."

"There's no time to stand by," he said. "We need to know if these guys are friendlies."

"I'm on it," Skipper said. "Just give me thirty seconds."

"We might be Alpo in thirty seconds."

I gave the signal for Mongo to start his movement to join Clark and Singer, and I prayed the giant could move in silence. He did, but I did not.

As I pressed the toe of my boot into the earth, a dead twig cracked beneath the stress, and it sounded like thunder inside my head. I froze, and my heart thundered in my chest. Daring a glance, I put eyes back on the nest and saw both dogs pulling against their leads and staring directly at me.

One of the handlers commanded, "Back!" And the dogs returned to sniffing the nest.

I swallowed the boulder in my throat and pushed myself backward, moving as slowly as possible. Just as I felt the slope of the ground beneath me fall away into the saddle, my earpiece crackled. "Alpha Two, there are no friendlies on the mountain."

Clark asked, "Are you certain?"

"Affirmative. Whoever they are, they're not ours."

At that instant, both dogs burst into ravenous barking. They were focused on me with intensity like I'd never seen from man or beast. The gig was up, and I keyed my mic. "Blow the mountain."

Skipper said, "But the drone isn't in place. Verify blow the mountain anyway."

The sound that came out of me felt more like a cornered animal's growl than a command. "Blow it!"

Chapter 31
What Have We Here?

The coming roar of the explosives we'd rigged would be enough to deafen every living creature on the mountain, including the threatening dogs, and the shock waves that followed would leave the men in its wake feeling as if their lungs had just collapsed inside their chests. There was no time to prepare for the blast. All we could do was turn our heads downhill and open our mouths so the punishing wall of pressure from the C-4, grenades, and ammunition wouldn't demolish our sinuses and eardrums.

Relaxing and correctly estimating the passage of time while awaiting such a torturous event is impossible. We were left lying prone and praying we wouldn't be showered with flaming debris when the explosives cooked off.

Time is relentless and often agonizing, but no matter how slow it seems to pass, it never stops. Instants became hours, and seconds became days as we waited for the blast that didn't come.

I keyed my mic again. "Skipper, blow the mountain, now!"

Her bewildered tone punctuated her insistence. "I did."

"No, you didn't. Nothing happened."

Mongo and Clark exchanged looks of ultimate disbelief, and Clark yanked his sat-phone from a pocket. He dialed a number, pressed send, and buried his face back into the earth. But still, nothing happened.

Trying to piece together what had gone wrong, my mind ran in ever-widening circles of questions without answers, and fears without consolation, until I took inventory of what few assets we had. "Skipper, blow the diversion charge!"

Almost before I finished the order, a rolling, billowing wall of thunder rose from the west and shuddered the trees. There was no time to look back at the dogs and the English-speaking squad. Instinct would overwhelm their senses, and they'd have no power to stop themselves from turning toward the sound of the explosion that was meant to draw innocent men from their coming death. Instead of fulfilling its mandate, the diversionary charge served only to cover our hasty escape.

Each of us knew there was nothing left on that mountain for us except death, so we leapt to our feet and sprinted through the trees, underbrush, and detritus of the rain forest. Gravity added fuel to the fire that our legs created and sent us accelerating out of control down the slope of the mountain. Aside from rifle fire from our rear, I only feared colliding with a tree as my feet pounded the earth and my body careened southward.

My brain should've been piecing together our coming return to the ocean, but instead, it wouldn't stop conducting inventory of what we left behind. Our gear in Fingers's den had been discovered, the dogs had our scent in their noses, and a team of . . .

Were they Americans? Was their English inflection and dialect familiar? They were Americans, but who were they? And why didn't our C-4 turn the mountaintop into dust?

I tried to yell into my mic as our descent grew into unadulterated chaos. "Skipper! They were Americans! Find out who they are!"

I couldn't understand my own words, so expecting Skipper to hear and decipher the garbage spewing from my mouth was irrational at best and hopeless at worst.

Her voice echoed, but the sounds of my lungs screaming for air and my legs absorbing the agonizing shock of the out-of-control downhill run drowned out whatever she was saying. I hoped she heard the words *Americans* and *who*. At that point, nothing else mattered.

Nothing about my situation qualified as stable. Everything was falling apart, and my goals had changed from preventing the next world war to merely staying alive. If our feet would carry us to the ocean, our chances of surviving would increase exponentially, but there were still five miles in front of us and a pair of working dogs behind us.

Despite my dire need to reach the water and stay alive, two haunting words kept thundering through my head: *We failed.*

The containers survived. The mission of the perpetrators of the coming atrocity didn't change. Fingers may never walk without a limp. Hunter may have paid the price of my failure with his life.

As my body labored to stay on its feet, everything in my world changed in a flash. Actually, in dozens of flashes from muzzles of rifles I never expected to encounter. The edges of my periphery were dotted with belching orange flames filling the air with missiles of lead, and I was propelling myself through little more than a semi-controlled fall down the seaward side of Cuba's steepest slope.

I had only two options, and neither was good. I could continue bounding down the hill, raise my rifle, return fire, and learn to dodge bullets, or I could lean back, let my body hit the ground, and take my chances at coming to rest in a position from which I could fight and survive. As if we'd coordinated the maneuver before our run began, the four of us threw ourselves backward, raised our rifles, and returned fire in a horrific show of marksman-ship. If our rounds hit anything near our foe, it was sheer luck . . . or the hand of God. At that point, I'd welcome either.

I finally stopped tumbling when I collided with a mahogany tree. Having no time to acknowledge or accept any damage to my body, I rolled prone and returned fire into the last place I remem-bered seeing muzzle flashes. I was disoriented, confused, and prob-ably injured, but dealing with incoming fire was paramount. Everything else could wait.

I heard the distinct report of three other M4s firing in time with mine, so I believed my team was still alive, even if we were pinned down and wasting ammunition.

The tree provided both cover and concealment, so I took ad-vantage of both. By some miracle, my night-vision nods had stayed on my head, and I scanned the area in search of my teammates. Clark appeared in green relief against a boulder the size of a compact car. Beyond him and farther down the slope, two more friendly rifles fired into the darkness, and I silently thanked the keeper of the stars for keeping my brothers alive.

The firefight raged on, and as haphazardly chosen as our posi-tions were, the incoming fire waned until three or perhaps four shooters remained. At least, that's what I thought happened, but I wasn't just routinely wrong. I was wrong in the extreme.

That reality fell on me in the form of someone's knee in the small of my back and a muzzle pressed against the back of my head. "Drop your magazine, and squeeze off that last round."

In defiance, I dug a foot into the ground and tried to roll onto my side, but my captor was not only obviously well trained, but also big enough to keep me pinned to the ground.

Changing tactics, I released the grip on my rifle and lowered my hand to my sidearm in hopes of putting a round through the bot-tom of my holster and into the aggressor's thigh. Except for being underwater, the position I found myself in that dark night was nearly identical to my predicament in the lagoon on St. Thomas the night I shot off Anya Burinkova's toe. It had worked in the lagoon, so for the sake of my life, I hoped it would work in the Cuban jungle.

My efforts were rewarded with one loop of a flex-cuff sliding around my right wrist and drawing tight. My captor then leaned forward, pressing all of his weight on my back, and grabbed my left hand. He forced my hand across my shoulder and through the other loop of the cuffs. In an instant, I was restrained with my left hand across my shoulder and my right twisted behind my back from beneath. I had been in, what I believed to be, some of the most painful and dangerous situations any human could endure, but the guy on my back was a special kind of asshole. I didn't know human arms could be pulled so far without separating joints or breaking bones, but I was being schooled by my superior.

My fight was over, and I was a prisoner, but maybe my teammates weren't, so I yelled as if crying out to the other side of the world. "Watch your six! I'm busted!"

For warning my team, I caught a butt stroke to the back of the head, and although the shot rattled my cage, I didn't go out. With my arms twisted beyond human endurance, I still refused to surrender, kicking, twisting, jerking, and howling like a beast on fire. It took only seconds for my captor to feed me a mouthful of a mahogany tree to shut me up. As long as I was conscious and alive, I was determined to make him regret rolling me up.

With my face full of blood from my torn lips and nose, the man threw me to the ground and sent a powerful kick to my hip. The blow started my body rolling like a log down the incline until I finally collided with a tree that had to break at least a pair of ribs, if not more. The coming night wasn't going to be pleasant, and I was certain I'd never see the Caribbean Sea again.

As I lay grinding my teeth together and trying desperately to swallow the pain my body felt for the second time in twenty-four hours, I realized that trees had become both my savior and tormentor, all on the same mission. Whether the man ripped the nods from my head or I lost them on the roll, they were forever gone, and I was left drowning in the darkness with the sounds of my teammates—my brothers—fighting for their lives. No matter how hard I blinked and squinted, the ebony night refused to give my eyes the slightest hint of what surrounded me. My situation was dire, but despite the pain, I had to stay conscious and piece together the scene with only my ears.

Labored footsteps approached from the east, and something hit me like a ton of lead. When I was finally able to catch my breath again with my ribs driving their broken termini into flesh, I twisted enough to recognize the load that had fallen on me was Mongo, our three-hundred-pound Goliath. If they'd taken him out without half a dozen bullet holes in him, we were facing a more formidable force than I could imagine.

Finally, a second body hit the ground beside me, and Clark moaned as the air left his lungs. They were stacking us like cordwood, but I couldn't imagine why. Why wouldn't they just kill us where we lay and then walk away?

My ears rang as if I were inside a church bell, but I heard one of the breathless men say, "That's all three of them."

Three? Did he really just say all three of them?

I had no doubt I was one of the three. Mongo's size gave his identity away, and the third man thrown on the heap was, unquestionably, Clark, but the men who'd taken down a giant, scooped up a Green Beret, and rolled me up like a Persian rug had made the worst mistake of their lives, and I wouldn't have to wait long for the men to claim their reward.

I counted at least six pairs of boots around us, and maybe more. We were outnumbered, but only by a head count. A pair of men yanked at Mongo's body until he rolled off of me, and then they grabbed me by my hair and beard. They dragged me from the base of the tree and set me up against an uprooted stump.

I was battered and weary, but I'd never be submissive. I kicked at the men until they pinned each of my feet to the ground and pressed pistols to my kneecaps. "You want to keep playing? Go ahead, and you'll find out how it feels to have nine-millimeter holes through your knees."

I jerked and twisted. "Who are you? Tell me who you are!"

Finally, a man knelt between my boots and grabbed my face with one hand while shining a massive light into my face. "Well, what have we here? What's your name, little boy?"

I spat in his face, and he crushed the light across my jaw, sending blood and spittle spraying through the air. He grabbed a handful of my hair and bounced my head against the tree trunk several times until I was barely able to stay awake.

"Are you ready to play nice now, little boy? Tell me your name, or I'll tear you apart, piece by piece, until you do."

I know that voice. Keep him talking. Stay alive, and stay conscious.

A second flashlight replaced the first one the man had destroyed against my face, but this time, my inquisitor wasn't holding the light. One of the kneecap gunmen was holding it, and I could make out the features of the man only inches from my face.

"I know you," I said. "What's your name?"

I pored through my mental Rolodex, trying to link the familiar voice with the face I know I'd seen before.

Where have I seen him? Whose voice is that? Why is this guy so familiar to me?

I squinted against the light and studied the man's features until, at last, it hit me. "You're Hal Grimes. You're that son of a bitch from Brinkwater who left my men to die on the Khyber Pass."

He furrowed his brow and leaned in even closer, studying every angle of my face. I'll never know if he remembered me because his head exploded into pink mist, covering me in blood, pulverized bone, and grey matter. His men, frozen with panic, stared to the east until each of them met the same fate as Harold Grimes, senior operator for Brinkwater Security.

Minutes later, Jimmy Singer Grossmann cut the flex-cuffs from my wrists and waved a pack of smelling salts beneath Mongo's nose. The giant returned to the realm of the living at the same time Clark shook the cobwebs from his head.

I looked up at our sniper, the man who'd likely saved all of our lives. "Really? You shot a guy in the head three inches from my face?"

He pulled a rag from his pocket and tossed it toward me. "Clean yourself up, man. You're a mess. Oh, and one more thing . . . You're welcome."

Chapter 32
The Cavalry

We pieced together four sets of night vision from the bodies Singer created and conducted our squad-level battle-damage assessment.

Mongo pressed a pair of meaty fingers against my ribs. "Yep, they're broken, and there's nothing we can do about it until we find some duct tape."

Clark was light-headed but as coherent as he ever was. We got some water down our throats and tried to figure out what happened to get us ambushed on our descent from the heights of Cuba.

In the middle of our discussion, I froze. "Where are the dogs?"

Every head spun to the north, and every ear perked up.

Clark said. "We have to go back up there. We don't have any choice."

I winced as I imagined the pain of climbing that mountain with broken ribs. "As badly as I want to disagree with you, I can't. If the dogs weren't chasing us, they're sure to find the explosives, sooner or later. We've got to set them off before we lose our one shot."

Amidst groans and sighs, we forced ourselves to our feet.

I said, "This is going to suck."

Clark laid a hand across my shoulder. "Embrace it one more time, young Jedi. Just one more time."

I brushed his hand away. "Anyone have comms left?"

Mongo pulled out a collection of plastic parts from his pocket. "I've got most of a sat-phone, but God only knows where my radio is."

"Mine, too," I said.

We patted our pockets and felt inside our ears, but we were alone, deaf, and silent in the tar-black Cuban wilderness.

Singer said, "There was one spare commo kit left in the gear, if the dog handlers didn't pilfer it."

My stomach twisted into knots. "If we don't get in touch with the *Lori Danielle* soon, Skipper will launch every asset she can get her hands on to find us, and we don't need any more Americans on this chunk of ground tonight."

Clark said, "Maybe one of Singer's dead guys has a sat-phone we could borrow. Something tells me they're not going to need theirs anymore."

Picking the pockets of dead men is but one of the brutal necessities of war, but necessity or not, it was an atrocity I'd never accept as a task of a God-fearing man. Everything about it simply felt inhuman.

Halfway through the search, Singer held up a device. "I scored a Sat-Com radio, but no phone."

"That's better than nothing," I said. "But I'm not a fan of talking to Skipper on anything somebody else could intercept."

He shoved the radio in his pocket and continued his search.

With every twist of my body, I gasped in pain. There are few injuries short of a broken spine that come with the same degree of life-altering pain as broken ribs. Every breath, every stride, and every nod of my head felt like someone was trapped inside my body and trying to claw his way out.

With our search complete and our situation unimproved, Clark said, "I'd love to know who these guys are . . . or were."

I stopped in my tracks. "They were Brinkwater Security guys. The same crew that left you three to die on the Khyber Pass."

Clark's eyes turned to saucers. "What? We killed a team of American contractors?"

"Their passports may be American," I said, "but they weren't on this island in the name of the Red, White, and Blue. Whatever they're doing here, it has something to do with the Russian weaponry and the assault on Gitmo."

"How could you possibly know that?" Clark demanded.

"I know it because of the look in the head honcho's eyes when he discovered I was an American and I knew his name. If he were here and on the good guys' team, he wouldn't have tried to dislocate my shoulders and have his men drill holes in my kneecaps."

He shook his head. "What have we stumbled into down here?"

"I don't know, but it's bigger than any of us and deeper than any conspiracy I've ever heard of."

He glanced up the slope. "We've got to get up there and end this. We're the only ones who can."

We started the long trudge back up the mountain toward what promised to be the end of our finest hour that no one would ever know about, the prevention of a war that never happened, and a long line of deeds that would keep our flag flying high and give our enemies one more reason to believe we would always fight when challenged and never back down in the face of an enemy threatening the way of life we've come to hold dear. We *would* finish this, or *it* would finish us.

The ten minutes we spent galloping down the mountain became forty-five minutes to regain. Between my broken ribs and my team's physical exhaustion, every stride felt like a marathon, but continue we did until the mountaintop clearing came into sight.

"Do we risk heading back to the nest?"

Clark wiped the wall of sweat from his brow. "I think we have to, but not you. Singer and I will check it out. You and Mongo get up there and figure out why those charges didn't crack off. We'll meet back here in fifteen minutes."

I wasn't sure why Clark suddenly took over, but that was no time to discuss leadership styles. Mongo and I made our way to the eastern end of the clearing while Clark and Singer crept toward our den beneath the fallen trees. When we reached the sat-phone-triggering device after low-crawling for what felt like a mile, Mongo studied the connections carefully while I whimpered like a child.

Mongo disconnected the sat-phone from the detonation device and programmed the timer for thirty minutes. He slid the phone to me and rose to his knees, scanning the clearing. Without a word, he motioned for me to get on my feet and move down the slope. As badly as walking hurt, it was indescribably better than crawling on my belly. We slinked back to our rendezvous point where Clark and Singer waited.

"Any luck with our gear?" I asked.

Singer shook his head. "No, they cleaned us out, but the nest was booby-trapped with a couple grenades and some tripwire."

"Good catch," I said. "You kept the grenades, right?"

He bounced the pair of fragmentation grenades in his palms, and I grinned. "That's the best news we've had all night."

Mongo groaned. "I'm not so sure about that, boss."

He pointed toward my pocket. "We recovered our sat-phone."

It was Singer's turn to put on a smile. "Now, *that's* the best news we've had all night."

Mongo checked his watch. "I hate to cut our celebration short, but we've got eleven minutes before this place turns into Mount Vesuvius."

Clark reclaimed command. "Let's put as much distance between us and the mountaintop as we can and then call the ship. We move as a unit, and Chase sets the pace. Nobody gets left behind. Now, move out!"

Hopefully, for the last time during the mission, I gritted my teeth and embraced the suck, and we picked up speed descending the slope.

After five or six minutes, the distant roar of rolling thunder echoed through the darkness, and I came to a stop. "What was that?"

Singer said, "It sounds like thunder, but there was no forecast for storms tonight."

Clark squeezed his eyes closed and listened intently. "That's no thunder. That's an explosion. But it's not our explosion."

Mongo checked his watch. "No, it's definitely not ours. We've still got four minutes, and we're still too close for me. Whatever the sound was, we can't do anything about it."

We settled back into our rhythm of bounding and running and sliding down the slope as the minutes ticked off.

Mongo said, "Thirty seconds."

We didn't break our stride when eighteen pounds of C-4 and two dozen grenades turned the mountaintop into a wasteland of burning military hardware.

Still moving as quickly as my body could tolerate, I thumbed the sat-phone to life and heard Skipper say, "Go for CIC."

Without preamble, I breathed into the microphone. "The explosion was us."

She said, "Which explosion? There've been four in the past five minutes."

"The one on our mountain," I said. "Where were the others?"

"We think they came from Guantanamo Bay, but we can't be sure yet. Communications are down, and the base is on emergency generators. But that can wait. Where have you been? We've been trying to reach you for two hours."

"It's a long story, and I don't have time to tell it right now. We're on our way back to the beach. We should be wet within the hour if we don't get intercepted. Listen closely . . ." I paused to catch my breath, then continued. "Somehow, Brinkwater is involved. Find out all you can about what they're doing down here, and get word to the other team on the north side of the island that there are hostile Americans on the island. You got all of that?"

"I got it," she said, and the line went dead.

As dawn drew ever closer and the sky traded the all-encompassing darkness for the first signs of morning's light, I could smell the salt air of the Caribbean Sea and almost taste the salt water on my lips. For the briefest of moments, I almost forgot I had a pair of broken ribs in my side, but that moment was fleeting as the beach came into sight below us and the sound of automatic-weapons fire filled the air.

Bullets pierced the trees around us and whistled past our heads until we took to ground once more and brought our weapons to bear on the gunmen on the beach. We scampered for cover, and I conducted an ammo count, estimating each of us had fewer than a hundred fifty rounds. Fighting off a barrage of fire from at least three Russian PKP machine-gun emplacements would be impossible, even if we had heavy weapons and endless ammo, but definitely impossible with our M4s and six hundred rounds.

We watched carefully for any break in the fire, and we sent wave after wave of 5.56-millimeter rounds into the mouths of the machine-gun nests, but the lead kept pouring from the beach, with no end in sight.

Clark yelled from behind a tree. "Get us some help, or this isn't going to end well."

Skipper answered on the first ring. "I know, and help is on the way. Just keep your heads down. We'll get you out of there."

Before I could respond, a burst of machine-gun fire tore a chunk from the boulder I was using for cover and ripped the sat-phone from my hand. I pressed myself against the back of the stone and yelled, "Keep your heads down. The cavalry is on its way."

Waiting is not something battle-hardened warriors are good at, so my words went mostly unheeded. My team kept raining small-arms fire on the beach and ducking back behind cover in rapid, re-peated cycles until our solid black Hughes 500 Little Bird climbed from the wave tops and turned broadside to the beach. Her General Electric M134 Minigun belched 7.62-millimeter hell into the bunkers at six thousand rounds per minute. Smoke boiled from the gun as the barrels burned white hot and the lead kept coming.

After one strafing run down the beach, two of the three ma-chine-gun nests were silenced, but the third was still firing, and her guns turned seaward to bear on the Little Bird.

Singer sprang from cover and charged the beach with fury in his eyes and fearless resolve in his chest. As he ran, he pulled the pins from the pair of grenades that had been the lethal teeth of the mountainside booby trap. Ten feet from the machine-gun nest, he dived through the air and hurled both grenades through the slit in the sandbags. He landed on his belly in the sand and threw his hands over his ears. The grenades roared their murderous yawp, and fire leapt from what had been the final barrier between my team and the security of the sea.

With our M4s at the ready, we advanced on the beach, carefully scanning the area for threats, and the chopper touched down at the water's edge. We backed toward the Little Bird with our muz-zles still covering the tree line. When we reached the chopper, I looked up to give Disco a nod of appreciation, but instead of the old A-10 Warthog driver in the cockpit, I saw a mass of golden blonde hair fall from beneath a flight helmet and a beautiful woman smiling down at me.

She said, "Hey, cowboy. Does your momma let you date? If so, hop in, and I'll take you for a ride you'll never forget."

"You must be Gun Bunny."

She slid on a pair of aviator sunglasses, replacing her helmet. "And you must be darned lucky that Staff Sergeant No-H and I showed up when we did. It looked like you boys had your hands full."

Epilogue

Gun Bunny brought the Little Bird to a hover directly over the spot where we'd left the SEAL Delivery Vehicle, and Clark and Singer slipped from the chopper's skids and into the crystal-blue water. Mongo and I chose to ride back to the ship with Ronda No-H and our new favorite helicopter pilot. The big man didn't feel up to riding the little submarine like a donkey all the way back to the boat, and I couldn't muster the wherewithal to cram my broken ribs back inside that underwater coffin.

We touched down on the deck of the *Lori Danielle* like a hummingbird with sore toes, and Skipper was there to hand out hugs all around. I begged her to postpone mine until Dr. Shadrack had a look at my ribs, and she reluctantly complied.

Skipper conducted our debriefing in the sick bay while the good doctor taped me from neck to naval and declared, "You'll live, but you won't feel like it for a week or so."

Skipper folded the first sheet of her yellow legal pad across the top. "So, here goes. First, Hunter is out of surgery, and he's going to make it, thanks to Disco and our favorite seagoing doctor."

Dr. Shadrack took a small bow. "I'm honored to have been able to do my small part, but Fingers saved his life. If he hadn't discovered the internal bleeding and kept pumping Hunter full of fluids, he wouldn't have lasted an hour after the injury."

"That's great to hear," I said. "Where is Fingers, anyway?"

Skipper said, "He's still with Hunter in Miami, and he won't leave his side, no matter what we say. It looks like Hunter's got himself a brand-new guardian angel with a green beret."

"We should all be so lucky," I said. "So, let's have it. Can we tie a bow around this thing and call it done?"

Skipper said, "Maybe. Let's start with Brinkwater. Chase, you were mostly right about Grimes. The part you missed is that he's not with Brinkwater anymore."

Mongo laughed. "Thanks to Singer, Grimes isn't with anybody anymore, except maybe a little pointed-tail, pitchfork-carrying, fire-and-brimstone broker."

Skipper shivered. "Yeah, well, that's out of my hands, but it turns out Harold Grimes and a bunch of his flunkies jumped ship at Brinkwater and opened their own operation. Somehow, they finagled their way into a security contract at Gitmo, and I guess contracting money just wasn't good enough for them. It seems they got in bed with some jihadis and a couple of former communist party guys in the Kremlin. I know, I know. Those two factions don't mix well, but apparently, each thought they could blame the other if anything went wrong, so they partnered up to close Gitmo permanently and make it look like it was done by a bunch of revolutionaries. The explosions we heard around the same time as yours were bombs planted by Grimes's guys on the base and fashioned to look like mortar and artillery attacks. The battle-damage assessment showed a lot more detonations than we heard."

When she slowed down to take a breath, I asked, "How did you figure all of this out?"

"I didn't. The Marines get credit for piecing together what happened on the base. The connection between Grimes and the jihadis was divulged by a person—or persons—unknown at Lang-

ley. You can take that for whatever you want to make of it. Personally, I don't think it was CIA. My money is on the NRO."

"The National Reconnaissance Office? Why would they have
their hands in this cookie jar?"

She rolled her eyes. "Oh, Chase. You're so cute when you pretend to be naïve. Now, here's the best part. Your buddy, Dmitri
Barkov, turned out to be the first honest Russian I've ever met.
Well, besides Irina and Tatiana, of course. Everything he told us
was spot-on. And thanks to his intel, the other Board-directed
action team took out the containers on the north side of the island . . . sort of."

I pressed a hand against my ribs. "Sort of? What does that
mean?"

She shrugged. "Let's just say they have a combat controller of
their own—not one as cool as Hunter, of course—and he called in
the fire mission to a submarine—who will remain nameless—off
the coast of Key West, and weapons boys on the sub parallel-
parked a couple of cruise missiles right on target."

I grimaced. "Are you telling me we could've called in a fire mission and not had to have gone back up that mountain?"

"Yep, you could have, but you lost all of your commo gear, so
you got to play Jack and Jill went up the hill, *again*." She flipped
through her notes. "That's all I have for now. We'll do the formal
debrief with the Board as soon as I can get all the players in
place."

The party broke up, and I slid from the edge of Dr. Shadrack's
table.

Skipper caught my arm as I stood, then checked over her shoulder as if she were going to tell me a dirty joke. When she turned
back to me, she slid a sat-phone into my palm. "Press redial, and
just listen."

She left me alone in sick bay, staring down at the phone, so I pushed the button and stuck it to my ear. After four rings, an unmistakable voice filled my ear. "My Chasechka. You are alive."

I swallowed the lump in my throat as I thought about how surprising Anya's revelation was. I'd been near death more in the previous forty-eight hours than I had in the rest of my life combined.

"Yeah, I'm alive. And apparently, so are you."

She made a sound that could almost be considered giggling, if I didn't know she was incapable of such sounds. "Yes, Chasechka. I am alive, and you were worried for me, yes?"

"Yes, I was a little worried. It's good to know you're safe. I'd love to hear the story of how you escaped, but we'll save that for another day."

She sighed. "Is always promise of another day. I am glad inside heart that you are safe. Everyone is also safe, yes?"

"Not everyone," I said. "Hunter took a bad fall, and he'll be in the hospital for a while, but he's going to make it. Other than that, everyone you know is okay."

She hesitated for several seconds, then said, "Is nice to hear your voice, my Chasechka. We have serious conversation waiting for us, and is important. You will make this happen, yes?"

I paused in reflection. "I don't know, Anya. My life is with Penny, and I love her more than I could ever put into words. And I—"

"I know all of this, and I sometimes dream I could be her, but is silly dream of silly child. I know it cannot be, but is still important for me to see you and tell to you this thing. Is important, Chasechka."

"Okay, Anya. I'll think about it."

"Do not *think*, Chasechka. I need for you only to—"

"Hang on a second."

I covered the mouthpiece and looked up to see Skipper pointing toward the deck and mouthing, "Clark's back with the SDV."

"I have to go, Anya. We'll talk again soon. I'm glad you're okay."

"I am glad for this also, and tell to Hunter I hope for him to be okay soon. Goodbye, my Chasechka."

I cleared my throat and said, "Just Chase, okay? No more Chasechka," but the line was dead.

Clark and Singer surfaced the SDV in the moon pool, and the crew placed the craft on her cradle. After showers, mounds of breakfast, and checkups from Dr. Shadrack, we crammed ourselves in the combat information center for the official debriefing with the Board. The space was far less comfortable than our op center back at Bonaventure, but Clark said, "It's not so bad. You know what they say . . . You can bring water to a horse, but you can't put lipstick on a pig."

We stood in stunned silence, staring at our handler, until he said, "Oh, you know what I mean."

Before we could throw Clark overboard, Skipper brought the monitors to life with every member of the Board in place.

The same gentleman who launched us on the mission took the floor. "Congratulations, gentlemen . . . and ladies. Freedom gets to ring one more day because of your efforts. The Board and I thank you for what you accomplished over the previous few days. Without you . . . well, I'd rather not think of what might've been without all of you. You won't get it, but each of you deserves an outpouring of gratitude from every American who woke up this morning. Such is the nature of what we do."

Each of the Board members took turns saying the same thing with slightly different words, but it was nice to hear their praise. When the rounds had been made and every detail of the mission laid out, the original speaker cleared his throat.

"It's an ugly business we're in, but thank you for making the necessary sacrifices to keep the wolves at bay. I think I speak for everyone here when I say patriots like all of you don't devote their lives to the preservation of freedom in expectation of financial reward, but we believe you'll be pleased with the compensation that was deposited into your account early this morning. And we just have one more question . . . Have any of you ever been to Iceland?"

Author's Note

I sincerely appreciate you reading my work, and I hope you enjoyed *The Gambler's Chase*. As many of you know, I never write with an ending in mind. I write entirely by the seat of my pants, never knowing what will happen next, and certainly never knowing how the story will end. That is an exciting, and sometimes terrifying way to write. This story contained more than a few moments of terror for me, but we'll get to those moments shortly. For now, let's talk about the hardware.

The most fascinating new piece of equipment we were fortunate to enjoy in this story was, of course, the SEAL Delivery Vehicle (SDV). The SDV is quite real, and at the time of writing, is still in service with Navy SEAL teams. The brave warriors who operate from these vessels are specially trained and equipped specifically for missions involving use of the SDV. During my research, I talked with a few SEALs who said they never wanted SDV duty, but the men who served in these specialized SDV units were proud to be part of such operations. Much of the technical data came from a former operator we'll call "Frogman Jim." Of course, he never divulged any classified information about the SDVs or their operations, but his willingness to answer questions and provide information was incredibly helpful in making the operation of the SDV in this novel as realistic as possible, with one huge exception.

While researching this novel, I visited the U.S. Navy SEAL Museum in Fort Pierce, Florida, and I highly recommend spending a day at that magnificent facility. You'll be glad you did. They have an SDV on display at the museum, and I just had to crawl inside. Readers often assume I was Chase in my youth. That couldn't be further from the truth. I've never been Chase, but I must confess that I'm my own inspiration for Mongo. I'm not a little guy, so I had to know if I could put our favorite giant inside a real SDV. I got in, but there was no way I could've put two other humans in the compartment with me. Because of Mongo's size, I had no choice other than to hang him on the outside of the vehicle. This is illogical, impractical, and would've been extremely uncomfortable. In the real world, there's little chance that would ever be done. That's part of the literary license we writers put to use to make our unrealistic story lines possible. I needed Mongo on the mission, and I couldn't come up with any other way to get him ashore. I hope you'll forgive me for stretching the believability of that scene.

Another piece of hardware that played a significant role in this story was the Russian Klub-K Container-launched 3M-54 Klub/Caliber SS-N-27 Sizzler. Although this weapon system exists and is terrifying, it probably didn't exist during the time this story took place. The world got its first look at the system in 2017, but it was a perfect piece of equipment to make this story even more chilling, so I ignored the timeline and shipped a few of those monsters to Cuba. I recommend doing a little research on the Klub-K if you're curious. It's a fascinating weapon system.

The M134 General Electric Minigun mounted on the Hughes 500 Little Bird was a fun little addition to the climactic scene on the Cuban beach. I did not have to stretch the ferocity of the M134. It is just as deadly as I described it, and if you ever get a chance to pull the trigger, don't pass it up.

As is the case with many modern thriller stories, my premise was extremely unlikely. However, many of the geopolitical scenarios happening around the world today would've been considered unlikely not so long ago. Some of my favorite bad guys are the Russians. I'll admit that they're an easy target, and I enjoy writing dialogue in Russian accents, so I'll likely continue to pick on the former Soviets for years to come.

Please understand that I hold absolutely no ill will toward the Russian citizens. Just like here in the U.S., the opinions, emotions, and expressions of the population are not well represented in the actions of their leaders. My only target is the evil of totalitarianism and socialism, and certainly not the Russian citizens. Freedom will always be the good guy in every story I write. I believe humans were created to live free of oppression and equally free to take crazy leaps of faith like becoming a professional novelist. Those leaps don't always work out, but the freedom to leap at will is engrained in the American spirit, and is, in my opinion, one of the things that make our country the greatest nation to have ever existed. In short, I'm not picking on the Russian people. I'm picking on the ideology of their leaders.

Now, let's talk about Cuba. We've covered my feelings on socialism and oppression, so it's not a challenge to guess where I stand on the politics of that beautiful island just ninety miles from the shores of Key West. I have enormous respect and admiration for the resilience of the people of Cuba. They are some of the most hardworking people on Earth, but unlike here in America, their hard work will never result in financial freedom or security for themselves or their families. The heartbreaking reality of life in Cuba was driven through my soul like a spike, back in late December of 2022, when we discovered a tiny, inflatable raft with two Cuban refugees aboard while cruising in the Strait of Florida about forty miles north of Havana. I'm incapable of imagining how terrible life would have to be to blow up a raft and run from my country, not caring where I landed, just determined to be any-where but where I was. Much like the Russian people, I have nothing against the citizens of Cuba, but I despise the oppressive regime under which they are forced to live. I will always believe it is a horrific shame that such wonderful people must live under such terrible conditions, only ninety miles from our shores.

I get a lot of emails from readers asking why I do such painful things to my characters. I wish I had a reasonable answer for them, but the truth is more complex than the questions. I honestly never know when someone is going to get hurt or killed in my stories. Because I sit down every day and write what falls out of my brain without any pre-planning, it's just as shocking to me as it is to you when I get characters hurt or killed. Fingers, the former Special Forces medic in this story, is based on no one I know, and when I wrote him into this story, I had no idea how impactful his role would be. Without him, Stone W. Hunter would've died in the jungles of Cuba. Characters come and go at fascinating and bizarre times while I'm writing, but I love when it's their time to shine. I felt sorry for Fingers, but his determination to continue the mission after a hip dislocation showed remarkable character and grit. I love those traits in fictional characters, but I love them even more from the real-life heroes who keep us free and pro-tected. Athletes call it playing hurt, but the warriors who stand toe to toe with evil on our behalf call it "just another day at work," and that's true character and sacrifice for their fellow man. Playing hurt when an athlete earns a seven-figure salary will never be the same thing as strapping on a flack vest and embracing the suck of combat while every muscle aches and every joint cracks. Heroes don't catch touchdown passes or hit grand slams in the bottom of the ninth. They get up every day, tie their boots, and stick their muzzles in the faces of those who would destroy our country, demolish our way of life, and trample our freedom. Those brave, young men and women do it seven days a week, three hundred sixty-five days a year, for a fraction of minimum wage, while deployed to places most of us can't pronounce or find on a map. Those are the people who should get the multi-million-dollar endorsement deals and show up on the front of cereal boxes, but they don't do it for recognition or for riches. They do it because they love you and me and freedom more than they love air-conditioning and Xbox and being home for Christmas. I pray that I live a life that deserves such sacrifice, and I hope you do the same.

Thank you again for reading my work. I'm honored beyond words to be on your Kindles, your nightstands, and your bookshelves. I love being your personal storyteller, and I hope you'll let me continue to be just that for years to come. I'll do my best to keep entertaining you, making you question what's possible, and sharing my passion for celebrating the brave, honorable men and women of our military, the clandestine service, and everyone who's ever taken up arms against an enemy bent on robbing us of our freedom and liberty.

—Cap

About the Author

Cap Daniels

Cap Daniels is a former sailing charter captain, scuba and sailing instructor, pilot, Air Force combat veteran, and civil servant of the U.S. Department of Defense. Raised far from the ocean in rural East Tennessee, his early infatuation with salt water was sparked by the fascinating, and sometimes true, sea stories told by his father, a retired Navy Chief Petty Officer. Those stories of adventure on the high seas sent Cap in search of adventure of his own, which eventually landed him on Florida's Gulf Coast where he spends as much time as possible on, in, and under the waters of the Emerald Coast.

With a headful of larger-than-life characters and their thrilling exploits, Cap pours his love of adventure and passion for the ocean onto the pages of the Chase Fulton Novels and the Avenging Angel - Seven Deadly Sins series.

Visit www.CapDaniels.com to join the mailing list to receive newsletter and release updates.

Connect with Cap Daniels:

Facebook: www.Facebook.com/WriterCapDaniels
Instagram: https://www.instagram.com/authorcapdaniels/
BookBub: https://www.bookbub.com/profile/cap-daniels

Books in This Series

Book One: *The Opening Chase*
Book Two: *The Broken Chase*
Book Three: *The Stronger Chase*
Book Four: *The Unending Chase*
Book Five: *The Distant Chase*
Book Six: *The Entangled Chase*
Book Seven: *The Devil's Chase*
Book Eight: *The Angel's Chase*
Book Nine: *The Forgotten Chase*
Book Ten: *The Emerald Chase*
Book Eleven: *The Polar Chase*
Book Twelve: *The Burning Chase*
Book Thirteen: *The Poison Chase*
Book Fourteen: *The Bitter Chase*
Book Fifteen: *The Blind Chase*
Book Sixteen: *The Smuggler's Chase*
Book Seventeen: *The Hollow Chase*
Book Eighteen: *The Sunken Chase*
Book Nineteen: *The Darker Chase*
Book Twenty: *The Abandoned Chase*
Book Twenty-One: *The Gambler's Chase*
Book Twenty-Two: *The Arctic Chase* (2023)

Books in the Avenging Angel – Seven Deadly Sins Series

Book One: *The Russian's Pride*
Book Two: *The Russian's Greed*
Book Three: *The Russian's Gluttony*
Book Four: *The Russian's Lust*
Book Five: *The Russian's Sloth* (2023)

Other Books by Cap Daniels

We Were Brave
I Am Gypsy (Novella)
The Chase Is On (Novella)

Made in the USA
Las Vegas, NV
04 May 2023

71585718R00163